One for the
Money

Ellen M. Foss

Copyright © 2020 by Ellen M. Foss

Library of Congress cataloging – in – publishing – data
One for the Money / Foss, Ellen M.
2020922751

ISBN: 978-1-7348904-2-6

First published in 2020 in the United States

Acknowledgements

I want to thank my husband for his years of patience, as he listened to me developing my Characters, Plots and Story Lines.

Thank you, Barbara McGarvey, for all your input and editing support.

Proofreader, Tamra Sherman, Thank you.

Thanks again to all my friends for your continued support and encouragement. You know who you are.

Love, romance, heartbreak, attempted rape, anger, and broken friendships. Plus, murder? All for Dan's quest for money and power. Now in the shadowy underbelly of Hollywood's dark side, he franticly tries to marry his way out of his hell.

CHAPTER ONE

"Come on, Mother! Wait up! What's the big hurry anyway? Why can't you just slow down?"

"I can't sweetheart. I'm meeting Dan and he's due here any minute and I'd like to touch up my lipstick before he sees me. I certainly wouldn't want to give the man the start of his life, it might scare him away forever. Raynie dear, I'm sure by now you've noticed, along with everyone else, that I can hardly wait to be in Dan's company?"

Raynie's beautiful face turned sour and she tartly retorted, "Ohhjeeeezus, Mother! How can anyone who has eyesight have missed it? I mean, your sentimental drivel is pretty damn obvious and to be honest, at times it's almost to the point of sickening."

Squinting to see Raynie clearer Jackie removed her sunglasses so she could get a better look at her daughter. She was surprised to see her frowning face. Her own happiness was immediately replaced with concern for her daughter and she asked, "Raynie, is everything okay? Don't you like Dan? I can't tell if you're joking or if you're serious."

"Oh, Mother, of course I like him."

"Then why the long face and the contrary remark?"

"Mother... Come on, you just beat me at three sets of tennis," Raynie paused, then rolled her eyes as she begged, "Jesus, Mother, isn't that enough to put anyone in a cranky mood?"

"Raymeana, you are attempting to change the subject. So pleaseee, let's hear it young lady. What's your problem?"

"Dammit Mother, you know I hate it when you call me that."

"Well sweetheart, I'll try to remember that in the future, and since we're on the subject, maybe you can show me that same courtesy."

Raynie gave her mother an unsure look so Jackie continued, "I've asked you repeatedly to call me Jackie instead of Mother. Regrettably sweetheart, my needs have not slowed you up one bit, now have they. So, now that we have that off our chest, let's get back to the subject at hand. While you're at it, why don't you also fill me in on what's going on in that head of yours? Raynie something has been bothering you for a while...and I can't quite put my finger on it, but I know your attitude has something to do with my relationship with Dan."

Jackie could see Raynie struggling with her response. It appeared she couldn't decide whether to be honest or not. To Jackie, it seemed obvious her daughter didn't want to open up and talk about her feelings, but that was not going slow Jackie down. After Raynie's longer than necessary pause, Jackie decided to push the conversation further. "Honey, do you think that Dan's too young for me?"

"God... Mother noooo..., I'm sorry, Jackieee, and before you go there, no, you're not too old for him either." She kicked the ground and plucked the strings of her racket before she heeded, "I'll try to do better in the future..., about calling you, Jackie, Mom... Okay?"

"Okay. But...what Raynie...?"

"Oh, oh yes, and of course, I like Dan and I'll also try to show it more from this day forward."

"Thank you Raynie. Now, was that so hard?

"No, Mootherr...Jackie."

Smiling at her daughter as she shook out her towel Jackie asked, "Sooo, do you really think he's nice?"

"Yes, I do. He's good natured and fun. Plus, he's handsome in a regular sort of way and from what I can tell, he's even intelligent. Which together is usually rare in Hollywood. Add that to the fair amount of money he has; I'd say that you have quite a catch there." Shrugging her shoulders Raynie asked, "so tell me Mother; what's not to like...what more can a woman ask for in any man?"

Jackie started to answer then decided against it. She concluded that it was probably best to leave Raynie's evaluation untouched. Right now, she rather they stay on neutral ground and away from any heated discussion that Dan might walk in on. At that very moment, the gate to the tennis courts flew open with a loud clang and in walked Dan. At once he could see that the noise startled both Raynie and Jackie. Embarrassed, he smiled sheepishly as he continued his stroll full tilt in their direction. As soon as he reached the ladies, he threw his arms open and encircled Jackie then Raynie. He laughed out loud as he pulled them both closer to his sides, and gaily spouted, "Hey lovely ladies! This must be my lucky day. Not only two of the most beautiful women in Hollywood... and of course my favorites by far, stand here alone and unguarded." He tweaked his pretend mustache and added, "and at my very mercy."

He laughed loudly at his own joke and then continued in the same jocular manner. "Okay... Let's see; turn around." Pushing them both out and away, he twirled his finger around to indicate a signal to turn. "Come on, turn. Both of you turn around; I want to see your backs. I need to check to see which of you has the knife protruding; then I can easily tell who beat whom this time around?"

Smiling at Jackie, Raynie immediately twirled around and walked away as she defiantly answered Dan with a dirty look.

"Wait; stop," hooted Dan. "I'm only telling the truth. You can't hold that against a guy; can you?"

Shaking his head while he tipped it to place a kiss on Jackie's cheek as he pleaded, "Come on, baby; tell me. Am I really the bad guy here... cuzzz I don't think so? If the truth be known, I've never witnessed such competition between two people before, especially between a mother and daughter. It's almost scary."

Without cracking the smile she was trying hard to suppress, Raynie turned to face them as she grumbled, "Mother, can't you do something with him, as well as with that repulsive jovial disposition that he can't seem to contain?" With her hands on her hips and an exaggerated annoyance she added, "And for your information, Mr. Smarty Pants, Mother won as usual." Feigning further annoyance, she lunged out and gave him a shove. Then, moved several steps in the direction to where her belongings laid. Over her shoulder she called out one last remark. "We may be competitive, but you'll have to admit, we're also the closest mother and daughter you've ever met."

"Yes, true, true, I can't argue the point, so I guess you have me there, Ray. Admittedly you are by far the closest mother and daughter I have met to date."

When it registered that he had called her Ray, she halted in midsteam. Jerking her head around, she threw him another dirty look. This time it was for real, since the only person she permitted to call her *Ray,* was her father. All her friends knew this, which she assumed included Dan.

Oblivious to the purpose of Raynie's piercing glare, Dan smiled as he rambled on, "Hey Sweet Cakes, it's my sense of duty to inform you since I am such a gentleman and one who hopes to be your stepdaddy one day, that you are a sourpuss today!"

She groaned, "Dammit Dan, leave me alone. I would like to wallow in my own self-pity a bit longer. I believe it's the only thing that's going to pacify my blues."

He flinched as he exaggerated a step backwards and yelped, "OUCH! WOW! I can certainly see we're going to have to work a whole lot harder than this, if we're going to get any kind of smile out of you today."

He glanced over at Jackie, and then shifted uncomfortably when he noticed the unhappy look on her face. His first impulse was to wink in an attempt to seduce her back into a more playful mood.

He could tell he'd gone too far and was paying much too much attention to her daughter.

"Jackie my sweet..., I don't think either of us want to take the blame for that dreadful sour look that's covering Raynie's face." He smacked a loud kiss above her watchful eye as he apprehensively probed. "You do agree, don't you... my love?" He stood there with an expression of expectancy; and self-consciously moved from one foot to the other as he awkwardly asked, "By the way Jackie, have I mentioned how much I love you today?"

Jackie immediately changed her mood and beamed with pleasure.

From afar Raynie finally gave in and attempted a weak smile. Yet as slight as her smile was, she knew it was still illuminating, an eye-catcher, as Jackie always said.

Jackie watched Raynie move swiftly away to retrieve her extra tennis racket and balls. At the same time, she moved one step closer to Dan's side and grinned happily as he bent down to kiss her again. This time his lips were aimed in the direction of her lips and spread slightly more for a passionate kiss. This act immediately brought back her confidence.

Raynie tried to ignore the two while actively moving around the court picking up the rest of her belongings. The items were strewn all around the clay court. As she moved about the court, she nonchalantly glanced in the opposite direction away from where Dan was kissing her mother. For a moment she gave in and looked back, she noticed Dan's eyes were back on her and she immediately turned and hurried away while she suggestively swayed her tennis skirt with each movement of her hips. After a few steps, she reached up and pulled the bungee from her long blond hair so it would blow softly in the gentle breeze.

Jackie observing her daughter and her actions frowned unhappily. Yet, her motherly instinct was to swell with pride. Yes, her Raynie was not only smart, but beautiful as well. She could have easily been a movie star if she wanted. But instead she loved being behind the cameras.

Jackie shook her head sadly. She had been so worried about her daughter lately. As hard as she tried, she couldn't help but think about Raynie's attraction towards Dan. In all honesty, she could understand her feelings. After all he is almost perfect. Yet she couldn't prevent the slight hint of jealousy that kept creeping into her thoughts. Especially when the three of them were together, then it was almost impossible to avoid the jealousy. She tried, but the truth is, she could see that Dan felt a little of the same attraction for Raynie. Although she was quite sure not enough to put a blemish on their relationship. She turned and smiled thankfully into Dan's astonishing looks and weighed her observations. *No, I shouldn't worry, I know he loves me as much as I love him. Naturally, our affair is going to trouble Raynie; that's understandable. Dan is the only man since her father, and I divorced.*

As for the silly attractions, Dan's a sexy guy and Raynie's a vibrant young woman, they're bound to be attracted to one another. *But still,* she pondered, *that doesn't mean either will act upon it.* If Jackie harbored any doubt of Dan or his intent, she was positive she didn't have to worry about Raynie because her daughter would never do anything to hurt her.

At this time Jackie realized Raynie was moving back in their direction, so she busily snatched up her own equipment as she continued to think: God, I hope I'm wrong about their interest, but I don't think so. I guess I'm just going to have to deal with the fact that Dan is a reckless fifteen years younger than me, and only five years older than Raynie, so the attraction may be inescapable. *Or...* maybe I'm completely off the mark and simply being foolishly suspicious. Still, in all, she didn't believe so and no matter how she tried to gloss it over, she couldn't deny the look of desire in Raynie's or Dan's eyes. She had witnessed it too many times.

Annoyed at her self-doubt, Jackie attempted to halt her flow of thought and silently began to admonish herself. *Jackie, stop. You can't go around presuming every woman you see is after Dan, particularly your own daughter. You have to be wrong, although....*

Suddenly, Dan grabbed her by the hand like an adult would a child's and led her across the courts toward the exit. At the same time, he cried out, "Come on Raynie; let's get a move on. You're dawdling and I've been away far too long already."

All three reached the exit at the same time and Dan proposed, "Let's say we go directly to my place and join the barbecue? I've left several guests in Mike's incapable hands, so... in reality, they're going to have to fend for themselves, at least until I get back with you two. What do you think? Is that okay?"

They both stood there gawking at him as if he were some kind of madman. After all the tennis they had played, they certainly didn't look presentable for a party. Even if it was a pool party.

"Come on, don't panic! You two can shower there. I'm sure you both have bathing suits and wraps in the guest closet. If not, we'll find some."

Raynie quickly began to beg off the invitation, but Jackie immediately jumped in and pleaded, "Come on Raynie, please come help us celebrate. It'll be fun. And you know very well that this is Dan's greatest film success so you must be there. The celebration would hardly be the same without you."

Raynie couldn't help but note the persuasive appeal in Jackie's eyes, and loving her mother as she did, she rarely denied her wishes. Nevertheless, she really did not want to go, but what the heck. "Well okay, but I can't stay long. I have a lot of things to do, plus a script to go over."

"Great! Well, ladies if you'll please follow me to the limo, we can be on our way." His limo was a new black four-door Mercedes Benz which was quite impressive. It contained just about every goodie a person could buy. Jackie genuinely liked the car and immediately began to squeal like a teenager, "Can I drive? Please. Dan, please let me drive."

Ignoring the excitement in Jackie's voice Dan responded, "Soorry." He grabbed the belongings from their arms and literally threw them into the trunk of the car. Thereafter he rushed back to their sides as he playfully mimicked a dutiful chauffeur and opened

Jackie's door. He moved swiftly to Raynie's side, then with a bow accompanied with a French accent he politely advised, "Entry my Dame."

Once he himself was in the driver's seat, he immediately jammed the car in gear and sped off to join the party, along with his best friend and roommate, Mike. As soon as the car hit the streets, Dan playfully shouted, "Just hold on Mike, we're on our way."

Raynie adjusted herself comfortably as she felt the softness of the seat. She took a deep breath and inhaled the car's newness. She loved the fresh smell of new leather, and again she reached out and touched its smoothness. Satisfied, she sat back and buckled her seatbelt.

Sitting on the soft cushion with the sun beating through the windows, she soon began to feel lethargic. With her body so relaxed she changed her position to slouch further into the seat to better enjoy the peaceful ride. Discreetly she eyed her mother's profile, and within a minute she became miffed and crossed her arms. Why can't her mother be like other mothers? Why does she always look so damned beautiful? There should be a law that a person had to look their age. Afterall, a person close to fifty should at least look forty, or better yet forty-five. Dan looked his thirty-three years, and she certainly looked her twenty-eight, so why can't her mother look her age? Instead, she looks a gorgeous thirty-five.

Immediately Raynie's mind moved to her father and her parents' recent divorce. She still couldn't believe her father left her mother, especially for a younger woman. Maybe her mother had been right when she said he was insane. Yet, if I keep in mind where we live, and what kind of business my father's in, then I would have to give him credit. Yes, if she took all that into consideration, she would have to admit; he did last a lot longer than most before he married his trophy wife. She muttered under her breath, "Damn California and damn you, Father, for working in an industry of glamour and heartache and damn your precious Pamela and her staggering youth."

For Raynie, her parents' divorce was an obstacle she never dreamed would come between her and the man she loved. She was sure that her mother wouldn't have given Dan a second glance if her father were still in love with her. But he wasn't, and her mother was an opponent she's never been able to beat. So, there's little chance that she'll ever come close to knowing Dan in any way except as a friend. She pushed herself up to sit straighter in her seat. She hoped this move would block the view of Dan and his grip on the wheel. She hated that she had this attraction for him. It was foolish and she knew it, but, then there were other times when she wondered if Dan was meant for her. Maybe she was missing her one and only chance for happiness?

At last they pulled into the long expansive driveway that lead to the front entrance of what everyone called, Dan's mini mansion. By this time Raynie was ready to bolt; lately it seemed she had an aversion to crowds. She decided this feeling was simply because it was getting harder for her to pretend that she held nothing more than friendship for Dan. There were times when she was sure everyone around her could see her desire for him. Several times in the past months she caught herself staring into the mirror, while searching for any visible signs of her true feelings. Once or twice she even wondered if there was any evidence in her voice; her fear that everyone knew worried her greatly. Now all she wanted was to run. But leaving was out of the question; for Raynie knew it was customary if not mannerly, to stay for at least an hour. After such time, she could politely claim a headache and leave without reparation. Hollywood is a warm and friendly place if you play by their rules, but it can be very unforgiving if you don't. Of course, that *is*, unless you are at your peak then anything goes.

Jackie and Raynie bathed quickly and changed into their swimsuits, and then promptly hurried down the stairs to join the party. The music was loud, and the gathering seemed to be in full swing.

Raynie and Jackie stood for several minutes watching the crowd from the stairway. Finally, Raynie stepped closer to her mother and whispered; "It looks like everyone's having a good time including Dan."

Jackie grinned at Raynie, then without a second's hesitation, headed straight towards her man. She was very aware of all the beauty that surrounded Dan and his pool, and she intended to stake her claim as soon as possible. It was a well-known fact that Dan was a very eligible bachelor, and she had no intention of losing him to some twenty-year-old Hollywood bimbo.

Raynie continued to stand by the stairs and analyze her mother and her obvious assertion for several minutes. Finally, she headed across the room and out to the patio to find a sympathizer.

Almost immediately she spotted Mike who was deep in his pro-claimed post as head-chef for the barbecue. Verging upon him and the grill, she could see his intense preoccupation with his chef's duties. From what she could detect from his apron, he was fully immersed in his position. The apron was full of sticky reddish-brown barbecue sauce along with most everything else within arm's reach. She watched quietly from the sidelines and finally, she couldn't help but laugh at his comical movements. He had globs of spattering everywhere and was continuing to add to the mess while attempting to plaster the meat with the sticky substances.

Raynie waited a minute longer, then laughingly suggested in a warm, but directional critique. "Hey Mike, I know you're quite good at this, but I hear putting the sauce on the meat instead of around it, is usually what makes it taste so good! Do you think we otta try that?"

Mike immediately turned around as he uttered, "Ahhh, the only voice that can possibly sound that mouthwatering has to belong to no other thannn...Miss Raynie Dey, herself."

"Why thank you, my dear devoted and trustworthy confidante. I have always known that you, my friend, is where I come whenever I need the day's woes gently garnered, and then one by one flicked obligingly away."

He reached out and took her hand in his and kissed the tips of her fingers lightly before he gallantly proclaimed, "Yes, my lady, you are correct once again, for I am truly and always have been the loyalist of your servants. But my sweet damsel in distress, I am woefully troubled. For you see, I have lost my white horse. Whilst I would still love to be of service, I have also misplaced my shining sword. Sooo... as you can see, I am somewhat befuddled on how, pray tell, I shall come to my lady's aide in her dreadful time of need."

"Ahhh..., but my loyal servant, your wit is as sharp as your sword as well is your tongue. So, you see, my true and loyal friend, inadvertently, you have once again come to my rescue, and now I am well on my way back to the warmth and security of Camelot."

At that instant, they both erupted into laughter and Mike murmured gently, "Rough day, huh Raynie?" Then almost immediately his tone changed to mock a reprimand. "Raynie, I want to know why you can't simply give it up? Can't you get interested in some new fellow? If not, get out and have a one-night stand. Or better yet, get involved in some wildly lascivious office romance. Anythingg... just as long as you get...you...know...who, off your mind. If you can't do it for you, then do it for me, I love to hear about luscious, scandalous sexual encounters. Besides, my dear, you know I think you're much too good for..., you... know... who."

She placed a kiss on his cheek while she evaluated his proposal before she answered, "Thank you for caring, Mike. I wish it were that easy. But, as far as affairs go, you know I've had my share. Unfortunately, this time I don't think that's the answer."

Her face grew serious and she squeezed his hand between hers. "Mike, I really want you to know that it means a lot to me that you're always here when I need you. I don't know if you realize it or not, but you're the only person I can talk with about this. And in all honesty, sometimes I feel I'm going to go mad if I can't end this absurd obsession with...." She stopped abruptly before she finished her sentence as she gave an overstated look around the vicinity, then whispered, "You... know...who?"

Once again both instantaneously exploded into lighthearted laughter while Mike admitted, "I love you, Raynie. And I really wish I could help, but unfortunately, I'm stuck in the middle, so my only advice isss; GET OVER IT, GIRLFREIND!"

Raynie grumbled, "Mike, I'm tryin. Honestly." Scrutinizing the room, she probed, "I haven't seen Louis. Where is he? He did come, didn't he?"

Mike began to answer when a loud screech came from behind him. This instantly startled him into silence and quickly they both turned to see what on earth was going on. The young lady who did the screeching was in the midst of stepping back, away from the grill. While another guest was courageously grabbing a blazing piece of chicken off the rack and throwing it to the ground, he immediately began stomping it until the fire was out. After the disturbance, all talk of her or Mike's situation ceased since several of the other guests decided to stay and join their vigil at the grill.

Following lunch, Raynie stood half listening to the conversations around her. At the same time, she slyly observed Dan and her mother who sat across the room with a group of people from the studio. It seemed Dan was extremely popular lately. Since the current success of his last movie he's had a group of wanna-be's, constantly following him around. Recently she noticed the group had grown a bit larger. She assumed it was because of last month's announcement, that he was establishing his own production company. She considered whether she should join the group or not, and then decided against it when she saw Dan encircle her mother's waist and pulled her closer to him.

Wistfully, Raynie watched Jackie kiss Dan on the cheek and felt a touch of envy. She wished it were her waist Dan's arm was attentively encompassing and she who was placing the kiss upon his cheek.

She suddenly jumped when Mike walked up behind her and whispered, "Lovely couple, uh?"

"Yes, too lovely. Look at him! He looks like a giant next to Mother. I'm sure he stands taller by five inches or more."

"That's why they look so good together, Raynie. What's Jackie, about five foot-seven or eight? She probably weighs no more than a hundred and ten pounds. Yet she looks even tinier than that standing next to Dan. Admit it. They complement each other, just like they should."

Raynie inhaled a deep breath and immediately exhaled a muttered, "Whose side are you on anyway?"

"As I said earlier, I am unbiased, and I hope to stay that way."

She cracked a crooked grin and whispered, "Chicken ass." Then unhappily admitted, "They do make a fine-looking couple, I guess I can't argue that." Suddenly she began to giggle as she squeaked, "Mike, they look like Ken and Barbie, especially Mother with all her blond curls. Tell me, how does it always fall just so around that exquisite face of hers. And then if that's not enough to contend with, her lovely face at any given time of year, boasts a healthy shade of tan. All in all, I'd have to say she is a carbon copy of *Malibu Barbie*: simply perfect. Perfect teeth, perfect lips, all to go along with her perfect body, and worse yet, all of its real. Not one bit of its cosmetic surgery." Laughing she asked, "What's a girl to do with a mother like that?"

Mike sighed and kissed Raynie on the forehead before he vowed as walked away, "Love her Raynie and just be happy that you have her."

When she stood alone, she sighed again and gave her mother one last appraisal before she moved her attention towards Dan. Mumbling to herself, she asked, "I wonder how much Dan resembles Ken?" It was easy to see Dan was deep in conversation with several guests since his hands were waving about in every which direction. She smiled slightly, as she watched him move about with his usual gusto. At that moment, she noticed his lanky body was more than merely a little attractive in the dark gray trunks he wore. This observation immediately made her feel uncomfortable and she started to turn away, but then she noticed a hunk of his coal black hair had fallen across the right side of his face. He looked adorable. His hair was always falling just so. This, she thought made him look a little vulnerable which was even more irresistible.

For an instant, she had the urge to walk over to where he was standing and lightly brush the unruly hair aside, but instead she stood fast and continued her vigil. As far as she was concerned, he looked far more like a leading man than any producer, but in this industry that wasn't that unusual. Everyone looked like a movie star. From what she had heard, so did she.

Suddenly she released a light sigh that sounded more like a small moan, while at the same time noting that everyone else in the room was having a great time. *And here I am*, she thought, *close to the point of taking an early leave; for now, I really have a colossal of a headache.*

Hiram Bernstein, who was standing near her moved closer. His eyes showed his concern when he asked, "Raynie, you look pale. Are you okay? Can I get you something?"

She at once scrunched up her face and pretended a half smile as she shifted into her act of a weary and headachy guest, and when she spoke, she did so in a strained pain-filled voice as she explained, "I have a humdinger of a headache, Hiram. I think it's going to become a migraine. I guess I better get home and rest before my dinner date this evening." She laughed halfheartedly and exaggerated her pain, "I'm sure my date would appreciate me looking my best this evening."

She knew this would be an acceptable excuse. Anyone here would easily understand and not hesitate to pardon her for an early departure; after all, this is the industry of beguile and pageantry. Looking one's best is always of the utmost importance.

CHAPTER TWO

The next day Raynie received an early morning call from the studio. They wanted to know where in the hell she was. She didn't pick up the phone but listened to the message as it recorded on her machine.

Why'd she take those damned sleeping pills last night? She should've gone straight to bed, but instead she sat alone staring into the empty fireplace. After an hour or so, she finally gave up and ate a light dinner of shrimp and pasta. Then she followed it with a glass of wine and a couple of sleeping pills. "Damn," she mumbled, "how could I have forgotten to set the alarm?"

She sat on the edge of the bed still groggy and in a sleepy stupor as she continued to mumble to herself, "Come on, Raynie, wake up." Cheerlessly she stumbled out of bed and croaked one last "Damn," as she threw on a pair of jeans and a wrinkled tee shirt while she grabbed a sports coat to dress it up. She rushed to the bathroom, quickly brushed her teeth, and rinsed her mouth with some minty wash, then headed back to the bedroom to finish dressing. She stooped to pull her Reeboks on with no socks while she skipped, hopped, and jumped her way across the floor to the living-room.

She didn't even stop long enough to pet Nikkei, her long-haired Persian who was still snoozing comfortably across the edge of the sofa. As she left the room she glanced over her shoulder and the cat lifted her head and gave her the evil eye, then an ever so feeble, "Meow." Raynie quickly cooed, "Mommy loves you too, sweety pie." Then she grabbed her car keys and raced for the door. After slamming it shut and cutting off all view of what might have been a more demanding cry, Raynie sang, "Poor neglected kitty."

Once she pulled out onto the street, she remembered that she wouldn't be back until after midnight. "Dammit, I'll have to call Shannon and ask her to feed the cat again."

Shannon Hicks, her neighbor, was one of her closest friends. It seemed she was always bailing her out one way or another. Raynie shook her head and wondered where Shannon found the time or the energy. She was always involved in some kind of project or in the midst of leaving town for some great vacation spot with one of her many male friends. The girl had more friends than a road has turns decided Raynie. In the three years she had known her, Shannon has had a date almost every night. Usually, it was with some new and remarkably handsome hunk. Raynie glanced at her watch, and made a mental note, "I'll have to call her after lunch." She knew that generally Shannon slept in till noon, and typically had a long leisurely brunch, at which time she would start preparing for her next date or excursion. "Yes, I think that girl lives the life of Riley."

Raynie pondered the possibility of living such a lifestyle then determined that maybe she should hit her father up for an allowance. Maybe she too, can live the life of leisure. However, by the time she reached her exit off the 405 Freeway, she had decided against any such request. Afterall she had always insisted that she wanted to make it on her own. To be a strong and independent woman. Of course, you really can't count the house Daddy bought her, or the trust fund from her grandparents.

Minutes later when Raynie pulled through the gates of the studio, she couldn't help but notice people wandering around in costumes of an earlier period. They were dashing about everywhere;

she forgot there was a 6 a.m. shoot on the lot this morning. From the looks of it, the movie's crew along with a couple of its stars were all headed in the direction of the commissary. "Shoot," she mumbled. As she immediately maneuvered her car in the opposite direction. Luckily, she found a parking space soon after. She pulled her car as close to the curb as she could get it so not to block on-coming traffic. As she jerked on the emergency brake she read, "**NO PARKING ANYTIME.**" It was spelled out pretty damn clear, and she wondered, how in the hell anyone could possibly miss the damned large red letters? "Maybe that's why Security is so dispas-sionate about my defense," she muttered to herself.

Raynie patted the steering wheel, then purred, "Don't worry baby; maybe we'll just get a ticket instead of the usual tow." She giggled as she opened the car door and admitted, "Maybe the sign should read, **RAYNIE, NO PARKING ANYTIME**, since she parked here every time she was late, which seemed to be at least once a week. God, last week it crept up to two."

But for right now, it really didn't matter, because she was too late to care about the sign or worry about being towed. She needed to get to her post and as soon as possible. She reached in and grabbed the clipboard that still lay on the BMW's weathered seat. She twirled around and took off in a dead run for the set's entrance. She was glad they were shooting inside today and not out on loca-tion somewhere. The smog was already evident, plus it felt like it was going to be another L.A. scorcher.

Raynie started to pass the table which, at any given time of the day was filled with a variety of munchies. This time it was stacked high with breakfast goodies. She slowed her stride so she could sur-vey the table's bounty and swiftly picked up a cheese croissant and a cup of coffee. Without so much as a second's hesitation, she turned and headed for the room full of cameras, lights, and produc-tion people.

The complete crew was standing around chatting while waiting to begin the first shoot of the day. With this evident, she hurried to the other side of the room and the chair marked Director. She slid quietly into the one next to it, which read Production Manager. Finally, she breathed her first sigh of relief, as a loud voice bellowed from the other side of the stage. "QUIET, QUIET EVERYONE, QUIET." The sound resonated and echoed throughout the building. This announced to everyone that filming was about to start.

For an instant Derek turned and threw Raynie a pointed scowl, then immediately returned his full attention back to the task at hand. His eyes were focused on Thomas, the handsome star of the hit show **Detective Alley,** as the star walked onto the set. With his entrance, the cameras commence to roll, and her day began.

This was one of the worst days Raynie had encountered since production began eighteen months ago and by the end of it, she was ready to pull every single hair from her head. Fed up beyond control, she turned and asked her assistant, Marsh, "Why is it, when a day starts out shitty, it feels the need to end the same way?"

The star and the co-star of the show had begun quibbling right after the first shoot and were now carrying it through the last take. Agitation was visible and Derek frustrated, shouted, "It's a wrap!" At this point both actors immediately took off again, right where they left off before the shot had begun. Derek's eyes met Raynie's and she voiced, "I don't know what to say." To herself she whined, *why can't these guys ever get a clue, neither one is good without the other?*

To the two squabbling men she shouted, "The day's over. Give it a rest. OKAY!"

Derek nodded his agreement but neither actor looked up or acknowledged that Raynie had spoken. *The moronic thing is,* she thought, *their disagreement is so trivial that it's ridiculous.* But as Raynie approached, she tried to keep an open mind. To a star, something trivial often meant empowerment or ratification of who they were. Yet, understanding them or not, their behavior was still annoying, and sadly she was the one who usually got stuck with handling their silly controversies. This time Thomas, the star of the show, felt his costar was trying to upstage him. Last month Thomas had hit his fortieth birthday, and since then he has had a particularly sensitive time dealing with the much younger and extremely popular actor. Lately he had found fault with every scene the two were in together. He even rejected several vital parts he and his costar were supposed to film together, saying the shoot favored the younger actor. However, today their bickering was making Raynie's job extremely difficult. She had no patience left for their infantile behavior, and by the end of this day, she was about to scream at the two overindulged stars, *that maybe they can use their acting skills to act like grownups.*

Marsh Elliott, the Assistant Production Manager, walked up to stand beside her as they both watched the persistent vendetta. Finally, he asked, "What is it with those two? It seems they never, ever stop. Why?"

Derek Gizzer, the Director, stood up and shot another quick look towards Raynie and Marsh while he shook his head back and forth in disgust. It was clear to see what he was thinking when he threw his hands in the air and marched off the set. W*hy me lord*, was written all over his face?

Of course, Derek's exit left Raynie and the others to referee the calamity and with this added stress Raynie began to experience a strange awareness. It was a feeling she first noticed a couple of months ago, and now she threw out a question to no one in particular, "is this why I feel like I'm running a daycare for unruly children?"

Miffed, she continued to observe the two actors in silence while hoping they would stop, but they were oblivious to anyone except each other, and they continued their petty quarrel. To Raynie, it was obvious that neither wanted to give the other the satisfaction of triumph. With this observation, Raynie finally raised both arms towards the heavens as if she too was begging for God's help, then gave in to an unsuccessful attempt to control her anger as she belted out a loud, "DAMMIT, STOP! JUST STOP!" The sound echoed throughout the near empty building.

Both actors jumped and immediately suspended their conflict. Their faces instantly turned red when they turned on their heels to confront her. Angrily she continued. "Okay, now that I have your attention, I have one simple question. Which one of you feels that this is so important that you might want to owe me? And I mean, owe me big."

The actors stood there. Neither uttered a sound for a complete minute. Then simultaneously they quickly glared at each other, spun around sharply, and left the stage.

Marsh exhaled, along with an astonished tone whispered, "WOW! WOW, Raynie, I'm damned impressed." Almost immediately his smile changed to show a new-sprung admiration, then confusion. In that same instant his expression altered and formed a bewildered glare as he asked, "How in hell did you do that? They never listen to me like that. Why would they listen to you like that? Come on, Raynie, how'd you do that?"

"Simple, my love. They're well aware that the show has recently lagged in popularity. The ratings show it's been steadily slipping for the past two months. This may suggest the show could possibly be tired and in need of some new blood, and you know as well as I do, no actor wants to be out of work. So, since they both think I'm sleeping with Mr. Moneybags himself and have some pull, they tend to listen to my threats a little more readily. You see; it pays for me to occasionally remind them of this. It helps to keep 'em in line."

Aghast, Marsh cried, "Oh, Raynie... how appalling! Who would start such an awful rumor?"

Raynie snickered mischievously as she turned to walk away. Then over her shoulder she winked and offered, "Like I said, it helps keep 'em in line."

He evaluated her message before he ran after her. As soon as he caught up, he asked, "You... You mean you did this... you did it yourself? You started the rumor that you're sleeping with Mr.... Why, he must be a hundred years old, who would belie..."

She smiled but said nothing as she turned to enter her office and with no hesitation, she closed the door between her and the astounded Marsh.

By the time she finished her work and finally walked out into the cool night air, it was close to nine o'clock and she was exhausted. But her day wasn't over yet; she was expected and should have already met her father for dinner at 8:30.

She thought, *I need to put it in gear and get to The Polo Grill, post haste.* She wondered; *is there a quicker way to get to the Beverly Hills Hotel?* Answering herself she grumbled, "Nooo, it's a good half hour away."

Hurriedly, she rushed to her car and dialed her father's car phone. No answer, "Damn."

She dialed the restaurant and waited. The phone rang at least twenty times before someone finally picked up the line. Raynie began to speak, but before she could say a word she was asked to hold. When the man's voice finally came back online, he went directly into the usual spiel. He introduced the name of the restaurant and their famous chef. Finally, he stopped long enough to ask what he could do for her.

By this time Raynie felt exasperated, but she bit her cheek and asked nicely, "Can you please check to see if Mr. Raymond Dey has arrived yet."

She could hear the smile in his voice as he asked, "Is this you, Miss Dey."

"Yes," she answered.

His reply was warm and friendly, and suddenly she could hear his rich New York Italian accent as the tone carried through the phone lines. "Haay, Miss Dey, this is Jimmy, the Maître d'. Your Daddy said you'd be callin anytime. Yeah, I'd say he sure knows his little girl, right, Miss Dey? Anyhow, he told me ta tell ya, not to rush, ya understand? He said, just slow it down little one and take your time gettin here. Of course, he'll be waitin dinner till you get here."

Almost instantly, she felt every muscle in her body go lax. She smiled into the phone, "Please tell him I'll be there in thirty minutes. Thank you, Jimmy. You probably saved my life."

After she hung up, she smiled at the memory of Jimmy's voice when he first answered the phone. She hadn't recognized it at all; there was no trace of his accent. That must mean he's really doing well in his voice classes. She made a mental note to tell him so, as she mumbled to herself, "I hope he's doing as well in his acting classes. If so, Brando, beware."

Raynie headed straight for her father's table since she knew where he'd be seated. At once she noticed that another guest had already seated himself across the table from him and she smiled. Her father, no matter where they went, someone knew him, and they always had the need to acknowledge their presence.

"Hi Daddy. Sorry I'm so late, but I can see that you've been entertained by this nice gentleman." She smiled across the table in the stranger's direction, then added pointedly, "Until I could get here."

Her father leaped up and welcomed his daughter with a kiss on her cheek, before he commenced to proudly introduce her to the intruder. "Mr. Charles, this is my lovely daughter, Miss Raynie Dey. She is quite beautiful, don't you agree?"

Raynie growled an angry, "DADDY, PLEASE."

Standing to greet her, the handsome gentleman's smile was broad when he courtly declared, "I am so incredibly pleased to meet you, Miss Dey. Please won't you call me, Simon? All my friends do, and I hope I can add you to this list as well." Slowly he turned to face her father while he continued to hold Raynie's hand and added; "Ray, I am an excellent judge of beauty and I will most certainly agree with your assessment. She is definitely a knockout straight-away."

When he spoke, Raynie detected a slight hint of an English accent, which also held a definite ribbing resonance. Teasingly he declared as he smiled directly into Raynie's unfriendly eyes, "I would assume that you take after your mother?"

Ray burst into laughter and agreed, "Yes Simon, I'm afraid you are correct in your assumption. Very astute; she does indeed take after her mother. As a matter of fact, she's the spitting image of that beautiful and irresistible woman."

Raynie gave both men a dirty glare and asked; "Do you think that maybe the both of you can stop talking about me as if I weren't here?"

Simon immediately initiated an apology; "Oh; I am sorry, Miss Dey. Please excuse our deplorable manners. I am afraid we were being utterly thoughtless."

His smile grew broader as if he expected her to melt at the very sight. He pulled her chair out and waited for her to be seated while smiling like a silly schoolboy waiting for his request to be accepted. Yet she stood where she was and openly challenged his invitation.

Ray attempted to ignore Raynie's rude scowl as he graciously asked, "Simon, you will stay and join us for dinner, won't you?"

At that moment Raynie wanted to choke her father. But instead she screamed inside. 'Why! Why! Why does everyone I know, always try to fix me up? I don't want it, nor do I need it.'

She narrowed her eyes as she sharply looked at her father then back toward Simon and saw that he was still standing as he waited for her to be seated. She could tell that he recognized her dilemma; yet he stood by and continued to say nothing to ease her discomfort. In fact, she could swear that he was relishing the moment while he watched her squirm as he considered Rays invitation. He stood there looming over her the entire time, smirking. She noted, he was obviously enjoying the standoff.

Simon detected her awareness of his boldness, and his smile became even more impish as he began to weigh his opponent's discomfort. Her brilliant gray eyes dazzled him, but he did not falter or divert his gaze from her bitter stare. He stood fast and smiled directly into her bogus smile, which Raynie kept uncomfortably displayed across her beautiful face. He continued to taunt her with her father's unwelcomed invitation by not answering the question right away. Then she noticed he slowly changed his half-witted smile into a full-blown grin that easily read, Gotcha.

Suddenly, her fake smile turned to a surprised expression, and he could see that she was astonished by the fact that he could read her so easily. He couldn't help but take immense pleasure in this awakening, at least he had made some kind of an impression on the beautiful Raynie Dey.

Raynie taken aback took her seat and Simon started to move back to his chair as his eyes darted from her to her farther then back again. Slowly he airily replied. "Ray, I would love to stay...." When he noticed that Raynie was visibly miffed, he added, "But I can not. Besides, I can see that this is an occasion that belongs to the two of you and does not need a third party. So, if you do not mind, for now; I will decline your gracious invitation."

Her father stood and started to object, but Simon casually raised his hand and added, "Ray, please, I am quite sure. Moreover, since a man of my status should not be lurking around restaurants, pestering beautiful young women, I will take my leave while I am still considered a gentleman."

Suddenly Simon's expression changed, and his face became serious, the tease left his voice as he added, "All kidding aside, I do have several legal documents to read over along with a list of things to do before I fly out tomorrow. However, if you will permit, I would like you to entertain this lovely creature lavishly and sign it to my account."

Her father started to protest, but Simon shook his hand stately and announced, "Please Ray, do not deny me this pleasure."

Her father nodded his agreement and Simon continued, "I will inform the propriétaire' on my way out." He reached out and took Raynie's hand between his and gave it a slight shake. Followed by a whisper of a kiss as he whispered, "Take care, lovely lady," and hurried away.

Raynie sat there slightly flustered and didn't know what to say, but her father certainly did. "Ray, what the hell am I going to do with you? What were you thinking? Thattt...that, my dear daughter, is one of the most eligible bachelors in the world. And... and you let him walk away. I mean, what's wrong with you, young lady? Jesus Christ, Ray, I think he's even related to the Queen in some distant way."

Frustrated, her father sat back against his chair before he whined once again, "Jeeesus, Ray, he's related to the Queen. The least you could've done was be nice to him. I mean, couldn't you see that he was captivated by you?"

Raynie crossed her arms and declared, "Daddy, I am not blind, and I am certainly not desperate. So please stop trying to fix me up. I don't do blind dates. Not now! Not ever!"

"But Ray, this was not something I planned. Simon just happened to be in town tonight, so... I asked him to join us and that is all. And once again I ask you, young lady; couldn't you have been just a teeensy bit nicer. Geeez, I think the least you could've done, was remove some of those damned darts your eyes kept shooting his way. I mean, we're lucky he wasn't mortally wounded."

Raynie erupted into laughter. Soon after she began to choke on her words as she stuttered, "Da-daddy, you're exagger...ating. I, I w... was not th...that b-bad." Just as suddenly her expression switched back to a more earnest look. Leaning across the table she took her father's hand. Smiling softly, she attempted to not sound too wily while she professed, "Besides, Daddy, this is our night out and I don't want to share it. You know how much this time we spend together means to me. I certainly don't want to lose or share a single second of it if I don't have to. Especially with someone I don't even know. What's more, I've had an extremely rough day and all I want is a glass of wine, a steak and a few tender words from my daddy." Smiling her biggest, Daddy's little girl grin, she asked sweetly, "That's okay, isn't it? I mean, that I need my Daddy tonight and not some rich debonair playboy?"

"Oh, you little scoundrel... you. You know exactly how to wrap me around that lovely little finger of yours, don't you?" Woefully he asked, "What kind of chance does a father have against that?"

Laughing with pleasure at her triumph, she said, "Sorry Daddy, I'm afraid, I not only look like Mother, but I also think like her. You see, she taught me everything she knows about handling men, and that especially means you."

Faking exasperation, Ray grabbed his chest and pretended he was in a midst of a heart attack. While he sputtered, "Oh...oh Ray I'm afraid this is the end. I always knew you and your mother would be the death of me one day. How could I have let your mother influence you so? Now, what kind of chance do I have against the two of you? Zip, zero, nada, there's no way I can stand up to the both of you and live threw it. Yes, I can see it clearly, I'm in big trouble. I might as well give it up and go meet my maker right now, since I'm a dead man either way." Slowly he mocked a gasp and gulped a last breath while he clutched Raynie's hand tighter and struggled to choke his last request. "But couldn't you have been, just a teeny bit nicer?"

Laughing at his awful performance she bantered, "Daddy that was outrageously dramatic. Something I might expect from Mother; but never from you. From your act, I can only deduce that you watch way too much of that silly soap opera you're hooked on. Now please pour me some wine; I need to get rid of this awful taste in my mouth."

CHAPTER THREE

The following day while Raynie attempted to finish the last of her paperwork, she became startled by the rapid sound of footsteps. They moved briskly across the floor and were headed in the direction of her office. She was surprised because she thought everyone had gone to lunch. Momentarily blinded by the sunlight shining through the window she saw the shadow of someone as they rounded the corner and entered the room. Surprise immediately spread across her face and she leaped out of her chair and disdainfully yelped, "What are you doing here! I mean, I thought you were leaving town?"

"You are absolutely correct, pretty lady. However, since you would not have dinner with me last night, I figured I would try for lunch today."

When she didn't respond Simon nervously added, "Um, here." He shoved a huge bouquet of various colored roses in her direction, "I brought you roses. See, some are yellow roses; I hope you like yellow...roses. But if not, I bought pink, white, and red ones too. Which, do you like best?"

"I like red," she answered without feeling.

He ignored her dispassionate answer and let his smile grow brighter. She noticed today his grin held less arrogance and seemed to lack the confidence it boasted the night before. She studied him as he moved shyly from one foot to the other as he waited for a broader response. After a few seconds, he nervously pointed to the roses in her arms and repeated, "Roses... for you."

By this time, she couldn't stop herself. She tried hard to stay displeased, but she couldn't stop the giggle that escaped her lips. Nor could she fight the enormous laugh that followed. Suddenly she was laughing wholeheartedly while attempting to converse, "Yes, Simon, I can see and thank you for your thoughtfulness. They're really beau...tiful, I adore roses." Just as quickly as it started, her laughter subsided, and she struggled to gain control. She noticed his self-consciousness was clearly evident and it made him look pitiful. He just stood there waiting for her acceptance while wearing a clumsy grin and she began to feel sorry for him. *His discomfort,* she concluded, *is so much more attractive than the arrogant manner he presented last night.* Yet this was something she had not wanted to admit, and the deduction created a strange uneasiness in her. Immediately she moved her attention back to his faults and reevaluated her impression. She decided he looked more like an insecure teenager who was awkwardly facing his first crush than the well-groomed playboy she had met the night before. When this thought hit her, it triggered another bout of laughter and it filled her voice while she attempted to thank him for the flowers. She thought her actions might embarrass him so instantly she felt bad, although once their eyes met, they both started to laugh senselessly. Raynie struggled to control her mirth but in the end, all she did was sputter. "Oh Simon, I'm so sor....ry. Si...Simon, really, I am, but you look sooo...damned comical...standing there."

Relieved, then encouraged, he made his move. "So, you will have lunch with me?"

Still laughing she burst a rapid, "No! No, I won't."

Raynie immediately started to explain again but stopped abruptly; she couldn't understand why she felt so giddy and it slightly embarrassed her. Her laughter dwindled and a soft apologetic smile replaced her silly laugh. For an instant, her expression grew serious and a touch of despair accompanied her answer. "No, Simon. I'm sorry, but I really can't. I have so much to do. And...."

He heard her uncertainty but waited for her to go on. When she didn't, he asked. "And...?"

"And to tell you the real-truth, Simon I'm really not interested in any kind of new relationship. I hope you'll understand. But frankly, I'm not looking for romance. So, if you don't mind, I'd rather not have breakfast; lunch, or dinner with you."

She could see his disappointment, so she went on with her explanation. "I'm sorry Simon; I don't mean to be so blunt. But I feel that truthfulness is always the best way to go. So, again, I'm sorry, but no."

He grinned broadly as he resolved. "Yes, and I agree, and as disappointed as I am, I must say that that is a commendable conviction. A relationship should always begin with truthfulness."

"Simon that's what I'm trying to tell you. We don't and never will have a relationship. Not now, or ever, friendship or otherwise."

"Now, now, Miss Dey, let's not be too impetuous. However, if you would rather wait, saaay, until after I return from my business in England, that will do simply fine. Still and all, for the record, I do intend to see you Raynie. No matter how long it takes me to wear you down." He wavered then added, "If you care to ask your father, I am sure he will attest to the fact, that I rarely fail to get what I want."

Simon reached up and pensively tapped his index finger to his pouted lips. After some thought, he decidedly continued. "Yet, before I do agree to see you or to get too involved, Miss Dey, I believe you must first work on those God-awful manners of yours. I am sure you know about which I speak since you had presented them repeatedly last night." He displayed what he hoped was one of his most attractive smiles, turned, and walked away.

Raynie stood there astounded. Unexpectedly she became angry. She couldn't believe his audacity. "Talk about rude," she mumbled in a stiff undertone, "I've only met the man twice and both times he's left me completely enraged." In a huff, she yelled, **"Who the hell do you think you are anyway?"** She stomped her foot and muttered to herself. "I don't care if you are related to the Queen."

She waited where she stood a second or two longer while she tried to decide whether she should call him back and give him a piece of her mind. But after she rethought that idea, she said, "Maybe he's right. Maybe I am overly blunt. Does honesty count as being rude?" she asked herself. Then thought, *if so, then maybe I did deserve to be put in my place.* Well, if she deserved to be admonished or not, she would have to admit, he certainly did a good job at it. She couldn't think of anything more he could've said that would've made her feel any worse than she did right now. She really should've been more considerate. The least she could have done was to have lunch with him. After all, he did come all this way just to see her. And she was hungry," She sighed before she grumbled. "Maybe he's right, and I'm simply not a very nice person."

Suddenly, her long face changed from its scowl to a tender smile when she noticed the roses he had left in her arms. She sighed again and uttered almost despondently. "Well, maybe if I wasn't in love with Dan, then maybe... Mr. Charles, you'd be exactly what I'd be looking for in a man. Yet maybe not, since you re truly obnoxious and way too cocky for your own good. *However,* she thought, *some women do think that is appealing. His audacious confidence may even appear sexy to some, but that's some women; not me.* She did a about face and headed back to her desk as she unhappily moaned, "But let's face it Simon, you're certainly no Dan."

CHAPTER FOUR

Jackie was meeting Dan and Raynie for dinner that evening, so as soon as she had awakened that morning she headed straight out the door for a day at the spa. In her mind this was a necessity; she had to do everything to help her look as good as her gorgeous daughter. So far today, she had suffered through the tedious task of a manicure, pedicure, and facial. Moreover, now here she was in the midst of enduring this dreadful wrap. She implored as she giggled and felt the full stress of her day, "God, to be young again."

A few years ago, her youth didn't seem to matter so much, but now when it was harder to achieve the look, it seemed so all important. Of course, a few years ago, everyone said she and Raynie looked like sisters, but now staring into the face of a much younger you, certainly did nothing at all for the ego. Not to mention how the mirror image constantly tore down your inner spirit. Particularly when the man you desire and hope to wed one day was much closer in age to your young daughters than your own.

Jackie examined her thoughts for a few seconds and decided she shouldn't worry about it. She certainly didn't need worry wrinkles to add to her insecurities. Besides, even if Raynie wanted her man, it didn't mean she was going to get him. The one thing she is confident about is Dan. She herself, has everything he wants, and that without a doubt, is lots and lots of money. She smiled maliciously, and a giddy laugh escaped when she recited, *Amongst other things.*

She chuckled at her wit and recalled the nights they've spent together. Their liaisons were the most fervent sexual passions she had ever tasted. Unexpectedly she felt her cheeks burn as her desires began to ignite. She twisted in an attempt to change her body to a more comfortable position, and immediately she made an effort to change her recollections to something less arousing.

Yes, there's no doubt, Dan has many desires, but not all are in the bedroom. He has an enormous hunger to be an entity in the Industry. However, for him to achieve this he will need far more than just money. He will also need connections, and who has more connections then her? Surely Dan is aware of her prominence in this sector. As well as being aware of how important these connections are to his future. There is no doubt, in this industry contacts are the name of the game. Therefore, if he wants to play, and she's sure he does, then she is his best bet, not her darling daughter. So, as far as she can see, Raynie doesn't have a chance. "Sorry sweetheart..., but Dan's mine. I guess you'll just have to get out and find your own man," she quipped.

Her last remark brought to mind what Ray, her ex-husband, had mentioned the other day. He said he had tried to fix Raynie up with the distinguished, Mr. Charles, and failed miserably. From what Ray said, Raynie was terribly rude and made it quite clear that she was not interested in dating Mr. Charles or anyone else. This, fact in-itself is no big deal, but since she is convinced that Raynie has an interest in Dan, she couldn't help but wonder what Raynie was up too. Maybe she should have a talk with her. Perhaps it's time they sit down and discuss her future or should she say, lack of future with Dan. Besides, Raynie's not getting any younger and she should be out securing her own man. A wealthy man with whom she could settle down comfortably with. I mean it's nice to have a career, but Raynie better think twice before giving up this chance with Mr.

Charles... he's an extraordinary opportunity, especially with all his incredible wealth and from the pictures in the newspapers and magazines she had seen, he's not bad to look at either.

She herself had never met Simon Charles face to face, but from what she's heard he would be well worth the effort. "Geez," Jackie uttered, "by Raynie's age, I was already married to Ray and six months pregnant." Despite that indisputable fact, she was also well on her way to her first million, and all because she knew when to use her beauty and when to use her head.

Jackie was puzzled by her daughter and her most recent actions. She tried to recall, "what is it that Raynie always says? Oh yes! "I want to be an independent woman and carry my own weight." Well, she will never get rich that way, and she better not waste her youth and beauty on such a ridiculous notion. *Yes, Jackie pondered, I definitely need to talk with our daughter. It's time to nip this ridiculous notion in the bud. It's time Raynie faces the realities of life. The only sure way for any woman to truly be independent is through extreme wealth.*

The attendant interrupted her thoughts with several knocks on the door and when she entered the outside light flooded the area. Jackie stayed motionless and refused to open her eyes. She remained as still as possible and pretended to be asleep. She listened to the sounds the attendant made, and after a minute, she wished the woman would leave. Eventually she heard the door close and she relaxed. Unexpectedly she became aware, then startled, when she felt the towel that covered her face lifted and removed. Immediately it was replaced with the heated weight of another steam-filled wrap. Jackie thought she was alone, and it angered her that this woman hadn't even warned her before she removed the cover. For this reason, when the attendant politely asked if she could bring her anything, Jackie rudely waved her away without wasting a single word on being congenial.

When she heard the door close again, she peeked around the corner of the towel to reassure herself that the woman was truly gone. Once she was satisfied that she was indeed alone, she laid her head back and returned to her self-aggrandizing meditation.

With the concentration of the warmth and the darkness of the room, it wasn't long before she could feel every bone in her body relax, and her mind began to drift swiftly back in time. Her thoughts eventually focused on Ray and their past relationship. However, she hovered in and out of a slumber-like state, and at one point, she startled herself when she uttered a slumberous, "Dear sweet, Ray."

She and Ray had always been close friends, even today after the divorce. But for some reason Raynie still had trouble understanding this relationship. She felt that since they were so devoted to one another that they must still be in love; therefore, they should be together. Raynie had always refused to see the real Ray and Jackie. If she couldn't bring herself to face who they really were, then she'd never be able to understand their marriage. Jackie sighed as she wondered if Raynie ever learned the real truth, would it break her heart. But for her and Ray, their marriage worked perfectly. They had always known exactly what they wanted, and together, as partners, they went after it. Neither one had ever been sorry for the arrangement.

Jackie impulsively opened her eyes and smiled at the memory of their first meeting as she cried, "Dear Lord. I was so young. I was just a baby, barely eighteen."

Ray had been so awkward when they first met, although he was extremely handsome in an unrefined way. Even though, in her opinion, he is much better looking today than he was in his younger years. The hint of gray at his temples has made him look so distinguished, and with the level of confidence he now emits, he is attractive if not alluring. Still and all, as a lover, he had never rated very high. Suddenly she giggled as she spoke softly, "Oh Ray; how shrewd you were, even at such a tender age, but not at all realistic."

At the time of their first meeting, Ray had only recently passed his BAR exams. Tragically, he was nothing more than a new-sprung, wet behind the ears, attorney-at-law, who had outrageous aspirations of managing the big stars of Hollywood. She laughed, "Silly-man; little did he know that you didn't just waltz into town, put an ad in the local trades, and find a client or two."

Lucky for Ray, soon after he arrived in Hollywood, he and Jackie met at a party and his career was soon initiated. Even though she was ten years younger than he, her youth had not been a disadvantage. She had grown up in Beverly Hills among the movie industry's elite, and this, to Ray's advantage, had easily infiltrated him into the business.

She, at barely eighteen, was already well seasoned in the ins and outs of the organization. Since her father was a well-known stunt man, a great deal of her success was attributed to him and his career, particularly after his accident. A stunt he had been performing backfired, literally, and paralyzed him from the waist down. This accident changed her father's career options greatly, not to mention hers. After his accident he turned into one of the top antiques and period car suppliers for the Industry. That's when she was introduced to the real world of Hollywood, along with many of the top movie makers of the world.

Of course, Jackie was always the first to admit; that being beautiful never hurt her success. In truth, at first, that was chiefly why she was continually invited to the best adult parties since the ripe young age of fifteen. By the age of sixteen, she had made the decision that changed her life; she had decided that dating older men were much more advantageous than dating boys her own age. From that day forward, all her energies went solely to a chosen few, many of whom were the powers of the industry. Together they helped set the course of her life. Indeed, by the time she met Ray, she had already filled a little black book with all the most important names in the industry, creating the perfect network for their future. This is what also gave them the power to thrive well beyond their dreams. She; at first, was surprised when Ray immediately recognized her potential.

Matter of fact, he was quite impressed with her and told her so from the start. Although she was still surprised when he happily relinquished his lead and let her direct his professional future. Her heart warmed when she remembered the first time he said, "Fortunately for us babe, these men showed you a lot more than a good time. They also showed you the ropes and how to use your looks and abilities for your own benefit." But if she herself ever had to sum it up, she'd say, *they taught her the value of trust, and how rewarding it could be to keep her mouth shut.*

Before Ray, this *trust* only brought her small compensations, but once she and Ray became partners, these same affiliations bestowed significant favors upon them and continued their generosity throughout their marriage. Today Ray's practice thrives along with their immense prosperity. What's more, never once had Ray ever held her questionable reputation against her.

Jackie groaned as she forced herself to turn over on her stomach, at which time she whispered, "I thank you all for my great *fortune.*"

After a bit, she thoughtfully concluded, "Now I intend to help Dan, the same way I did Ray. Together we will attain his dream to become a super presence in the movie world."

This is where Jackie knew she had Dan over Raynie, or any other young beauty. Simply because, more than anything else they can give him, he wanted success much, much more. Fortunately for her, this takes not only talent, but a lot of money. Of course, which she herself, holds the purse strings to. Much more important, it takes connections, and right now, she and her little black book is his only link to these all-important people. "Yes indeed, I needn't worry, for Dan will most definitely be mine one day."

CHAPTER FIVE

Mike Ryan has been Dan Aleut's friend; since before grade school and he wasn't about to turn his back on him now, even though he was convinced that his friend was on the road to self-destruction. But knowing Dan as he did, Mike knew he wouldn't listen to him or anyone else about this concern. Dan had always been focused on his movie career, so he was not about to change his course of action in any way. This path was chosen years ago, and his goals are all that are important to him. It seems at this point in his life, it no longer mattered who he hurt along the way. As a matter of fact, his new motto is, 'You may have to step on a lot of insignificant people to reach the top, but, one can merely hope to make as few enemies as possible along the way.'

Mike had always understood Dan better than anyone in the world. Yet he still couldn't grasp, nor did he like, his vast hunger for success. He knew it was this drive that was making him crazy, and with this recent course of action, Mike has feared his dream was going to be the end of Dan. Mike uttered to himself in despair, "Completely baffling, is the only way to describe this behavior. It's destructive."

The teapot whistle blew, and this brought Mike out of his reverie. He grabbed the pot and poured the boiling water into his cup. He angrily dunked the tea bag up and down before he finally challenged the empty room, "Dan, lately it's been getting harder and harder to see the soundness in your decisions and even more difficult, to overlook your harsh behavior. So, what am I supposed to do? I can't just sit by and say nothing? I have to speak my mind if you like it or not."

For the past months, Mike has attributed most of Dan's unusual conduct to the fact that he was finally close to achieving his lifelong dream. At last, he's the head of his own production company, but maybe it's this reality that's overwhelming him. Yet, this is what he's always wanted. "Still, I guess the actual achievement can be overwhelming," he muttered to himself.

He recalled when they were kids, they would ride their bikes through the orange groves of Covina to Pasadena, and halfway he and Dan always stopped to lay on the dampness of the tall green grass amongst the orange trees. They'd eat oranges and talked about their futures for hours at a time. Mike's dreams were always changing, but not Dan's; his always stayed the same. In those groves, they mapped out every detail of how Dan would reach his ultimate aspirations.

For Mike, those moments together were his most treasured memories. He had loved to hear Dan talk about becoming a famous movie producer. He painted such a colorful picture that Mike knew he would one day succeed. His stories never varied. They always ended the same, with him, rollin in the big dough. Yes, that's how he always ended his tales of success, *rollin in the big dough*. Nevertheless, at that time they were nothing more than two adolescents with barely a hundred bucks saved between them. Still, Dan was adamant about going to college and studying film making. He had his plans outlined from beginning to end, and if Mike ever questioned him about the much-needed cash his dreams required. Dan always glibly announced, 'I'll just marry some rich bitch.'

But soon after Dan started college, he decided Mike would provide the major portion of their financial livelihood since Mike's aspirations were in no way as high as his. That, Mike couldn't argue, so he reluctantly became the breadwinner for the two. But then, he never imagined what Dan's game plan would one day demand. Sadly, it didn't take too long to learn that in Hollywood, it was not only important but also imperative; to look the role you desired.

For that reason, Mike's position as the breadwinner became all important and he worked vehemently to help achieve Dan's dream. He contributed all he earned to portray Dan as a wealthy young businessman, and undoubtedly from the beginning, it was Mike's money that consequently raised their level of milieu and intensified their game. It was also he who provided the daily expensive necessities it took for Dan to look the part of the wealthy and aspiring young producer. As a result, it was Dan who always wanted more. He continually reminded Mike, 'We both have to do our part. In Hollywood, appearing wealthy is as vital to success as aptitude,' and as far as Dan was concerned, it was Mike's job to portray him as such.

Yes, it was true, money was the key, the only way to unlock the door to Dan's dreams. Yet it was Mike who had contributed the bulk sum of this vital element. Of course, as time went on Dan's success began to take more and more money. More money, than either of them ever dreamed it would. But still Dan demanded, "We stick to the plan." Dan was to portray the sensation, whereas Mike's job was to create and pay for the deceptive illusion. As a result, it was Mike who ended up dating the wealthy old women. When these many trysts were no longer bringing in enough to meet the demands for Dan's charades, he urged Mike to move to more libidinous relationships with much older and far richer men. Dan insisted that such intimacies would pay extremely well especially from men who were married for appearance sake only. Mike had to agree any rendezvous that required such discreteness, would indeed wear a higher price tag and so he moved in that direction. Fortunately for Dan, Mike from the start, was in demand. This enabled them to affordably travel with the people in the fast track of Hollywood, which Dan insisted only increased his odds for success.

For Mike, these relationships were like a living hell, and as time went by, he began to think less and less of himself. He called himself an escort, but he was a prostitute, and he knew it. That *is* until he met Louis Carver. Mike smiled when he thought of Louis's last name. Doctor Carver was a perfectly poetic name for his chosen profession, Plastic Surgery. At any rate unbeknownst to him, this wealthy lover has helped Mike maintain Dan's pretense for the past eight years, all without Mike working the streets. This fact delighted him, as well as restored his self-esteem. He no longer had to deal with ecstatic old men drooling over him, or elderly women crooning and strutting about like some proud peacock, all because they had some handsome young man displayed manfully on their arm.

Mike owed his liberation to Louis and he will forever be grateful. Sadly, for Dan, Louis will also be the man who terminates his cornucopia. He was positive Dan was going to be livid when he found out that Louis wanted their relationship to move forward, and he asked for a life-time commitment. That was last week. Yesterday, Mike accepted his proposal. Thus far, he had avoided telling Dan about his and Louis's plans. But now, there is no more escaping the confrontation. Mike had decided that he would sell this large estate and move into Louis's chateau. These turns of events will not make Dan happy. It will force him to move onward with his plan to get Jackie Dey to marry him. Up to now he's been playing it cool since he felt there was no urgency.

Mike shook his head at the thought of Dan's absurd plan. He felt his scheme was much too selfish, and therefore, dangerous. Marrying Jackie for her money has to be a lot better than his latest proposal. "This strategy of his is inconceivable," he uttered as he looked up towards the heavens; "How can Dan even consider a loan from those goons?" He's not just talking about a few bucks, but a great deal of filthy money. Shaking his head, he asked "Lord Jesus, please, tell me what has happened to his reasoning?" These guys are the most unscrupulous men he had ever met. Foolishly, he made the mistake of relating his feelings to Dan, right after he had brought the men to the house. At one point, he even begged Dan to see that any kind of deal with these guys would be disastrous, not to mention what the association might do to his career. But since his arguments fell upon deaf ears he eventually gave up. Dan refused to recognize the dangers, and the only impact the arguments had, was to make him angry. Now all he could hope for is that he had established some kind of fear in Dan, for caution's sake, if not enough to change his mind. Although knowing Dan, Mike doubted that. As usual he will probably do what's easiest for him. I guess Louis was right when he said, 'It's high time Dan Aleut grows up and faces life on his own. Then and only then, will he become less of a user.'

Dismally Mike realized how true this was and now he knew that Louis understood far more about his and Mike's relationship than he ever let on. Mike sighed and whispered, "Soon Dan will learn that all has changed.

Raynie inhaled the sweet scent of jasmine as she decided the evening was a perfect L.A. night. She was truly thankful that the weather was warm enough so that she could wear her new spaghetti-strapped dress. It was cut to the point of no-no, and she didn't want to coverup its effect with a wrap. She stood on the patio and watched the stars sparkle in the crystal-clear sky. After a minute she realized she was tense and made an effort to relax her shoulders. At last she released a satisfied smile; she was extremely pleased with herself tonight. Everything was good and she felt full of happiness, and she wondered, with all the night's beauty about her, if the universe was made for her alone. Instantly she realized how selfish that thought sounded, but the vastness of the heavens always made her feel so incredibly special. She gasped, "What a silly sentiment." She scrunched her eyes nearly shut as she pretended the stars were dancing across the heavens for her entertainment alone.

Almost at once her face grew more serious, and she glanced at her watch for the umpteenth time. It was close to eight; Dan should be here any minute. This would give them plenty of time to pick her mother up by eight-thirty. God, she wished the evening were over. The reservations weren't until nine-fifteen. That should give them ample time to make it to the restaurant. She would hate to be late and lose their reservation; with Dino's popularity she couldn't guess when the next seating would come available. The thought of waiting and prolonging the evening made her shudder. All she wanted was this to end as early as possible. At this time, Raynie heard a car pull into the driveway, again she glanced down at the elegant wristwatch that encircled her slim wrist. She was sure it was Dan, so she grabbed her wrap and headed for the doorway. The plan was not to give him time to make it to the front door where she would have to invite him in. It is going to be hard enough to spend the evening with him and her mother the way it was but being alone with him could prove to be even more unbearable.

She met Dan at the end of the open porch, and instantly he took her breath away. Luckily, it was dark enough so he couldn't see her face and the flush in her cheeks. It was about this same time a neighbor from two doors down yelled a merciful, "Hello, Raynie." Which distracted Dan long enough for her to make an escape to where Shelia and her dog Shabby stood. Raynie playfully stroked the bushy ball of fur and hoped the distraction would give her enough time to compose herself. After wishing the dog and her master a goodnight, she headed for the car.

By then Dan stood next to the passenger's side with the door wide open and when he started to push the door closed, he whispered, "Damn Raynie, you sure look good. You're as close to breathtaking…," he coughed his discomfort, and Raynie suppressed a smile while she thanked him. Quickly she shifted her body closer to the driver's side, then as quickly moved back to lean against her door, trusting this would block any sexual spark between them.

As soon as Dan entered the Mercedes, he threw the car in gear and started to back up but stopped and turned in her direction. His eyes held desire, and he openly stared in appreciation for a full minute.

Feeling awkward, Raynie dropped her gaze shyly for several seconds while she struggled with her conscience. She looked up and asked, "Shouldn't we be going Dan?", then fell silent again. Eventually, she moved her eyes back to stare out the window and made an extra effort to concentrate on her neighbor who now stood at the end of the driveway waving next to her yapping pup.

After they hit the freeway, it wasn't long before Dan asked, "Are you okay, Raynie, you don't seem to be yourself tonight?"

She threw him a vexed look since she knew damned well that he knew exactly what was wrong with her. He knew she felt bamboozled into this evening's dinner party and for that reason, she wasn't about to give him or her mother the satisfaction of enjoying it.

After a time, Dan broke the silence again when he said, "Raynie, you really do look good tonight. I wish you wouldn't do that; you know it upsets your Mother. Other women and their beauty make her feel less than it should."

She gave him an offended glare, then answered angrily, "Well, I think that's her problem, and you know as well as I, that my mother is beautiful. So, I can't believe for one minute that my dressing down is going to make her look any more beautiful than she already does."

"Dammit, Raynie, you know that's not what I mean. Jackie's clearly going through a rough time right now and you know it, especially since your father left her for a younger woman and all. She feels threatened so easily these days. Your mother's worried that she may have lost her touch. She's afraid that everyone thinks she's getting old, and she's no longer beautiful."

Again, Raynie cast another pissed off glance in his direction and immediately looked back towards the windshield and straight ahead. She didn't know where Dan got his theory, but as far as she knew he was way off base. Her mother always felt self-confident and altogether sexually appetizing. But she said none of this to Dan.

Instead, she fell silent and sulked. In time she asked, "Dan, do you really think I look *that* good?"

His smile was full of relief when he uttered, "Even better."

They both sat quietly the rest of the way. Yet Raynie couldn't help but pretend that it was she and Dan who were out for the evening, and her mother was the third wheel, not her.

When Jackie came out with Dan's arm wrapped possessively around her, she swayed happily and moved even closer. She leaned inward and against him as she held tightly onto his free hand. It was plain to see that she felt good about herself tonight, and Raynie immediately slipped back into second place, which was how she usually felt when Jackie was around. Heartsick she muttered, "I guess she really can't help if she looks completely gorgeous."

The sheen of Jackie's silk dress shimmered with each step she took and the various colors of greens in the design enhanced the greenish gleam in her mother's eyes. The dress fit flawlessly. It seemed to embrace every curve Jackie owned along with adequately displaying a fair amount of her cleavage; she was picture-perfect.

Raynie stepped out of the car and slipped into the back seat and Jackie slid across the front seat close to Dan. Jackie turned, smiled her warmest welcome and blew a kiss in her daughter's direction. Raynie could see her mother's expression was sincere and when she commented, "Darling you look absolutely beautiful tonight," she meant it. But through it all, she could see that Jackie knew she had accomplished exactly what she had set out to do. She would be the center of attention all evening long.

After Raynie received her mother's warm reception, she glanced in the rearview mirror. With the light from the bright moon, she saw the smile in Dan's eyes along with the wink that was meant for her alone. His look made her heart skip a beat, and once again she was happy with herself. She leaned back against the seat for the short drive to the restaurant and her mind soared with happiness. He did feel something for her; she had known he did. He's only hiding it, so not to come between her and Jackie.

Now, for the first time, she was beginning to feel eager to start the evening. For once it was over, she was sure Dan would drop her mother off first, and then drive her home alone. *Maybe by then, I'll have enough courage to tell him how I feel*, she thought.

The Veal Scaloppini was delicious, and the wine was superb, but the company was heartbreaking. Soon after they had arrived at Dino's, Raynie realized that she must have misread Dan and his message, since so far, he only had eyes for Jackie, and more than once, he kidded her about the prospect of becoming her stepfather. Each time this happened, she literally felt her heart break; and crumble into a million pieces. All evening she had been watching the love exude from her mother and the man that she herself desired, and the pain was agonizing.

All through dinner she kept a fixed smile on her lips. Her emotions swung from rages of jealousy to douses of envy. Shortly, her shame for these feelings began to overwhelm her, which in turn rendered a staggering desire to crawl away and hide. She loved Jackie and had no desire to hurt her… yet she also wanted Dan for her own and she had no idea how much longer she would be able to go on pretending she didn't. Moreover, when the maître d approached their table and poured wine in Jackie's glass, he added fuel to the fire with a comment on how delightful Jackie looked tonight. By this time, Raynie was awfully close to tears.

It was just before the flaming dessert arrived that Raynie felt the warmth of a hand positioned itself on the bareness of her back. Startled, she glanced up and gazed directly into the smiling eyes of Simon Charles.

He grinned down at her and pleasantly asked, "Please, I hope you will forgive my intrusion; but I did not want to leave this fine establishment without saying good evening." He smiled and nodded his head toward Dan and her mother and returned his gaze on Raynie. Lustfully he added; "My, my, Miss Dey. I must say, you do look smashing this evening." His eyes lingered on her cleavage, then moved boldly to smile suggestively into her now openly sur-prised eyes.

She felt a sudden rush of her heartbeat and for a brief moment wondered, *What in God's name is going on with me lately? It's like I'm in heat or something.*

She floundered then mumbled a quick, "Hello, ahhh, thank you," then as an afterthought she added, "Mr. Charles".

At this time from the corner of her eye she caught the reaction Simon's presence was having on Dan. She beamed as she reached out and touched Simon's hand and openly flirted with an implied, "I see you are as handsome and dapper as ever, Simon." She pushed her chair back and stood up and took a step forward. She wanted Simon to get the full impact of her radiance. At the same time, she continued with her playful come-on. "Simon, you're not intruding at all. It's always a pleasure to see you," with her gaze, she allotted exactly what his suggestive leer had given her. Their eyes lingered for several seconds before she moved her attention back to Dan and her mother. "Oh...I, I'm sorry. Please, excuse my manners. You, Si-mon, I no doubt, will recall, that I often forget myself, as well as my manners?" Smiling she added, "Mother, let me introduce you to my dear friend, Simon. Mother... this is Simon Charles, and Simon, my mother, Mrs. Jackie Dey." She paused as if she had forgotten Dan's presence then unmindfully clarified. "Oh and, of course, this is a friend of ours...Mr... ah; Mr. Dan Aleut."

Raynie immediately smiled with self-satisfaction when she saw Dan's face twitch uncomfortably. Encouraged, she turned her atten-tion back to Simon and announced buoyantly. "Mr. Simon Charles is from England and a very dear friend of Daddy's." With a wink, she playfully added... "and mine, I dare say."

Simon greeted them with a wry smile, at which time he accepted Jackie's extended hand and with a kiss he acknowledged, "Ray said you and Raynie were spitting images and I indeed will have to agree, you are both lovely, Mrs. Dey." Jackie faked a blush and thanked Simon adequately.

Simon moved his attention to Dan and appraisingly shook his hand while at the same time throwing several dubious glances in Raynie's direction. He wasn't quite sure how to take this person. She was definitely friendlier than the Raynie he'd met on previous occasions, yet this creature, as lovely as she was, was far nicer than the Raynie he'd met prior. But in-spite of her behavior being somewhat odd, it was a welcome change. For an instant he fancied, *Could, this possibly be someone impersonating the real Miss Dey?*

Surprisingly, Raynie's next question was even more paradoxical. "Simon, will you join us? We've already had dinner, but how about a drink or maybe even dessert?" She grinned, and then teased; "unless you have guests. I certainly wouldn't want to be rude by enticing you away from them." She reached up to brush his cheek with her fingertips, and while her tongue caressed her top lip she promptly moved on, "Although this may be far more rewarding."

Simon started to respond though Raynie didn't wait for his reply, she simply continued, "I would love to hear all about your trip. You are going to be in town for a while, aren't you, Simon? Or are you returning right away? I hope not. I've really missed you."

At this time Simon came to grasp the escapade she was feigning, but instead of it chafing him the wrong way, he began to play along. He immediately changed the game to his advantage, and without warning, he moved a step inward and wrapped his arm around her waist, as he pulled her tightly against him. Now she was so close he could feel the warmth of her body. Her soft breathing felt marvelous on his cheek and it immediately gave him a slight tingle, and for an instant, he wondered if this was what heaven felt like. With that thought in mind he moved the game one step further, and he reached over and kissed her lightly on the nap of her neck. He wasn't the least bit surprised when he felt her stiffen and step backward. But he lightly jerked her back and snuggled closer while he laughingly teased. "Raynie, my dear, we must not be vulgar. You really need to slow down. I do understand how you feel. You are as excited to see me, as I am you. But, still my love we must not be crude," He hesitated only a second before he moved on,

"*So...,* for now, I will decline your invitation and I will call you later this evening."

Raynie caught a breath but before she could answer, he continued, "No, no, do not insist. We, my love, will simply have to contain ourselves and wait until later tonight. What time do you think you will be home? Or better yet; why don't I make things less complicated and just meet you at your place... say... about midnight, I have my key?" He smiled as suggestively, as she did earlier; and threw her a melodramatic wink. With a quick pat on her left rear he quipped, "Until then, sweet buns." Instantly he bestowed a hasty nod towards Dan and her mother, and quickly hurried away. The entire time Raynie held her tongue and never uttered the words that she ached to screech. Once again, he turned things around so he had the upper hand, and she could do nothing. She stood there open mouthed and flabbergasted until Simon was well out of sight. Then she sat down as if she were in a stupor. Awkwardly she smiled across the table at the pair of bewildered eyes that openly stared back in amazement.

After a minute, Jackie excitedly leaned across the table and grabbed Raynie's hand and burst, "Oh, Raynie my dear, I had no idea. This is just wonderful. Is this the gentleman your father told me about? Mr. Money-Bags, himself." She giggled, "I heard he was handsome, *but* I had no idea, and how utterly charming... Raynie, I am so happy for you. He is a marvelous catch. I've heard so many impressive details about him, and my God, to think he's not only loaded, he's breath taking as well."

At that instant, Dan jumped in and testily asked, "What the hell is going on here and who in God's name is that jerk anyway? What does it matter if he's loaded or for that matter if he's handsome or not? He's probably married and has a woman in every port. It's plain to see he's a playboy." He took a gulp of his wine and concluded his barrage with a derogatory, "Conceited bastard."

Jackie looked sharply in Dan's direction while she visually winced at his snide remarks. Once she became aware of her reaction, she immediately grew embarrassed. Promptly her humiliation turned to annoyance, and she began to scold Dan for his heedless bad manners. She had hoped this would camouflage her lapse of self-control. "Dan Aleut, I would have hoped that you of all people, would have recognized that Mr. Charles is a gentleman. But sadly, I can see you need tutelage, and in case there happens to be any future meetings, I will advise you that it would be ill fortune for you to make an enemy out of Mr. Charles. You see, he not only has a great deal of money; he also has a great deal of power for which I understand he is not afraid to use. In fact, from what I have heard, many men have been ruined for a lesser remark." She threw him another knifelike glare then moved her attention back to her daughter.

Her voice softened when she spoke briskly, "Oh Raynie, if I remember correctly, he even carries a title." Then quickly she glanced back in Dan's direction and muttered, "*And,* he's in *noooway* near being married." At the end of her reproach, she gave Dan one more abhorrent look before she moved her full attention back on Raynie, as she smiled and asked, "So, tell me Raynie, how long has this been going on? Should I get my hopes up? Is there a wedding in the near future?"

Raynie said nothing at all but smiled profusely across the table at Jackie and the wounded Dan.

Several minutes passed. Then her mother could see that her daughter was going to be closed mouth about the relationship, so she decided to give up for now.

Still stung by Dan's earlier outburst, Jackie turned angrily to face him once again. Dan still wore a strange grimace, but when he realized that Jackie's eyes were upon him, he sheepishly grinned. Soon he recognized her apparent displeasure and immediately recoiled, then glanced to where Raynie sat. His face turned slightly red when he distinguished that she was delighted in his humiliation and that furthered his discomfort. At once, he shifted his vigilance back to face the inflamed eyes of Jackie. He could easily read the extent of her anger. She knew he'd been jealous of Simon's interest in her daughter and was extremely irate.

He searched for something to say but stumbled into complete blankness. His utmost desire was to save the evening from becoming a complete disaster, but all he could come up with was a simple, "I'm sorry. I guess I'm starting to get a little over-protective. I may be taking this potential fatherhood, a bit too serious."

The rest of the evening was spent finishing dessert in an uneasy silence.

At Jackie's insistence, they both dropped Raynie off at her house first. Her mother said it was so Raynie could be there when Simon arrived, but there was an unmistakable implication in the air. Raynie knew Dan was in serious trouble. She felt a little sorry for him, yet she couldn't help but take pleasure in his sudden burst of jealousy. She had a sneaky suspicion that he was deeply perturbed at the prospect of Simon making an appearance at her place. As for herself, she was relieved that neither Dan nor her mother appeared to be suspicious that Simon had no idea where she lived.

Jackie was completely preoccupied with the possibility of a relationship between her daughter and the wealthy Mr. Charles. Although from the back seat, Raynie could see Jackie pause long enough to throw an occasional disgusted look in Dan's dismal direction.

As soon as the car pulled to a stop in front of her house, Raynie jumped out and muttered a hurried and distracted good night. She hoped her rushing eagerly up the stairs as if she couldn't wait to make herself ready for her forthcoming lover would foster Dan's jealousy. All the while Raynie fought the key to unlock her front door, her face held a devious grin. She could feel the first trembles of satisfaction, for the evening was an undeniable success. It was obvious that she had accomplished far more than she expected she would. Maybe soon, her mother and Dan's relationship would be a thing of the past.

CHAPTER SIX

D an and Jackie drove in silence most of the way home. Dan wasn't sure how to break the ice, without further damaging the evening, so he felt it was safer to stay quiet. Nonetheless, he was confident that once they hit the sheets Jackie would be his again, and by morning he should have her eating out of his hands again.

Jackie shifted in her seat and Dan glanced sideways to get a quick glimpse. She seemed to have mellowed out, so unconcernedly he moved his hand over to her side of the car. He hesitated only a second before he laid his hand on her thigh and squeezed. He grinned as he murmured in a lustful undertone. "Hey baby, you sure look good over there... damn, Jackie, all night long you've been driving me crazy with desire." He threw her a look that suggested he was disrobing her where she sat. Then longingly he continued, "You know, you were by far the most enticing woman at Dino's tonight." He exhaled, "I can't say I'm surprised, that usually is the case." He waited a second, before he sucked in an exaggerated breath and very softly murmured, "God, woman; you're so dammed sexy it hurts."

Jackie said nothing, but she did turn slightly and offered him a promising smile. Once he saw her expression, he finally let himself relax. To himself he snickered, "Yes, Babe, just don't fight it; you will never win with me. I have everything you want and we both know that."

When Dan pulled into the driveway of Jackie's estate, the gates opened automatically, and the security lights flooded the area. Immediately Dan contemplated the same thought he had each and every time he entered the property, "I'm really going to love taking this place over."

He had all kinds of plans for the house, as well as the grounds, and once he gave it its face lift, he was sure he would be rewarded with a huge selling price. It was one of the most sought-after property's around.

Dan was quite aware that Jackie loved the large estate. Nonetheless, recently he decided he didn't like the idea of living in Beverly Hills. No matter how exclusive the area was, it wasn't for him. As he saw it, it was where the old regime resided. He *is* the new Hollywood and he wanted to be where the new influence and powers lived. "Maybe we'll do Brentwood," he had told Mike, "or if the mood strikes, Santa Monica. Or better yet, both!"

He maneuvered the Mercedes around to park closer to the curb. He purposely jumped out, and vigorously ran around to the other side of the car. Eagerly he opened Jackie's door so she could feel his body close to hers, and their passions could put this evening behind them. He immediately wrapped his arms around her to shield her from the cool evening air, while at the same time kissed her on the shoulder and neck. He moved to nibble on her ear as they made their way up the wide stairway to the front entrance. The maid immediately opened the door and stepped aside. When they started to enter, Jackie stopped and turned to face Dan and his aggressive advances. Her smile was sensual, and her voice was filled with pleasure, but cool as she politely whispered, "Dan, I want to thank you for a thought-provoking evening. It was stimulating to say the least.

However, I must admit, a bit strenuous, so for now it must come to an end, I need my rest."

She started to close the door when Dan moved one step closer and demanded, "What, come on Jackie... Jackie."

"Sorry; but no, Dan. I have a tournament tomorrow, so I need to be up very early. I'm sure you understand." Without further conversation she quickly placed a kiss on his cheek and abruptly closed the door between them.

Dan stood there with his mouth open, his eyes were wide with surprise. He was brimming with disbelief at her bold rejection. This wasn't how he planned the evening. Jackie's not acting like herself tonight. He pursed his lips and thought, *I usually have her eating out of the palm of my hand and with little effort. What's with her anyway? Damn, she's been acting strange all night.*

Angry, he turned sharply and retreated to the security of his car. He sat there for several minutes going over the evening before he muttered, "I wonder what this means? Our age difference usually keeps her pretty damned insecure and off balance about the relationship. That's why it's so easy for me to stay in control, but for her to be so utterly defiant... Well shit, it's completely unlike her. Hell... now what?"

It was early, and Raynie knocked the lamp off the table when she reached out to stop the scream of the telephone. When she heard the voice on the other end, she was actually surprised. She hadn't expected to hear from her father. She thought he was still out of town. "Daddy? Hello, uh...when did you get back? Is everything okay?"

He answered her questions and completed his good morning ritual all in one breath. Then his tone changed and filled with displeasure. "Ray, what is this I'm hearing from your mother? She is convinced that you are involved with Simon Charles. She even mentioned nuptials. Young lady we both know that's a bunch of hooey... so tell me Ray, what's going on? What kind of game are you playing and how is Simon mixed up in it?"

She bit her lower lip as she tried to wipe the sleep from her eyes. At this same time, she tried to think of a simple response, nothing came. So instead she said, "Daddy, why don't we meet for lunch at Chops this week? At that time, I'll fill you in over a bowl of Mandarin chicken and brown rice." As an afterthought she added, "and hopefully, that will put you in a better mood."

Perturbed, he grumbled angrily, "I doubt it." She heard him lay the phone aside, and a drawer opening. Suddenly he was back with a gruff, "The only day I am not scheduled for a lunch meeting is Thursday. Will that work for you?"

"That'll do fine. Let's say around twelve-thirty?"

"Okay, but I want you to know young lady that I'm not at all fooled by this ploy of yours. I don't know what you're up to, Ray, but I can tell you right now, you're the one who's going to get trounced on. Simon or your mother, are not people to mess with."

Suddenly his voice softened, and she heard his concern when he added, "Listen Ray, I know I've mentioned this to you countless times, but sadly, it looks like I need to remind you again. You should never attempt to take your mother on. I know you don't want to hear any of this, but *I* can tell you right now. If you try, you'll be the one who ends up sorry. You can also trust me when I tell you, it could be one of the biggest mistakes you ever make."

"Daddy don't worry about me, I'm fine. No one's going to hurt me, least of all, Mother."

"Well, try and remember one thing, little girl, it's going to take a powerhouse and a much more experienced woman than you, to beat your mother at her own game. Therefore, take my advice and don't try, you'll never win."

"Daddy, you just don't understand."

"No sweetheart, it's you who refuses to understand. I can guarantee you, you will never run across a stronger opponent than your mother. Therefore, if you keep that thought in mind, it may help deflate some of those angry aggressions you seem to harbor towards her lately."

"Good-bye Daddy, I love you and I'll see you on Thursday."

CHAPTER SEVEN

For Raynie, once again, Thursday turned out to be the day from hell. It started with the first shot that morning and ended with the last wrap-call that night. This of course, included lunch with her father. After which, she wished she would have stayed on the lot and eaten alone at the commissary, especially in view of the attitude her father had developed right after she met him. Sometimes she just didn't get it. Why did he always have to choose Jackie's side? She was certain that she would never understand her parents *or* their absurd relationship. They seem to always stick together, divorced or not? Don't they know that they're not supposed to even like each other? In reality, her mother should be pissed off at her father. Afterall he did leave her for a younger woman. In most marriages that fact would have meant curtains for any other feelings except animosity, so why not theirs? In most of the terminated relationships she knew, that was the case, so again, why not theirs? Why did they have to remain such good friends?

Incensed she mumbled to herself as she shook her golden locks and rolled her eyes in despair, "Dammit, why me? Why can't I have normal parents who hate one another?" She shoved the key in and unlocked the car door and hopped in while she continued her reprehend. "Why Lord, I ask you, why me?" Full of discontentment she stomped on the gas pedal and headed for home. She drove mindlessly through the heavy traffic while she worked on shaking her feelings of malcontent. Her state of mind took root right after her father's lecture and continued to fester throughout the day. Now, after all her dismemberment of what he called, *'his well-grounded accusations'*. She still concluded that he just didn't understand. Silently she argued, *This, isn't a childlike battle of wills between Mother and me, it's much, much more. I'm not acting like a spoiled brat either. That isn't it at all. Daddy, you simply can't see the whole picture. That's only because you never see a thing wrong with anything Jackie does.* "Daddy, why can't you see Mother through my eyes?"

Her thoughts flooded her mind. All those years, every boyfriend she ever had, had a crush on her mother. When they broke up, it wasn't her they asked to stay friends with, but always her mother. Now here she is, my mother, dating the one man I love. She stepped further down on the gas pedal and demanded openly, "Why does Jackie always get to win? Why can't it be me who wins? Why can't I end up with the prize? Why Daddy, why can't it be me? I love Dan!"

Of course, none of these assertions were answered since she didn't tell her father any of them, but in a way, she sensed that he already knew some of her true feelings. She could read it in his eyes, not to mention everything he said today. Yes, there was little doubt that he had at least guessed that she was infatuated with Dan. Yet, still, he was on Jackie's side. "Shoot, it doesn't seem like my feelings count a hoot," she muttered out loud.

This wasn't anything new *or* even a surprise for Raynie. Although at times, she still couldn't believe how closed minded her father was about her mother. He repeatedly refused to hear anybody's side of the story, only Jackie's, and today wasn't any different. He certainly didn't waste a single minute on showing her a teeny bit of sympathy.

Suddenly, she was jolted out of her melancholy trance when she realized where she was. She jerked the wheel and threw the BMW across three lanes of traffic: barely making the exit off the freeway. Unfortunately, it was too late to see the officer who sat astride his motorcycle under the overpass. He was blatantly holding his radar-gun straight at her. "Damn," she muttered, "I swear he's smiling. What an end to a perfect day in hell?"

Once she pulled into the driveway that led to her Topanga Canyon home, she began to feel a lot better. Her father had bought the house for her twenty-first birthday, and for some reason, she always felt safe and secure here. She turned the motor off and leaned back with a sigh of relief, then she remembered, *happy hour.* "Oh Damn, I'm supposed to meet Marsh at Rusty Pelican, Dammit." But after a minute she decided with this shitty day, and now the ticket.... she would skip the get together even though she *was* beginning to feel better. This, she was sure, was only because she was home, but still she felt *far* from being in any kind of party mood.

That evening while watching a rerun of Three's Company, Raynie ate a tuna sandwich on whole-wheat toast while sipping a cup of tomato bisque. After she put the dishes in the dishwasher, she moved around the house mindlessly. She was really feeling antsy and needed something to busy herself with to help relieve her boredom. But what? She looked around the living room, yet nothing seemed to catch her interest, so she gave up the pursuit and poured herself a glass of wine. She hoped the alcohol would ease some of her restlessness, and she took a large gulp, and plunked herself into an easy chair. Soon she realized it was hopeless; no matter how hard she tried; she couldn't relax. She searched through several drawers looking for a magazine and then remembered a new one came in the mail that day. She glanced around while she tried to picture where she had laid it. Finally, she found the new edition of MADEMOISELLE under a pile of credit card bills that were spread across the living room bureau. After snatching it up she swiftly read over each page barely showing an interest in any of the articles. Everything seemed to be about love or troubled relationships. Eventually she found something intriguing on sexual harassment in the workplace. She wondered if that could pertain to the industry's environment. But it really didn't matter since she soon became bored with the article's content. Spitefully she muttered, "It's always the same old story, with the same old ending." She tossed the magazine to the floor, and at once, picked it up and laid it neatly on the coffee table.

Restlessly she began walking back and forth across the living room floor. Yet this still didn't satisfy her need to burn off the excess energy. She felt a need for movement and considered a quick jog. She peeked out the window and decided against it since it was pitch dark outside. Instead she flopped herself down on the floor and did thirty push-ups. That didn't help either, so she grabbed the latest copy of Variety and shuffled through several pages before she stopped abruptly. She gawked in amazement at the large print that stared back at her. The ad really knocked her for a loop. She had no idea that he was that far along on his project. But here it was in black and white, Dan's announcement to the world, that he started his company's first production. The ad also read that he still needed to fill several key positions. Maybe she should talk to him about joining his crew. It would be great to work with him. She had no doubt that he'd jump at the chance to hire her. He knew she was one of the best Production Managers in the business. Her heart fluttered with hope then instantly changed back to dread. *Nope,* she thought, *there's not a chance in hell I'll ever get to work with Dan.* Yes, she gave her word when she promised her father that she'd ease up and leave her Mother and Dan alone. The best thing would be to stir clear of any unnecessary contact.

She stood there staring at the ad for several more minutes before angrily slinging the paper across the room. It knocked the little night lamp to the floor as it flew by and she groaned, "Dammit, not again." Disheartened, she sank downward and threw her body against the back cushion of the couch as she moaned once more, "Dammit."

Just then, a hollow knock echoed throughout the room, and in walked Shannon Hicks. She grinned at Raynie foolishly as she let the screen door slam hard against the jamb. She looked around as if she expected to find someone in the room besides Raynie as she asked, "Hi, ah, are you alone? I thought I heard ya talkin to someone?"

"Yes; I'm alone, I'm always alone."

"What's da matter?"

"Nothing's the matter."

"Reeaaally...Weeelll from where I stand girly, it don't look like it ta me."

This time Raynie didn't answer Shannon, instead her face puckered, and she wrapped her arms around herself protectively.

Shannon took another step forward and flounced her finger up and down. "Come on Raynie, knock that shit off and don't you start playin games with me either. You've been actin like this for months now and it don't look like it's gettin any better, so what gives girl? Come on, you might as well talk ta me, girly."

"I don't know maybe it's because it's a full moon," spouted Raynie. "Who can guess? Why are you here anyway? Why aren't you out on a date or something? Don't you have your own fucken life to live?"

"Whewweee, toucheee. Well, I guess you could say; I'm home for the same reason you are, you know, full moon and all. But, for curiosity sake, only, why do you movie people always have ta go around cussin all the time? Anyway, I asked you first, so what's the matter, Raynie?"

"Okay, Shannon, which question do you want me to answer first?"

"You choose."

"Well first off, I don't know why, but cussing is part of the job. If you think we're bad, you should hear some of the rock groups. Wow-weeee, now their talk would curl your pantyhose girlfriend. As far as my problems go, I would much rather hear about your enigma than mine. I mean really, why are you here, Shannon? You're always out on a date or running off to catch a plane for some mini vacation. So, why are you here harassing me?" As an after-thought, she laughingly added, "You little Jezebel, you."

Shannon couldn't help but to join in on Raynie's laughter. Soon Raynie stopped and softly inquired, "Why do you go out so much, Shannon? Don't you *ever* grow tired of it? I mean, a different man every night."

"Ohhh come on girl. It's not really a different man every night and you know it, and yes, I do get tired of it...sometimes. But I only got four more years left before I get married, so I wanta pack in as much fun as I can." Rolling her eyes back in her head she added, "Before that blissful day comes."

"Shannon, you're always saying that. How do you know when you'll meet the right guy and get married? Are you physic or some-thing?"

"Well, if you get comfy girlfriend, I'll tell you a story about this little black jezebel."

"Shannon you're not really, and I know that."

"I know you were just kiddin, Raynie. But just for the record, I'm probably the only twenty-four-year-old virgin, left in captivity..., Let alone L.A."

Raynie almost snapped her neck when she looked up. Her eyes grew wide with astonishment and she questioned sharply, "WHAT? NO! NO WAY." She gasped and inhaled a large gulp of air, before she continued, "Ya gotta be kiddin, right?"

"Nope, that's me, I hold the title, Miss Black is Beautiful and I'm still a virgin. And that's with a capital *V*."

"But all your dates, I mean." Dumbfounded, Raynie threw her arms up in the air and said, "I don't know, I don't know what the hell I mean."

"I understand. It does sound unbelievable. *But* everyone I date is just a friend, strictly platonic."

"Strictly...platonic? Wow! Shannon, how do you manage that? I mean, you know how guys are?"

"Raynie, it's easy; really. Men are great and a lot more under-standing than you'd think."

Seeing the disbelief in her friends' eyes, Shannon pushed on, "Really, they are, Raynie." Laughing she rendered precisely, "Especially when they hear my story...."

"Story?" questioned Raynie.

"Ya, the story about what's in my Paternal-forebear's will."

Raynie looked confused and asked suspiciously, "Your grandparent's will? Why, what's in it? And *pleaseee* tell me how it would affect your dates?"

"Well, I know you're aware that I'm gettin a pittance of an allowance which keeps me in food and water, plus an occasional trip to Nordstrom's."

Raynie cut in before Shannon could continue, "Well ya, but I'd have to say, it's a far cry from a pittance. I wish someone would bestow that much generosity on me."

"Well, mine has strings attached, girly."

Raynie waited, and when Shannon didn't move on, she shouted, **"SO! Come on, whatcha waitin for, tell me... what strings?"**

Without deliberation, Shannon revealed, "I have to be married by age twenty-eight *a n d* a complete virgin."

Raynie repeated Shannon's words questioningly, "A *complete* virgin?"

"Yeah; no sexual experience, what...so...ever. Nodda, nothing at all. No sex. No foreplay. No nothing. Where one is easy enough to prove, the other is next to impossible."

"Your parents did this to you?"

"Nope, only my Granddaddy. Furthermore, there's no mixed marriage either. He has to be as black as a moonless night. If I comply with all that is written, I get millions when I turn twenty-nine, but, only if I'm married, of course. If not, all the money goes to charities. Granddaddy specified several in his will. I've come to the conclusion that he had his doubts of my perseverance."

"Dear Lord, how awful for you, Shannon."

"No Raynie, not really. At first it bothered me...but now I rather like it. I guess you could say, I sorta bought into the idea. I mean, I have gobs of great guy friends. Plus, I never have ta worry about takin those god-awful birth-control-pills, that you're always tryin to remember to take. What's even better, I've never had ta run around town in the middle of a Sunday night, looking for an open drug store because I forgot to fill my prescription."

"That only happened once, and only because I was going out of town and you know it."

"Ya I know, Raynie. Well enough about me. What's up with you? What's your big problem, girl? Why the long face?"

Raynie took a deep breath and held it as long as possible before she exhaled the air just as slow. Getting up from where she sat, she walked over and poured a glass of wine for Shannon and another for herself. After she handed Shannon the beverage, she sat down and swallowed a large mouthful before she conceded, "Okay. Okay, since you spilled your guts, I guess the least I can do, is reciprocate."

Shannon pushed herself back and deep between the cushions of the davenport. At the same time, she hungrily rubbed her hands together and eagerly expressed her anticipation, "Okay, go ahead I'm ready...shoot."

Laughing at her emphatic eagerness, Raynie vacillated only momentarily before she sighed, then confessed, "Oh, dammit, Shannon, I'm in love."

Raynie waited to hear her response, but all that came was, "Ooohhh."

After a long silence Raynie shouted, **"Is that all I get, oohhh! What do ya mean by, oohhh?** Shannon, Jesus Christ, I just announced that I'm in love, and all you say is, oohhh?"

"I'm sorry, Raynie, I guess I was just so surprised by the news...I mean I didn't even know you were seeing anybody."

Raynie picked up another magazine and also threw it across the living room while she muttered a harsh, "Dammit, that's the damn problem, I'm not. It's all one sided."

Immediately Shannon's expressions alternated strangely between skepticism and surprise, then quickly moved to utter bewilderment. Meanwhile, Raynie tried to construe what her friend was thinking behind the many faces. Nonetheless, she gave up when

Shannon's expression finally stopped wide-eyed... then quickly moved to a graceless wide-open mouth look. Finally, Shannon moaned her dreadful fears, "Oohhh my God, nooo, Raynieee.... You're not involved with a married man, are you?"

Before Raynie could deny the accusation, Shannon jumped up and started to pace back and forth as she went on with her mournful cry. "Oh Raynie, Raynie, Raynie, what are we going to do, girl? You're surely gonna get hurt messin with a married man. How could you let yourself get involved in somethin like that?"

"Shannon! Shannon.... no.... No, I'm not seeing a married man. Or should I say he's not married yet, but he will be soon enough."

Suddenly Shannon's stressful look relaxed, and she spouted, "Well, then that ain't as bad, Raynie. You could still have a chance."

"I don't think so. You see, he's in love with the woman he's going to marry. He's not even interested in me." Raynie stopped after she heard the end of her statement and realized how ridiculous the words sounded. All of a sudden, she put her face in her hands and begged, "Ooh, Shannon, help me."

Shannon walked over to comfort her friend. After she sat and wrapped her arms around her shoulders, she rocked her back and forth. After a time, she whispered, "Who?"

Raynie pulled her head upright and faced Shannon's concern and mumbled, "Dan, it's Dan."

Again, you could see Shannon's mind working away, trying to put a face with the name and not having much luck with her effort. At that instant, her expression changed, and her eyes grew round and even bigger than before. They were so wide that for a second Raynie feared they were going to bulge out of their sockets. Then suddenly, Shannon sucked in a deep ragged scream and burst forth, **"you don't mean your *Mamma's Dan*... do ya; Raynie?"**

Raynie didn't have to say a word because Shannon could see the answer on her face. Quickly, Shannon stood up and started to pace the floor again. Nervously she pushed the hair off her forehead and muttered to herself. "This can't be so. That's far too crazy. Things like this don't happen in real life."

She stopped abruptly and turned back to face Raynie again and begged, "Please tell me no, Raynie? Please, please tell me I'm wrong; it's not your Mamma's Dan. Tell me I'm crazy wrong."

Raynie closed her eyes and sadly nodded her head yes. With her confirmation, Shannon fell back against the cushions of the couch and whispered, "Oh lordy sweeeetjeezzzzzus." Silence enveloped the room. Both girls stared blankly into each other's disconcerted eyes. Until Shannon finally broke the silence with one more astonished, "Jeezzzzzzus, girl."

CHAPTER EIGHT

It had been a week, and Dan was still steaming inside. He couldn't believe the audacity of Jackie and her newfound courage. What was she thinking dismissing him like that the other night? Ever since that evening, she's been nothing but cool towards him. "Damn," he muttered, "We haven't even slept together in a week."

Raynie was the Goddamn problem. Why couldn't she just leave him alone? Right now, he needed to concentrate on Jackie. He had to get her to marry him and soon, or he was going to have even bigger problems than he does right now. Shit, it seemed things were coming apart at the seams. For the hundredth time today he begged, "Damn, what am I going to do?"

Dan was sure that if Raynie didn't stop coming on to him that Jackie was certainly going to stay angry. This, of course, would hinder his window of opportunity for a marriage proposal. He needed to at least secure a *yes* before he could push for a date. Shit, why was Jackie blaming him and not Raynie for her blatant misbehavior? Besides, what did she expect? Couldn't she see what her daughter looked like? What guy wouldn't be attracted to her? Belligerently, he complained out loud, "I'd have to be dead not to feel something for her. She's damned hot." Without a doubt Raynie *was* sexier than any girl he's ever had. But none of that mattered. At the moment, he needed to concentrate on her mother, especially if Mike's serious and he really means to follow through with his threat to move out.

Dan still couldn't fully comprehend everything Mike had said last night since he had several vodkas before they met for dinner. The vodka was what made Mike angry in the first place. After Mike reprimanded him for what he called, '*despicable behavior,*' he ended the altercation with reiterating his and Louis's full intentions of selling the house as well as them moving in together. He still didn't believe him. Mike wouldn't just walk out on him. He's always been there for him, and now when he needed him most, he was sure he wouldn't abandon him, not now. It's a threat that's all, just a threat. "This has to be that faggot jerk's idea, Doctor, Louis Carver. What an asshole. I hate the rich bastard," he spurted.

Dan despised Louis and had always thought of him as a thorn in his side. He realized long ago that Louis was clearly a threat to his ultimate plans. He knew many times Louis openly undermined him and tried to turn Mike against him. He had said as much to Mike countless times, though Mike has continued to deny the accusation. But no matter what he said, Dan was sure he knew better. For he once overheard Louis tell Mike, 'Dan is nothing more than a user. Your loyalty and friendship are wasted on someone like him.'

Well, Carver wouldn't have had to put up with his and Mike's friendship if he had simply loaned him the three million dollars that he'd asked for a couple of years ago. It was common knowledge that Louis was loaded. A few million wouldn't have put him out in any way at all. Besides, it was only going to be a short-term loan, but the damned asshole refused to cooperate. He simply said, "No, not interested, Mr. Production-man."

This comment, along with his refusal of the loan, really burned Dan. If Louis had loaned him the money, his Production Company would have been well on its way to success. Right now, he'd be a wealthy man and out of their lives for good. Instead, here he is spending all his time trying to hitch some rich bitch with an attitude. Worse yet, recently he had been forced to turn to dirty money for his first production. "Shit," he cried, "shit."

Even though he'd been warned about these guys that held the cash he needed, he went ahead with the deal anyway. Still, he was somewhat surprised when they turned out to be the most corrupt men he'd ever dealt with, and their interest on the loan was ridiculously outrageous. This fact frightened him, but he wasn't going to admit it to Mike since he had been against the loan from the get-go.

Dan shuddered at the thought of, Visente and Paulo. But, as far as he could see, he had no other choice. It was either them or no movie. He unfortunately miscalculated his financial needs, and the first loan which was supposed to last until he got Jackie to the altar; was running short. Right now, it looked like he might be able to hold out for about six months if he pushed it. But, with Mike's recent bombshell, he wasn't sure. Angry, he pushed the books aside. He was sick of looking at numbers that didn't match. How could Mike put him in this situation? He knew they were almost there. Their dreams were finally close to a reality and here he is threatening to take his money and leave, not to mention selling the house.

Dan rubbed his hand through his thick hair then gave it a jerk. The pain felt better than the constant worry and it helped distract him for a few seconds. "What's it going to look like," he asked himself? "What will people think? What can I tell them?"

Dan still couldn't believe that Louis convinced Mike to sell the house. Where the hell did, they expect him to go? How did Mike expect him to explain the sudden sale of the house to the nosy motion picture clique? If he isn't married to Jackie before it sells, it'll be all over town that Dan Aleut needed money. Hollywood gossip had always been one of Dan's biggest fears. Since most people believed the house belonged to him, he was sure the meddlers would perceive the sale as a cash flow problem and rumors would fly. Mike should realize the importance of him presenting a solid front, it's a must in order to stay on top. "Why can't he at least wait until

I marry Jackie? Why would he leave me in the lurch like this? It has to be Carver's idea," he grumbled.

Jackie sat sipping a red wine while she waited for her lunch partner to show. He had called minutes before she left the house to say he'd be late, something to do with some union problem. She leaned back contented and watched the golfers move from one hole to the other in their small electric cars. She couldn't understand why they didn't walk the course if the game was supposed to be exercise, like most all claimed. She glanced at her watch. She was already hungry and wished Art would get here.

Men, why can't they ever be on time, she wondered. Dan was always running late too; I just don't get it. She smiled when she thought of Dan. She was really taking pleasure from the little game she had been playing. It made her feel good to watch him squirm. It helped rebuild some of her destroyed confidence. "For which he himself marred, in the first place," she chided. It was purely delicious to watch him lose some of that enormous ego of his, which also helped to compensate a little for the embarrassment he caused her at Dino's the other night. His anxiety has been apparent and this, she decided, was remarkably rewarding. The last time she refused his overtures the panic on his face was simply delightful. That's when she decided to prolong the game. Once she decided not to change her tactics, since the state of frenzy he's been in was so enjoyable, it gave her the feeling of being in control. Something she had feared she lost when it came to Dan.

Besides, Dan is going to have to learn that Raynie is off limits. No matter how much she throws herself at him, he must stop thinking of her as a woman and remember that she is a mere child.

Jackie swirled the Merlot in her glass and watched the intoxicating beverage as it circulated down the sides to the center of the glass. Meditatively she took a leisurely sip, then considered her options. Optimistically, this new film endeavor will keep Dan more actively involved than the last, *which* hopefully will fatigue him enough to at least curb his unquenchable appetite for fresh flesh. At least until she can secure a marriage proposal. "Now, if I could only find something to distract Raynie's interest in Dan."

Jackie had thought Simon was the answer, but after seeing Ray's expression when she inquired about him, she no longer believed that. Her mind lingered on the conversation she had with Ray. It was over a scrumptious lunch at the Palm. Suddenly she felt her stomach growl at the thought of food, and for a minute, she forgot about her problems and began to think about her hunger. She smelled the fresh baked aroma from the crisp rolls the kitchen was baking, and her mind bought the distinct taste of the Cobb salad she had eaten at the Palm. "Oh, how I wish I had a few bites of both this very minute," she chortled.

Jackie pushed herself upward to sit taller in her chair and rearranged her short skirt to her advantage. Moreover, she attempted to get her mind off the grumbles in her stomach and back on the conversation she had with Ray.

Ray had assured her that Raynie gave him her word. He said she promised she'd behave herself and back off on the flirtations with Dan. 'Maybe this will help refocus Dan's sexual attention back to me,' she thought. Yet, it really didn't matter whether Dan could keep his attraction in check or not, because Raynie gave her word, and that, Jackie could count on. Still, in all, it might be wiser if she pushed for a marriage proposal sooner than later. "But," she sighed and then thought, 'for now, at least I can relax and stop feeling inauspicious towards Raynie.'

Yes, her daughter's been a little scamp lately, but once Dan is legally hers.... Well, at least then he will be easier to control.

Jackie's new conviction came chiefly from her new suspicion that Dan needed her far more then she first suspected. His financial shortcomings were frightful and utterly inferior to hers. This fact alone should keep him in check. Although since she was not fully informed in all aspect of his monetary circumstances, it would be smarter to keep an extra tight rein on her purse strings. By doing this she should be able to guide him in the direction she has decided is best for him to pursue. Suddenly delighted with herself and her intuitiveness she deemed, "Everything is under control or should I say, everything's under my control, just as it should be."

Her exultation shot to its peak, then as abruptly, it began to fade. When her mind gave birth to one last troublesome thought, *his independence*, losing it is going to be extremely difficult for Dan to swallow. But unfortunately, there is no way around it. He will simply have to relinquish it along with that silly little Production Company he's so proud of. This is the only way for her to make him the celebrated Oscar-winning producer, he says he hungers for.

All of a sudden Jackie's seriousness dissipated and again she brightened. Art had arrived. He was approaching the host who stood at attention in the entranceway. She could see the warm friendly welcome that the attendant bestowed upon him. Art's presence always dominated any room. He was well known in the industry as well as publicly. It seemed no matter where he went, he received a fair amount of respect.

Jackie watched as Art made his way across the room. He stopped several times to chat with people before he advanced directly towards her. As he drew closer, she thought, H*e is as handsome as the day I entered his name in my little black book. God, that's been well over thirty years.*

When she first met Art, he was just starting out in the industry, and not at all like the lucrative men she usually associated with, but she knew he would be a great success one day. She giggled, "Especially with his powerful negotiating skills, which he used to get her to accept his initial invitation." She had made an exception to her rule that she only accepted invitations from prosperous men, but she had been right to gamble on Art. Today Art Sheltzburg's name was so well intertwined with every studio, in and out of Hollywood, that it was hard to distinguish where they ended, and where he began. All because of his inter-mediator expertise, which she fully intended to utilize for Dan's future advancement.

Art's smile beamed as he sauntered up to their table. He bent down to kiss her on both cheeks before he placed one softly on her lips. When he stood straight to face her, he whispered, "Jackie you are forever beautiful, and you still make my heart standstill..."

"Good evening Cinderella! Your prince charming has arrived to carry you away."

Surprised, Raynie glanced up. He suddenly became sorry he entered unannounced when he noted how much his sudden appearance had startled her. But he dismissed the feeling as soon as her face changed to displeasure. She grimaced as she demanded, "Simon, how in God's name do you continue to get on this lot without me being called first? You simply have no idea whether I'm available, or not."

He put his hand to his chin and scratched it while he thought about her question, then answered, "I can only guess, you know? But again, it may be my charm." When he saw her expression, he shook his head and said, "Nope, not that. Okay. Then maybe it's my name or that I know a few studio people in high places? *Or*" he laughed, "maybe it's the fact that I own a petty bit of stock."

Raynie frowned, "Then why aren't you with your cronies tormenting them with your stock options, instead of pestering me while I'm trying to do my humble little job?"

Smiling he faked an ill-fated look and said, "I knew that I was right. That Raynie, I met at the restaurant last month had to have been an impostor. Yes, she was much, much too nice to be the *real,* Raynie Dey. Indeed, there is no doubt, this one is far more like the ill-mannered young lady that I have become smitten with."

Raynie gave him a look that said, *get lost buddy*, while asking, "What do you want Simon? Why are you here?"

"I am here to take you to dinner."

"Sorry, not interested." She immediately turned her attention back to the worksheet she'd been tackling when he had first entered the room.

"Sorry? No. Sorry is not an option. Sorry will not cut it young lady. You do not have a choice, you owe me."

Glancing up, she gave him a questioning glare, "Okay, I'll bite. How do you figure I owe you?"

"Well..., last time I saw you, you asked me if I wanted to stay for dessert. And... if you remember, I was polite enough to beg off," Smirking at his own observation he continued, "since three *was* obviously already a crowd. However, I did play along with your dirty little prank. For what reason one could only speculate. But still in all, you do owe me a dessert. Furthermore, since we are on the subject, I would have hoped that you had better taste."

Miffed she cut in, "My taste, good or bad, is none of your damned business, Simon. And as far as going along with the ruse, you most certainly did. Didn't you? As well, I might add, turning the so-called ploy, into your seedy opportunity. I still can't believe that you took advantage of me and the situation like that. What kind of a person are you anyway? Don't you have any moral virtue, taking advantage of a poor innocent girl like that?"

Simon raised an eyebrow as he asked dubiously, "Innocent? So, is that what innocence looks like, nowadays? As for your query on my moral strengths, in all honesty, I would have to admit that the question has come up periodically and incredibly the answer is always the same."

"And pray tell, Simon, just what might that answer be?" she inquired sharply.

"Alright, if I must respond, I concede that unfortunately at times my moral strengths do waver. Admittedly, there are times it is stronger than others, and I confess on the evening you speak of, it was running a bit on the puny side. However, at this very moment, I fear that it must be in a very hearty state; since I feel inclined to caution you."

He coughed nervously then continued, "Raynie, I am a man who knows exactly what he wants... and usually gets it. So, darling Raynie, be forewarned. You... fighting me is only going to postpone your destiny."

Immediately after he completed his declaration, he realized that he might have gone a tad too far, since Raynie was looking at him as if she were about to throw something at him. So, he hurriedly added, "Since, I am afraid, I may have gone a little too far... I better clarify my statement. Sometimes, that is not the case.... I do not *always* get everything I want, only most of the time, but not always."

Raynie dusted off her hands like she just threw someone out of her office and answered, "Well, Simon, it looks like you just ran across one of those times."

Visibly, his confidence wavered, and his boyish charm began to dwindle. Soon it was replaced by the same forsaken look he wore the last time he came to visit her when he brought her flowers. Solemnly he implored, "Come on, Raynie, please? Please, go out with me?"

Raynie gave him a stern stare but said nothing. She could see he wasn't used to being in a situation where he was not in command, and she was enjoying his discomfort.

He waited, then realized that she was not going to give in to his boyish charms, so he quickly moved on to what he hoped was his big guns. "Now, Raynie, you and I both know I am not going to give up. So why not merely give in and have dinner with me once? I can assure you it will not be as painful as you think. I give you my word, I will be a complete gentleman. And if that is not enough to sway you, instead of calling it a date you can label it as, insurance."

"Insurance? Insurance, for what?"

"Protection that no one, say like Daddy, will ever find out about our little secret."

Raynie looked confused so he teasingly went on. "You know Raynie, how you used me to make a certain someone jealous."

She couldn't believe his gall, and, in a huff, she stammered. "No, you...you wouldn't, you wouldn't dare! Why, that's out and out blackmail."

"Let us not find out what I will or will not do. And as for blackmail..., well, if you do not know by now, you should be informed, a desperate man can never be trusted." He hesitated before he asked earnestly, "Raynie, please, can we be friends? Please, say you will have dinner with me. Then afterwards if you insist, I'll go away forever... maybe."

Raynie studied him for several minutes before a grin finally covered her face. Hurriedly she growled her answer, "Okay, you win, and I'm hungry, so why not make you pay?"

Chuckling with relief that he had not gone too far, he whispered, "Wonderful, that *is* absolutely wonderful! Any place you choose is fine; the more expensive the better."

Raynie snatched her jacket off the back of her chair, smiled warmly and added, "I assure you, expensive will be my primary preference. Come on, Simon. Let's get this over with."

When they reached the sidewalk, Simon took Raynie's arm and guided her happily to where his car was parked. When he stopped to open the door for her, she gasped as she exclaimed, "Simon, I had no idea. This is beautiful!"

Beaming with pleasure, he hurried over to his side of the bright red Lamborghini. After he was seated comfortably on the driver's side he asked, "Do you really like her? She's not too splashy, is she?"

"Oh, no, she's perfect. I was just surprised. I mean, I thought you'd be driving a rental car. Or maybe you would even have a chauffeur driven limo, but in no way this..."

Simon smiled with pride as he watched Raynie reach out and touch the dashboard. Afterward, she turned to face him and asked, "Does it belong to a friend? I mean, since you live in England, I wouldn't think you'd have a car like this sitting around for your occasional visits?"

"Well, Miss Dey, you are wrong on both accounts. For one, I have several cars here in the States as well as in England. Plus, I also have a bona fide residence at both points. I dislike living in hotels no matter how luxurious. I prefer my own habitat with my own things. You know like, Home Sweet Home and all. Most of my travels are from England to Los Angeles then back again, that *tour de force* has been easy enough to maintain."

Suddenly, Simon fell silent, he reached into the back seat and when his hand came up it held a magnificent long stem red rose. He smiled proudly as he handed it to the once again surprised, Raynie.

"Do you always carry roses in your back seat?" she asked.

"No, my sweet lady. That was bought with you entirely in mind."

"Simon, how did you know I would say, *yes?*"

"I told you that I would not have taken *no* for an answer. If I had to, I would have followed you around like an abandoned puppy until you finally agreed to spend the evening with me."

Raynie laughed at his confession. Unexpectedly, she realized that she was starting to like his unrestrained confidence more than she wanted to. Casually she watched his profile as Simon put the car in gear and pulled forward. Maybe she was wrong to have called his manners impertinent. Maybe it was only plain ole tenacity that he exhibited. "Well, whatever it is," she said to herself, "it is nice to be with someone who is so openly honest."

As soon as they entered the restaurant that Raynie let him choose, she became instantly unequivocally impressed. She had lived in this area her whole life and never knew this place existed.

The structure was small; but larger than it appeared from the outside. She figured it probably wouldn't seat more than fifteen couples at any one time, but the room itself was arranged so it gave you a feeling of spaciousness. It glowed with warmth and friendliness, and in the center of the room sat an angelic woman with hair that flowed to her waist. Her dress was layers of soft ivory colored silks that shimmered with each movement of her arm. The harp she strummed was the most impressive Raynie had ever seen and her harmony was as euphonic and romantic as the restaurant itself.

No sooner did the door close behind them, when a refined middle-aged woman, who stood behind a podium across the room, looked up and blurted out, "Oh dear, it's Simon." With no apology or excuse she immediately left the customer she was assisting and hurried over to where they stood. Raynie watched her animated movements and as soon as she reached Simon, she threw her arms around his neck and placed a loud smack on his cheek. Afterward, she grabbed his hands between hers and patted them fondly as she remarked. "Simon, my dear boy, it is always so very good to see you."

When she spoke, it was easy to hear the strong bond that resonated from the woman's well-cultivated French accent. Her welcome towards Raynie was gracious and friendly as well, but her attention was on Simon.

Happily, she placed another kiss on his cheek and praised, "Simon, I see you finally did it. You finally talked her in to having dinner with you."

Simon smiled as he blushed lightly at the suspicious look Raynie threw at him. Quickly he attempted an explanation. "Since we first met, I have asked my Aunt Claudette to hold a table for me whenever I come to town, just in case I ever succeeded into sweet talking an evening out of you. I hope you will not hold that against me."

Raynie shook her head and smiled. She was genuinely happy for the first time in a long time. She liked this place. She liked Aunt Claudette. And she was beginning to like Simon more than she thought was possible.

Hand in hand, they followed Aunt Claudette to a table that sat in front of the fireplace. After they were seated, Simon's aunt began to express her delight that they had chosen Le Bistro for their first rendezvous. She squeezed their hands at the same time and grinned broadly while she whispered, "You two enjoy the evening, and we shall do everything we can to make it a memorable one." She turned to walk away while at the same time, she snapped her fingers at a waiter waiting across the room. Who Tout-de-suite grabbed a wine bucket and rushed to their table side. Without a seconds' delay he opened the wrap around the wine bottle for Simon to approve.

Once the server had left them, Simon gave Raynie a glum look. A nervous laugh escaped his lips, and he began to apologize for Aunt Claudette's comments. "I hope my Aunt did not make you feel uncomfortable. She is very pleasant, but as you can see, she is also somewhat up front, not to mention being a romantic. I attribute her assertiveness to her French heritage, which may also explain the romantic side of her personality."

Raynie smiled goodheartedly as she nodded her head in agreement and graciously confessed, "Simon, I'm really sorry that I've been such a poop head since we met. It's a wonder that you're still around. Let alone going through all this trouble. This place is lovely, and your aunt seems genuinely charming. She didn't offend me in the least. So again, I want to thank you for sticking in there and putting up with me, bad manners...and all."

His smile was sincere, and she noted that he looked so handsome in the candlelight. When he spoke, he did so softly, "I must confess, Raynie, it is not something I do for everyone. I do have my limits on how much I will abide, but so far you have not been anywhere near the finish." He hesitated momentarily while his mind considered if he should go further. But soon his honest nature won out and he decided to push it to the limits.

"Raynie, I want you to know. I am not the playboy you think I am. I am, as they say, a one-woman man. I am not easily smitten; nor do I fall in love simply because a woman is beautiful. Luckily, I am smart enough to see and identify what I want. I also recognize that if someone is that significant, then they should be worth fighting for." He paused once again as he weighed his thoughts, and his expression became even more serious when he continued. "But, as I said, I do have my limits, and I do not play second best. Especially to an unattainable dream, such as your supposed love for Dan."

Raynie gasped, then turned a bright red as she grabbed for her purse and stood up to leave. At that same spilt second, Simon quickly reached out and held her hand so she could not run from the table *or* away from him. He could see that she was fighting back tears of anger, but all she said was, "You bastard. You goddamn bastard, how can you be so mean?"

"Raynie, please? I told you when we first met that honesty is always the best way to start a relationship and I meant that."

Angrily she spouted, "We don't have a relationship...and we never will. Sooo, Mr. Charles, let go of my hand so I can leave."

"No, Raynie. I will not let go of your hands and you *are* going to listen to me. So please sit down."

She looked around as she sank slowly and awkwardly back into her seat. She noticed the couple sitting at the table next to them were wide-eyed and gawking as they openly attempted to listen to Simon's conversation.

"Last month, before I intruded on your Mother and Dan's dinner party, I could see from clear across the room the longing in your eyes. I could also tell you were making an effort to hide it, but I assure you, since I, a stranger, could unquestionably read your moves, so could your loving Mother and Mr. Marvelous.

He took a deep breath before he went on, "I wholly believe that Dan, along with your Mother, was well aware of your feeling and your intentions that night."

Raynie at this point was not relinquishing any of her pent-up anger, and Simon realized that she still harbored distrust of what he said, so once more he made an effort to further clarify his account, but this time with less tact. "Frankly, my love, if you want to admit it or not, if a stranger could see the love and desire that rippled from those gorgeous eyes of yours, so could your Mother and Mr. Wonderful. I guess, what I am stammering about, *is*, I hate seeing you make a fool of yourself, especially over someone who could care less about you or your feeling."

"None of this is any of your damn business, Simon," Raynie snapped, harshly.

"Maybe not, but I am hoping you will one day be my business."

She was so angry she couldn't think straight and all she could come up with was the childish remark of, "over my dead body."

Simon bridled a laugh and instead smiled when he answered, "Let us hope not. I much rather have you warm and spunky."

He could see that she was still angry, but when she pushed back hard against the chair, he asked, "If I release your hands Raynie, will you stay? You won't run away, will you?"

Through her anger, she smiled a fake smile, but she could see that he wasn't going to fall for it. Finally, she released the breath she held along with some of her pent-up fury and agreed. "Okay, I won't run, so let go."

He asked, "Will you listen to me?"

"Why? You don't even know me, so what gives you the right to decide what I'm feeling and for whom?"

"I know you better than you think, my love, and I want you to know I am not here to judge you. Nor am I here to save you from the inescapable heartbreak you are so obviously headed for." He released her hand as he continued, "I am strictly here because I see in you everything I want in a woman. Of course, you are a little more temperamental than I like, but no one's perfect. But I have come to believe that you are damned close to perfection. However, for right now, I am asking nothing more than for you to sit and hear me out."

"All right Simon, what do you have to say that you think is so damn important, that you would kidnap me and hold me against my will?" As soon as the words were out of her mouth, she realized how ridiculous her declaration sounded. Immediately, her frustration grew beyond the point of control, and the tears that filled her eyes rolled down her cheeks. Before she realized it, she started to laugh uncontrollably.

Suspiciously Simon watched, then skeptically he joined her. After a minute, he cautiously asked, "Are you okay, Raynie? I really don't want you wigging out on me?"

Suddenly her laughter grew louder, and she could hear it as the resonances elevated close to hysterics. She tasted the tears that had begun to roll across her lips, and she struggled to get control. Eventually the laughter ceased, and she sat forward. Quietly she watched her hands fiddle with her napkin. After a bit she looked up and professed, "I'm sorry, Simon... I guess I've been holding that back for some time...." She lowered her eyes and said nothing else for what seem like a long time. Finally, she looked up and smiled again.

Immediately he could see that she felt embarrassed. He did not wish to add to her discomfort, so he decided it was best not to say anything. He would wait in respectful silence while she struggled to find the right words to express how she felt.

After some time, she whispered, "I'm really sorry. And... Simon, I... know you're right. I guess I've really been making a damned fool out of myself."

Earnestly he countered, "We all do, at one time or another."

After that they sat solemnly, neither adding to what had already been said. Both lugubriously sipped at their wine while Raynie made an extra effort to avoid eye contact. Shortly, and without fore-thought, Simon reached out and caressed her hand. Slightly uncom-fortable, he coughed when he realized what he had done then uttered, "Raynie, the only reason that you have built this relation-ship in your mind is because you feel it is safe. It is a natural im-pulse to want to protect oneself."

Confused she said, "I'm not following you, Simon. I don't get it."

"Yes, you do. You simply rather not face it. You see, I can tell that you genuinely fear love. I would guess that you unknowingly feel that an unattainable love is much safer. That way you can fantasize about it, but you cannot touch it, so consequently it cannot touch you. Which leaves you safe...with no chance for an actual heart-break. That is until now."

She said nothing for she didn't know how to answer what seemed to be an accurate observation. After his comment, she felt an intense sadness, and she wished she had left when she had had the chance. Now she was forced to face the true meaning of his words, and the fact that he was right. She painfully repeated the words to herself, "he is right." She had always run from personal commitment, especially once it moved to serious. If she were to be completely honest with herself, she usually only wanted who she couldn't have. She had always labeled her actions as autonomous. But her friends said it was because she was spoiled and tended to be more self-indulgent and reckless. But now that she was forced to face the undiminished truth, Simon was completely right. She is, and always had been running from personal commitment.

Surprisingly, her parents came to mind. After some thought, she decided that when they divorced it had destroyed the only love foundation she ever truly counted on. As far as she could see, pain and sadness usually followed love. If she thought about it and was completely honest, she didn't know a single couple who hadn't been divorced or at least in the midst of ending a relationship, except for Mike and Louis, of course, who were totally committed to one another. But since they're gay and couldn't marry, she didn't know if that counted.

After several minutes of silence, Simon tried to change the mood by severing Raynie's private thoughts and moving on to a more cheerful topic.

"Okay, we have been melancholy long enough. This session is over, Miss Dey. So, let us agree to forget the world, along with all its occupants, and work on being happy." Reaching over the table he lifted her chin so he could peer directly into her eyes, and at once it crossed his mind that her eyes were beautiful. They seem to change color constantly. But out loud he asked, "Okay, Raynie? Do you think we can start over? No more long faces?"

Raynie's smile was full of gratitude since she too was ready for some frivolous conversation.

Relieved Simon quipped, "Good, let's' listen to the harpist and have some jolly chitchat. We are here to discover one another, so let us begin." In anticipation he waited for her response and laughed lightheartedly when she finally asked, "Simon, what did you say you do for a living?"

Smiling ambiguously, he whispered, "Capitalist." When she arched a skeptical eyebrow, he laughed guiltily and confessed. "Yes, as you probably already guessed, I do carry a degree in psychiatry. Therefore, every now and then I do dabble in its craft. I find it stimulating and somewhat helpful in my business dealings. You can tell a great deal by reading people and their body language, you know."

Again, she arched an indecisive eyebrow while she grinned and declared earnestly. "And I would wager a hefty sum, that it's quite helpful in your personal life as well."

It was eleven o'clock in the morning and already Dan felt as if he had put in a full day's work. Frustrated, he gave the budget sheets an angry shove. He'd been working on them most of the morning, and in no way was he any closer to an answer. He punched the desk angrily, as he gathered the sheets and shoved them as neatly as he could in their file. Pushing the chair back he stood up and glanced at his watch again. He had an appointment at 2:30 with Javier Visente, and his nerves were shot. Nonetheless, he didn't want Javier to see him this stressed.

Earlier he almost paced a hole in the damned carpet, while at the same time he popped his knuckles into soreness. Despite all this nervous activity, it didn't help ward off one fraction of his anxiety, and he still felt a fiery agitation in the pit of his gut.

"Maybe I have an ulcer," he grumbled. "Man, that's all I need. Shit, how did I ever get in this mess?" He stared out the window while he went over the past months. What had he been thinking, messing around with guys like Javier Visente and Paulo Pieta? But at the time there was no other way. He needed the cash to move forward. "Shit." Now here he is again, at the same place, with the same problem..., "Shit!" Yet, this time, it's even worse since he couldn't stop production now if he wanted to. Dammit, he'd be ruined if he did that. News like that could be all over town in a matter of minutes. His career would be in the toilet before it really ever got off the ground. "Shit," he muttered again. "Hollywood's such a heartless place and its fucking people, even worse. They never forget. Close down a shoot, for any reason at all, can easily ruin a man, especially if it gets out that it's down because of a lack of funds. Or even worse, mismanaged funds." Damn...if that got out, he'd be black balled. He'd never get another fucking picture. Every person, who claimed to be his friend today, would be a stranger tomorrow. He growled, "They'd all skitter away like rats in the night. Dammit, there's positively no fucking loyalty in this town."

Well, as far as he's concerned, he isn't going to give them the satisfaction of his ruin. He has no intention whatsoever of shutting down. He will simply get more money from Javier. That'll keep things rolling for a time, plus make his life a hell of a lot easier. Then once he marries Jackie, that'll put an end to all his money worries. "Damn right." he mumbled, "As soon as that happens all my worries will be over. I'll have all the money I need to pay off my fucking loans and get these damn goons off my ass."

Dan walked over to the bar in the corner of the room and poured himself a soda water with lime. He wished it could be something stronger, but he needed a clear head when he talked with these morons. They are the only way to the money he so desperately needed, and he wanted a clear head.

Startled, he suddenly turned when he heard an unexpected noise from behind. He could feel his whole-body jerk, and his heart jumped when he saw a person move forward and towards him. Finally, the silhouette passed through the blinding sunlight, and he relaxed when he realized it was only Mike. He had been extremely jumpy lately. He guessed it was because of the dealings he's had with these hard-nosed thugs, he hoped it wasn't noticeable to anyone but himself.

Mike's expression registered concern when he saw Dan's body visually jerk, and he asked, "What's the matter, Dan? Are you all right? Are you feeling okay? You look awful. Have you been up all night?"

"Great! That's exactly what I need to hear right now. Is that all you have to do, go around making people feel worse than they already do?"

"I'm sorry. I didn't mean to disturb you. I didn't realize you were working at home today. Are you having production problems again?"

Dan sneered and yelled, "What the hell do you want, Mike?"

"What I want is to help if I can. Is there anything I can do? Is it something to do with the movie like some major shooting catastrophe? Maybe it's that horrid leading lady again. Is that it. Is she making your life miserable again?"

Dan couldn't help but laugh at Mike's suggestions, because it seemed like those were daily occurrences in the industry. Nothing to get too upset over and certainly nothing to spend time discussing with some layman like Mike. As a result, Dan dismissed what he thought was a silly question. "No, the damn movie's doing just fine, and unless you got a couple of million dollars, you can't help."

"Oh Lord, Dan! Are you still having money problems with that damned film? I can't believe how much cash you've put into it and you just barely begun shooting."

Mike crossed his arms as he chided, "Dan, why won't you go back to work for one of the studios? Why do you have to have your own production company? Maybe you're trying to move too fast. It takes a lot of money to run any company and even more for a production company."

"Fuck, Mike, listen to what you're saying. This isn't something I decided to do yesterday. This was always the plan. Now, just because you decided to jump ship on me, doesn't mean that I have to give up my fucking dreams."

"I'm not jumping ship on you; Dan and you know it. But I have a life of my own and Louis is my focus, not supporting you and your damned ivory-tower dreams. Which, if I may remind you, I have done since... since forever. Besides, I thought you had planned to be married to Jackie by now. To quote you per verbatim." 'Then all my money worries will be his-tor-y.'"

"Hell, Mike, I'm working on it. I've just hit a snag that's all. But I have things that need taken care of now, and I can't wait for Jackie any longer, so I'm going back to Javier for more damn money."

Mike's face displayed complete horror, and Dan raised his hand immediately to ward off any further comment as he scoffed, "I don't want to hear it, Mike. It's only enough to last until I marry Jackie."

"Well, that certainly answers my question on why you're so damned jumpy. Dan, what are you thinking? Or are you thinking? Have your brains disintegrated? These guys are dangerous; they kill people, have you forgotten that?"

"They only mess with you if you try to screw them out of their damned money, which I am not. Dammit, Mike, I don't have any other choice, it's either them or I shut down production. That is something I am not about to do."

"Dan, I really think you should reconsider. It may be best to halt all production, at least for a while. Maybe if you talk to Jackie, she'd loan you the money."

Dan's face turned an uneven shade of red and moved to purple as he stepped forward, screaming, "Hell no! Dammit, Mike! I don't want you mentioning this to anyone! Do you hear me dammit? No one! And that especially means your dear little friend, Raynie. I don't need her running to her mother and spilling her god damned guts about how Dan's broke. Dammit, Mike, you know fucking well that I have to look successful to be successful. If there's even a hint that I have money problems, this whole damned town will drop me like a hot potato. You know fucking well that I've waited my entire life for this chance, and I'll be dammed if I'm going to lose it now. Do you hear me, Mike? Do you understand what I'm saying? No one is to know anything, nothing, or Javier's not the only one who's going to kill somebody."

"Dan, would you please stop talking to me like that? You know it scares me when you talk crazy. *And...*, people are more understanding than you give them credit for. That is, if you'd just be honest with them. Dan, if you'd just be forthright, you'd see that it's true."

"Mike, I'm warning you! You better keep your big mouth shut! If you do that, then I won't have to worry whether anyone understands or not. Now get the hell out of here. I don't have time to stand here and listen to you and all your tedious concerns." He turned his back on Mike and yelled, "AND CLOSE THE FUCKING DOOR ON YOUR WAY OUT!"

Mike closed the door and leaned against it for support. He could feel his knees shake and he asked, "What's going on with Dan? Is he losing his mind? Is he having a break down?" Mike had an eerie feeling of doom and it was frightening. He wanted to talk with someone about Dan's recent behaviors. But who? There was no one he could freely speak with, except Louis, and Louis really wasn't interested in anything Dan did. He felt that Dan was a user and he deserved whatever befell him. Disillusioned, he groaned, "Louis will never understand Dan or our friendship."

It had become quite clear to Mike, that if anything, Louis was jealous of the relationship. He couldn't count how many times he tried to explain his and Dan's bond. Yet, Louis didn't want to hear it. He chose to believe that Dan used him from the start. Mike still couldn't believe the mooted look Louis threw him when he tried to point out that when he and Dan were kids, Dan had always stood by him. Even when he announced that he was gay, all Dan said was, 'You're just figuring that out. I knew that years ago.'

Dan's act of friendship was the nicest thing anyone had ever done for him, and he repaid the favor the only way he knew how, with his complete loyalty and his total support.

Over time things changed and Dan was different now. He realized that his questionable principals should no longer be his concern, but he still worried. He wanted to help him if he could, despite Louis's disapproval. Mike rubbed his forehead and asked, "Lord, why can't the two men I love most in the world get along?"

In reality, the relationship between Louis and Dan was hostile at its absolute best. It was near impossible for either of them to be in the same room without some mishap developing. But neither would say why.

Suddenly Mike heard Dan's footsteps moving closer to the door, so he grabbed his gym bag and rushed towards the front door. There was no doubt in Mike's mind that if Dan caught him standing outside the office door, he would have jumped to the conclusion that he was eavesdropping.

CHAPTER NINE

"Come on, Jackie! Say you'll marry meee... *pleaseee*! I know you want to. I know you know we are meant for each other. Just think, we could have a Christmas wedding. That would be great, don't you agree? Come on, please, just say you'll think about it; we could be each other's Christmas gifts from Santa. Better yet, we'll be able to start the New Year off as Mr. and Mrs. Dan Aleut. Come on baby... pleaseee say yes. I love you and I can't stand the thought of living without you a day longer. I want you as my wife... I want you, nooow."

He waited while he watched her gratified expression. They had just finished making love, and Jackie was lying on the bed stark naked and beaming. He studied her face and her look showed nothing at all except contentment. He couldn't tell what she was thinking. He held his breath since there was no hint in her eyes either way. *Damn!* his mind screeched. *What the hell is she waiting for? What more does she want, I'm already begging?*

This was the fourth time he had asked her to marry him in six weeks. Jackie's first excuse was: 'No, it's too soon.' The next: 'I don't know if I'm ready yet.' Then the third time she said: 'Well maybe, but I'd like to think about it a little longer.' *Shit what did she have to think about anyway? She wasn't getting any younger,* he grumbled silently to himself.

At this point, Dan was getting desperate. The last time he talked with Javier, he was informed that their patience was running thin. They had anticipated a return on their money by now. This implicated threat only intensified Dan's efforts to get Jackie to marry him. He had to marry her immediately, or soon he'd be found floating face down off the shores of Santa Monica.

Jackie reached up and touched the hair that fell across Dan's forehead. In a husky voice she whispered, "Christmas, huh? Well, let me see. I guess if I try really hard, I can imagine seeing you with nothing on except a big shiny red bow." She ruffled her full head of hair, and added in a seductive southern drawl, "Now, I'd say, that's an image that could get a sweet little girl's bloomers in a tether."

Dan jumped up and shrieked, "Does that mean, yes? Are you saying you'll marry me? Ooh Jackie, I love you. Please say it means, yes."

"Yes, Dan, yes I will. I will love to marry you."

Dan was so excited he leaped out of bed and ran around the room while he yelped like a crazy man. Then suddenly, he dashed across the room and threw open the window and began to yelp even louder, "YIPPEE, SHE SAID YES! YES, SHE FINALLY SAID, YES! JACQUELINE DEY SAID SHE'D BE MY WIFE!" As soon as he realized he was standing stark naked in front of the large open window he made an awkward attempt to cover himself. Then self-consciously, he ran back to the bed and pulled the cover over their heads. Jackie was giggling hysterically as Dan desperately tried to kiss her laughing lips. He was thrilled she was finally going to be his, and now all his money worries were going to be gone.

In the middle of their kiss, Jackie suddenly pulled away from Dan and his firm grip and asked, "But, why does it have to be a Christmas wedding? I was thinking more like February. It's a nice month and much more romantic."

Before Dan thought about what he was saying, he blurted out a loud, "No! No Jackie, it can't be later. It has to be by Christmas."

At once, she pulled herself out of Dan's arms and eyed him questioningly. "Why does it have to be by Christmas, Dan?"

Dan instantly searched for an answer she would accept, then promptly grew frustrated and excitedly stumbled through an explanation. "Jackie, it's..., it's the best time of the year. It's festive. Think about it, baby. All the colorful lights, music, and parties. It'll be like everyone in the world is celebrating with us." Realizing he was sounding immature and desperate, his voice grew insecure and slowly died out, "the...they'll celebrat...."

Her face was filled with doubt when she murmured, "I had no idea that you were so sentimental, Dan. That's so sweet."

Eagerly he laughed as he recognized a way out, "Yes! Yes, I am Jackie, and Christmas and New Years are my favorite times of the year. And I... I want to share them with you. I want us to pick out our first Christmas tree together, as man and wife. I want to share all the holiday joys with you as my wife, Sweetheart. It'll mean so much."

Dan could see his justifications hadn't convinced Jackie yet, so he hurried on. "And if you think about it, time wise, it makes perfect sense. It'll be an excellent time for a honeymoon. To be completely honest, I can't wait a minute longer than that, Jackie. I swear I need you now." Suddenly his face transformed from the desperate mask he wore to a grinning lecherous old man. He was trying to lighten the mood, and he began to slur his words and wring his hands in anticipation. "Plus, my pretty little girl, you have to remember, I'll be on hiatus. So, let me reiterate, *honeymoon*. It'll be a perfect time for *honeeey-mooooning*. Just imagine hours and hours of uninterrupted sex, sex, sex and more sex."

Suddenly he grew serious again and he took her hands between his and begged. "Oh, please Jackie, don't make me wait any longer. If not December, then how about November? I need you to belong to me as soon as possible. It's cruel to make me suffer like this."

Almost instantly his confidence rekindled when he saw the change in her expression, and he became nonchalant. "Come on Jackie, I know you don't want me to die, do you babe? Because that's exactly what will happen if you make me wait longer than December. There's no way I can continue to live without you as my wife."

Jackie reached over and kissed his lips as she attempted to reassure him. "Oh, Dan my darling, I'm sorry. I didn't realize how important this was to you. I've been making you wait unfairly. Please forgive me. I too, can hardly wait for you to be mine. She laughed as she kissed his nose, forehead, then moved back to his lips again. Finally, she whispered tenderly, "Sweetheart, you're so damned cute when you're passionate. If this means that much to you, then how could I possibly deny you a December wedding."

Dan smiled before he kissed her because she had no idea how true his last statement was. Visente and Paulo were at the point of no more excuses, and Jackie was his only way out.

The next few days were chaotically hectic. Jackie only had six weeks before her wedding day, which she and Dan decided would be December fifteenth. With this date they could be in Bermuda for Christmas and enjoying their wonderful honeymoon. She could hardly wait to sit and watch the moonlight as it hit the pink coral beaches. Just the thought of walking along the rocky shores at dusk made her shiver with desire. The sheer prospect of making love on the sands of some hidden cove gave her goose bumps. "It'll all be so romantic," she giggled.

Her chuckles soon turned to laughter when she pictured Dan's face at the time, she informed him that she had reserved a couple of motor scooters. She thought he was going to have a heart attack he laughed so hard. She tried to explain that she was serious, and that these would be their only mode of transportation besides a taxi. Yet he kept gasping, 'No, no. No, Jackie! I want a car.' But giddily she clarified that tourists were not allowed to drive anything except scooters on the island. All other modes of transportation would have to be either in a cab or bus. Even if they could have a car and driver, she had no desire to have a chauffeur hanging around on their honeymoon. So, scooters and cabs are the chosen means of transportation and will be on hand for their convenience. She thought it was perfect, but once Dan realized she was serious, he wasn't at all thrilled about it.

Once she realized how late it was and jumped down off the stool, she snatched her purse and keys from atop the juice counter and hurried out of the gym. She had spent the last hour and a half on a vigorous work out, but right now she needed to get home to shower and change before she met Raynie for lunch.

Neither Jackie nor Dan had told anyone about the accepted proposal. She had wanted to tell Raynie first. She really wanted her daughter to be happy for her. But Jackie had strong doubts that she would be, especially since Raynie appeared to be avoiding her and Dan lately. Maybe she was being too sensitive, and Raynie's many excuses were real. Maybe she wasn't really trying to avoid them at all. She could be spending all her free time with that marvelous Simon Charles. "Boy, wouldn't that be great," she declared out loud.

The first time she saw the two of them together it was obvious that Simon was truly infatuated with Raynie and this delighted her. Wouldn't it be wonderful if Raynie was over her obsession with Dan? It certainly would make the wedding a lot more pleasant, she concluded.

When Jackie pulled to a stop at the red light, she saw her reflection in the glass of the corner department store. From where she sat, she thought she looked youthful, but in reality, she knew this was her last grasp for the brass ring. She wanted her daughter to be elated and a part of her happy day, not opposed to it. She sighed and murmured, "Oh Raynie, be happy for me. I love Dan, and I know I'll be good for him and his career. You're young. You'll find someone else, someone that's meant solely for you like Dan is for me." Yes, there is no doubt, Raynie will have many more chances at love and happiness. As for her this is probably it, her very last chance for happiness.

At that instant Jackie felt a warm tingle deep inside her. This was her first love. She never experienced the real thing before. Even though her marriage with Ray was good, it was for no other reason than convenience for Ray as well as for herself.

Unexpectedly, Jackie heard the blare of a horn. When she looked up, she realized that the light had changed to green, and before she could react it had changed to yellow. She stepped hard on the gas pedal and made it through the light. When she glanced in her rearview mirror, she witnessed the angry face of the lady behind her along with her protruding gesture. At this time, she decided she best put Dan out of her mind, at least until she arrived home safely.

When Jackie pulled into the driveway, she was surprised to see a matching pair of black Mercedes convertibles parked just inside the gate. Leaping from her car she eagerly ran over to the vehicle nearest to her, which adorned a big red bow. She screeched, when out of nowhere Dan suddenly appeared and screamed, "SURPRISE!"

Jackie reeled from excitement, and without any forewarning she vigorously threw herself in Dan's arms and began kissing him. After her last kiss, she pointed at the car and asked, "What's this Dan? What's going on?"

"Why my lovely fiancée', I am dropping off my wedding gift for you."

Jackie started to protest, and Dan immediately interrupted. "Jackie, I don't want to hear any objections. I know I'm early, but..., since you are forever asking to drive my car, I bought you your own. Now I will no longer have to deny you the pleasure."

"But Dan; you didn't have to buy me a wedding present. I mean I love it... but this isn't necessary, I already have three cars."

"Well, now my love, you have a fourth, one as sleek and sporty as you."

She colored slightly with pleasure and murmured softly between a passionate kiss. "Let's not forget, beautiful and sexy too."

He laughed and returned her kiss while he chanted several times, "Jackie, I love you, love you, love you."

"Ohhhh sweetheart, I love you too, and thank you for my gift. It is incredibly thoughtful and beautiful. Every time I drive it, I will remember your very words. Glancing at the auto's interior she took note of the clock and hastened, "Oh my, look at the time. Dan, I have to go, I'm running late as it is."

Dan opened her hand and kissed the soft center, then dropped the keys onto her palm as he whispered, "Enjoy," He turned and walked nonchalantly over to his car. After he sped off, Jackie stood there several minutes feeling delirious before entering the vehicle. She rubbed her fingertips around the steering wheel and inhaled the inside's untainted fresh leather, "I'm the luckiest girl in the world," she exhaled. In a dream-like state she unfolded her other hand and inserted the key in the ignition. At this time, she noticed the sheen of what appeared to be a diamond bracelet. The bauble dangled loosely from the key chain; the precious stones were brilliant. Uncontrollably she gasped, "My God Dan, they're dazzling."

It took Jackie several minutes to compose herself before she put the car in gear and drove slowly up the driveway. She parked the car in front of the house and decided to have her maintenance man, Kenny, bring in the Jag from where she had left it at the gates entrance. She smiled at her gift as she opted to drive it to her lunch with Raynie. However, the bracelet was another story, it'll have to stay home in the safe, at least until she talked with Dan about his extravagance. There is no need for him to shower her with gifts of jewelry; she had more than enough the way it was.

Raynie sat silent for several minutes. With Jackie's unexpected news, she had a clear impression of being slapped, which was unfathomable, since she'd never been slapped in her entire life and had no idea how it felt. Forcing herself, she focused on her mother's expression, it was evident that she was apprehensive. It was difficult but Raynie attempted a forced smile. At last she choked, "Aaah, um, congratulations...Mother. I...I know this is what you were hoping for...buuut don't you think it might be a little too soon. I mean, you and Daddy, your divorce only became final a few months ago. You need time to..."

"Sweetheart, Ray and I have been divorced for much longer than a few months. Beside Dan and I are not children. We do know what we're doing, and Dan wants a Christmas wedding."

"Well... that's something. At least that gives us a little more than a year."

"No Raynie, this Christmas, not next year. Dan doesn't want to wait. The truth is, he wants to make it even sooner, but I said no."

"Mother! But why...why the rush? Dan's in the middle of production; he doesn't have time for a pit stop, let alone a wedding."

"Raynie, please..., and you know as well as I do, that they stop all shooting long before Christmas. Dan will be on hiatus long enough for us to have a wonderful honeymoon."

At the mention of the word honeymoon, Raynie's face turned bloodless, and panic surged through her entire body. The full force finally struck her; her mother was going to marry Dan, *her Dan.* Suddenly Raynie had an impulse to scream; *no, no, no he's mine.* But she fought to control the first signs of hysteria before it took hold.

Jackie watched as Raynie sat speechless, so she too remained silent. She was angry with her daughter and her reaction. She feared if she spoke, she'd say something she'd be sorry for, so she bit down on her lower lip to help her self-control.

Raynie's mind was wild with wrath, and she wanted to scream at her mother, *to stop acting like a silly teenager. Just because she's afraid of losing her man isn't any reason for her to rush into marriage.*

Raynie closed her eyes and concentrated on what Simon had told her that night at the restaurant. Dan is someone she wanted only because he was unattainable. She stayed focused on that thought for several seconds before she felt the muscles in her body begin to relent and loosen. When she opened her eyes, she saw her mother's concern, yet her face also showed a hint of anger. Smiling a phony smile, she asked, "So what's first? What do we do? How do people get married? Mother, can I please be your Maid of Honor?"

"Oh, Sweetheart thank you! Of course, I want you as my Maid of Honor. There's no one in the world I'd rather have stand next to me."

Raynie grew somber and stopped her rampage of questions to ask, "Mother, are you really sure about this? Are you really, really, certain? If you're sure this is what you want and it's the right time for it, then I'm happy for you. All I really want is for you to be happy, Mother."

CHAPTER TEN

Raynie rushed from the elevator and swung the glass doors open to her father's suite of offices. She threw a halfhearted smiled at Kelsey as she passed her desk, but ignored her when she leaped up and yelled, "Raynie... Raynie no, he's on a phone conf..." She never heard the rest of her declaration since she already slammed the door to her father's office, cutting off all sound from the other side.

Her father's hand went up to suspend her interruption. Anger covered his face, but never touched his voice. Raynie halted abruptly then stood frozen in her tracks while he finished his conversation. Eventually he firmly set the phone back in its cradle. His aggravation was evident when he asked, "What the hell is going on, Ray? You better have a damned good reason why you stormed into my office without being announced."

Raynie sat down as if she were in some kind of trance, and whispered, "Daddy, Mother's getting married. She's marrying Dan."

The look he gave her made her feel like some five-year-old who was informing her daddy that someone was picking on her. He stared at her for a long time before he said, "Ray, I think it's time you get Dan out of your head and stop acting like some silly little adolescent with a crush on her gym teacher."

Raynie was dismayed; she really thought he would understand. *Yet,* she thought to herself, *why should I be surprised? They always stick together.*

But his remark was not going to alter her purpose, she was bent on being heard. "Daddy, I was sure you might have guessed my feelings for Dan. But I want you to know it's not like that any longer." Lying, she continued, "Dan, no longer means anything to me other than my mother's boyfriend. However, I can't help but feel that Mother is rushing into this marriage. Daddy, I really don't think she's over you yet. I don't think she's being rational. She hasn't been right since the divorce."

Her father stood and walked over to the window. After a few minutes, he turned back to face her. His look was stern, and his voice held an intolerance she rarely heard. "Ray, I've known your mother for well over thirty years and I've never seen her when she didn't know what she wanted. So, you will excuse me, young lady, if I doubt you and your presupposition now."

"Daddy, I'm not saying she doesn't know what she wants. But she's thinking with her libido; she's not using common sense. She's reacting to the fact that you left her for a younger woman. In a sense, she's getting back by marrying a younger man"

She could see the smile he was holding back when he asked tenderly, "Would you like to translate precisely who you deem is thinking with their *libido*?"

Raynie immediately turned a deep pink and she felt her cheeks burn with embarrassment, but she stood her ground and whispered, "I..., I just think it's too soon. She's nowhere near over you or the divorce."

"Maybe it's you, that's not over the divorce, but as for your mother, Ray, she is doing fine."

He weighed his thoughts for several seconds and then swiped his hand across his chin. His eyes were riveted on her face as he walked back to the front of his desk. Leaning back against the desk as if he were half-sitting and half-holding himself up with his arms, he studied her face.

Uncomfortable with the intensity of his stare, Raynie shifted in her seat. She said nothing more as she waited for her father to come to terms with his thoughts. Shortly after that, she recognized he had come to a decision.

Grimacing he said, "Ray, I have always loved you more than any other person on earth. And sweetheart, I can say, I would rather die than hurt you, but you need to grow up and you're not going to do that until your mother and I stop over-protecting you."

"Daddy, what does any of that have to do with Mother getting married?"

"Well, maybe nothing at all, but it does have something to do with you and how you perceive your Mother...and our divorce."

Ray waited while he watched his daughter labor to understand his words. Then quickly he moved on before she could interrupt his confession. "See baby,

I didn't leave your mother for a younger woman. She left *me* for Dan."

Raynie didn't wait or weigh her father's divulgence before she shot, "That's a lie, and you know it, Daddy. Why are you saying that? Mother didn't even know Dan at the time?"

"You're right to some extent, she barely knew him. But in Dan, she saw a conquest and a man she wanted to procure, and she asked me to release her so she could openly pursue him. Jackie, always liked a challenge and I certainly out-lived that portrait years ago."

"But Pamela! You married Pam as soon as the divorce was final. You were dating her since you left Mother."

He sat his full weight on the desk and crossed his arms, then released them when he became conscious of the action. "Honey, Pam and I have an agreement, the same type of arrangement your mother and I had all those years. Our marriage is one of collaboration. We both have our needs and we both give to the relationship what is expected."

"I don't understand. What could Pam give you besides sex?"

"Well, since you decided to go there first, yes Raynie, Pam gives me a sexual relationship. But, far more importantly, she gives me companionship. She's a dear friend and a person I can talk and share my life with. You see, I like having a woman in my life. I dislike dating or living alone, and Pam fills that void in my life. As far as I can see, she more than fulfills her part of the bargain. She's not only beautiful, but she's intelligent as well as entertaining, which is a plus in my profession."

He stopped and shifted his frame to a more comfortable position while adding, "I guess I should feel some kind of embarrassment for such a weakness, yet for some reason I don't."

Sarcastically Raynie spouted, "And what, may I ask do you do for Pamela, Daddy? Money? Prominence? Just what does a thirty-year-old woman want from a fifty-eight-year-old man?"

Smiling and ignoring her impudent attitude he answered. "All of the above." He stood and went back to sit in his chair behind the desk.

"You see, Pam had aspired to be a great actress. To attain her dream, she was forced to give up her family when she was eighteen. Her family is very affluent and believes that acting is beneath their station. When Pam left West Virginia to pursue her ambitions, they adamantly refused to support her, monetarily or otherwise. Basically, they disowned her, so I guess you can say, I gave her a family of sorts. Furthermore, by reason of my long-time contacts within the industry, the one thing she unquestionably gets from the relationship is an occasional part in a movie. You see, Ray, Pam's a smart girl, and she realized soon after she came to Hollywood that she lacked the talent it took to make it on her own. So, with me at her side she at least gets to dabble in the craft she loves, not to mention to rub elbows with some of the most celebrated celebrities at the most important events in the industry. That fact my dear daughter, pleases her immensely."

Raynie sat there stunned by her Father's offensive disclosure. She didn't want to believe her father was that simple and needy, but he said it himself. To her, he had always seemed so strong. He was extremely successful, and she merely assumed that you had to be strong to be so dominant in the industry, especially from what she knew of Hollywood. She knew it wasn't an easy town to succeed in, so he had to have something going for him. Yet, he had admitted he was weak. Suddenly her eyes lit-up and Raynie screeched. "Daddy!... Daddy, did I understand you correctly? Did you say that Mother and you had a similar arrangement?"

He chuckled lightly with relief then declared, "I knew it would sink in eventually. Yes, sweety, when your mother and I met we came up with a similar agreement."

"But...why? You and mother loved each other, why would you need an agreement?"

"Sweetheart, your mother and I do love one another, but we have never been *in love* with each other. That's why I'm happy for her. If she's finally found someone she really loves, that's something I've never been able to give her. I think it's great, and I only wish her the best."

"I don't understand, why did you get married if you didn't love each other? Was mother pregnant with me? Were you forced into marriage?"

Ray laughed in his usual easygoing way. Pushing his chair away from the desk so he could lean back more comfortably, he answered her question. "Neither your mother nor I have ever been forced into anything. No Sweetheart, she was not pregnant. Plain and simple, we both had a desire to be extremely successful, and we knew together we could accomplish our dreams."

His expression began to change, and Raynie guessed that he was recalling the early days of his life with Jackie. After a time, he shook his head to help clear his memories and to bring him back to her and the moment. She had noticed when he focused on her again, he appeared almost flustered and when he started to speak, he made an unconscious noise that sounded like a giggle. "Good, God, Ray, your mother, she was something else. I had never met anyone like her before...or since. And me, well I'm afraid I'd have to admit, I was a complete yokel. But Jackie she saw me differently; she recognized my potential. Admittedly, she was younger but nevertheless far more sophisticated than me..., far beyond her years. I guess one might say, she not only knew the ropes, she knew just how to climb them, which is exactly what *we* did..., together. What's more, we prospered remarkably beyond our dreams." His voice fell low when he added, "Thanks primarily to Jackie..., and her *little black book*."

He realized Raynie had heard his last words when he saw her bewilderment. He coughed in an uncomfortable manner and immediately explained. "Your Mother's little black book listed some of the most significant names in the movie industry, who, by the time we met, had become more like close friends to Jackie..., than professional companions. Yes, I guess I'd have to admit that for me, Jackie was heaven sent. You see, everyone she knew was in the right position to make life a lot easier for a country bumpkin like me. Now don't take me wrong. I had the ambition and was willing to work my ass off, but without a single contact..., well you know Hollywood. Anyway, with Jackie's guidance, and our talents, we soon became a hot commodity. By the time we were married I was well on my way and Hollywood's lawyer of choice. As I said, financially, we grew beyond either of our aspirations." Smiling, his voice grew tender; and when you came along it was like icing on the cake."

Raynie sat speechless. She was stunned. She thought she knew her parents. She thought that their love was like a storybook romance, and in a way, she guessed she was right. Because in reality, it was a fictional love story. Nothing more than a made-up plot with a bunch of erroneous players, a cast of characters pretending to be what they weren't.

On that point a new thought came to light. Slowly she moved her gaze towards her father's and without further contemplation Raynie asked cautiously. "Daddy, are you saying that my mother was a prostitute?"

"Raynie, what I'm saying, and I hope you will keep this in mind, is that everyone prostitutes themselves in one way or the other. I guess what I'm asking of you, Sweetie, is that you don't judge your mother too harshly. She is a strong woman. Accept her for what she is: a powerful, deliberate woman. She has always been independent enough to go after and achieve what she wanted. Instead of your mother riding the shirttails of some sugar daddy, or marrying for money, she used what she had to get where she wanted. And I, for one, fully respect her for it.

Raynie didn't know what to say. She didn't want to believe what her father was saying. When she came to him, it was for solace. Now here she was, drowning in a river of truths and realities. What is she to believe..., or think? What is she supposed to feel...? Right now, all she could sense was the heavy burden of reality that was dragging her under the heavy tides of verity. No wonder Daddy always told her not to take her mother on. She wasn't this sweet moral woman of good breeding that she always pretended to be. She was a harsh calculating woman of the world. She was no better than the girls she'd seen walking the streets of Hollywood. Her mother, the woman she loved and trusted, was no more than a pros...

Her thoughts were interrupted by a soft knock on the door and Kelsey stuck her head in and asked, "Mr. Dey, should I call and cancel your two o'clock lunch appointment? If not, you really should be leaving, or you'll be late."

Raynie jumped up and reached for her purse as she said, "No! No Kelsey, he's ready to leave right now, I'm on my way out." When she turned and ran from the room, she heard her father's voice calling her name. But she had no intention of answering him nor going back to him and his pool of distorted truths. Their life as a family was nothing more than lies.

When she reached her BMW, she welcomed the warmth of the heated car. She hadn't realized it was getting cold outside or maybe it was only her father's air-conditioned office. But suddenly she recognized it was only she who was cold, not the weather, not the office, only her. All she really wanted was to start her vehicle and leave, but she felt like every bit of strength had been drained from her body. There was nothing left, but an empty shell. She was void of all feelings down to her very core. "There is nothing left to give," and the thought crossed her mind; that she should sit there and wither away into oblivion. This thought was a welcome embrace.

Staring into space for what seemed like hours, Raynie finally admitted defeat and gave up the effort to wipe out her father's words. Grimly she started the engine and headed for home. On the long drive through the heavy rush hour traffic, she thought about her life and family as she had always known it. When she came to her exit, she ignored it and continued to drive until the anger began to lessen and a new awareness started to replace it. Once she had gone over word for word what her father had said, she was surprised by her sense of compassion. She knew her mother and she wasn't a bad person. Finally, relieved, she uttered her decision. "The one thing I am sure of, is that Mother has always loved me. She's always been my loyal supporter and a wonderful friend. No matter what she was in the past, she's what I know and love todFor this reason, I'll try to do exactly as Daddy requested and not judge her or her choices... past or future."

Jackie was having the time of her life. The wedding plans were all falling into place, and everything was going smoothly. Still she couldn't get over the change in Raynie, it was surprising to say the least. The difference was astonishing, and she wished she knew how or why it all came about, but her attitude seemed to have changed overnight and it was uplifting to see. Even her behavior towards Dan had changed. She was actually treating him as her friend and nothing more. No more flirting, and not a single snide remark about the wedding. She's been nothing less than a perfect daughter and Maid of Honor.

Jackie's observations soon moved to Raynie and Simon. At once her expression grew serious, and then changed to a dream-like smile, as she decided, "They would make a beautiful bride and groom." She giggled, "Almost as exquisite as Dan and me. Unfortunately, it looks like I'm going to have to do the work and guide my lovely daughter in Simon's direction."

Raynie didn't know it, but she had asked Ray to invite Simon to the wedding. She thought that was at least a step in the right direction, but still a long way from becoming a couple.

Jackie couldn't believe how hard Ray fought her. He said she was playing Cupid, and he thought Raynie might get angry with them for their interference. But as far as she could tell, Ray inviting Simon to the wedding was the only way he was going to get an invitation. It was only the day before yesterday that she had suggested that Raynie ask him and she simply shrugged it off with a, 'I'm sure Simon has other plans Mother besides attending my Mother's wedding. Matter of fact, I think he mentioned he was going to be out of the country.' Well, Simon had no such plans. To the contrary, he was hoping for and eagerly accepted, the invitation. For this reason, Jackie decided Raynie will forgive her and Ray, for their intrusion into her personal life.

Jackie inhaled a deep breath and released it long and whimsically as she thought, "Well now that that's settled, let's get back to me and my wedding."

With only two weeks before the wedding, she needed to tackle the long list of small details such as changing her passport to Mrs. Jacqueline Aleut. She hugged herself and whispered, "I can hardly wait. I love you Dan and I'm going to love being your wife."

Things were so different this time. When she married Ray, she wasn't nervous or excited in any way. She went into it as one would a business deal and as a result, the wedding jitters weren't there. But this time her wedding was complete, jitters and all. She was feeling like a young bride who finally caught her Prince Charming.

The phone rang several times before she heard her maid pick it up. Jackie waited anxiously to hear if it was Dan. The maid was sounding uncertain and kept repeating, "No, no, no, Meister no, you got da wrong numbar. Dis is da Dey residenta. Suddenly, she heard Carmen lay the phone down while she continued to mumble, "Ay cheewawha such a crazy man. Sensoria' Dey, dis man, he on a phone. He asked for money, ta pay for car. I tell him, no. He not listen."

Still feeling euphoric Jackie walked over to the phone and picked it up, while at the same time she whispered, "That's okay Carmen, I'll handle it from here. You go along and finish with your cleaning."

Jackie smiled into the phone and said a friendly, "Hello, this is Mrs. Dey. What can I do for you?"

Jackie listened to the well-spoken gentleman on the other end as he informed her that he was the manager from, Beverly Hills Benz, Mr. Ashford Little. Her mind immediately began to drift back to her list of last-minute details, she was still smiling absentmindedly into the phone when she realized the gentleman had stopped talking and was waiting for her answer.

With no uncertainty, she restated what Carmen had said earlier, "I'm sorry Mr. Little, but fortunately, you have the wrong Mrs. Dey. The only Mercedes I have was a gift and I own it. So, if you will excuse me, I'm terribly busy." She moved to lay the phone back in its cradle and heard a hurried, "Please, Mrs. Dey, is Mr. Aleut there, can I please speak with him?"

She hesitated, then answered sharply as her patience ran out. "Mr. Little, I will not say this again you have the wrong number, so I bid you good day sir." She could still hear his rambling when the phone finally clicked in its holder! After she hung the phone up, she reached for it again. She decided to call Dan and tell him what had just transpired, but the phone rang as her fingers touched the receiver. She was surprised, but very delighted to hear Raynie's voice on the other end, "Hi, Mother, how about lunch and a shopping spree?" At once, Jackie forgot all about the annoying Mr. Little and his phone call.

Jackie peered out the window and watched several of the guests arrive. The wedding was going to be small, but undoubtedly it would be beautiful, as all weddings are. Jackie nervously played with her engagement ring, but then slapped at her own hand and muttered, "Stop, Jackie." She couldn't repress her butterflies; they had been fluttering around in the pit of her stomach since early this morning. She was very aware that this was the most apprehensive she'd ever been. This knowledge made her feel a little on the foolish side and she thought, *I never would've dreamed that at my age, I'd be behaving like some giddy bride.* Even though, she was conscious that this was expected of any bride at whatever age. Still she felt it was a senseless frame of mind to be in, especially minutes before the wedding she's wanted for months.

"I really hope the strain doesn't show on my face," Jackie sighed. As soon as she said the words, she hurriedly walked over to stand in front of the full-length antique mirror that stood erect in the corner of her bedroom. She inspected every part of her exterior and then smiled with satisfaction. She was simply ravishing in the exquisite evening gown. She had decided that an evening dress was more appropriate for a second wedding. Raynie didn't agree with the choice; she pushed for a full-blown wedding gown and at one-point Jackie almost gave in to her wish. Now she was glad she hadn't because her reflection looked radiant.

Again, she felt the jitters as they quivered in the middle of the knot that laid heavy in the pit of her stomach. "Damn," she shivered slightly. *I'm positive... I will be the focal point of Dan's attention. I know his eyes will only see me. So, why am I so worried?* Out loud she voiced, "Jackie, this is your wedding day. Enjoy it. Stop acting foolishly. Soon all your worries will be in the past and Dan will be yours."

She heard a light knock at the door and turned to croak a dry throated, "Come in."

Raynie opened the door slightly and peeked in. She asked softly, "Can I come in and visit, Mother?"

"Pleeeease," screeched Jackie, excitedly.

Smiling tenderly at her mother's obvious nervousness Raynie slowly entered the room, and for the first-time, Jackie viewed her daughter in the gown she had chosen for her. She was stunning and when Raynie moved forward she appeared to float above the floor. Jackie whispered, "breathtaking. Raynie, you are absolutely magnificent." Now she realized why she was so concerned; her daughter was beyond ravishing. Jackie suddenly wished she had chosen a less appealing color for Raynie and her two bridesmaids.

Raynie asked, "Are you ready, Mother?"

When Jackie stiffly nodded her head, Raynie rushed to her side to hold her close before they moved towards the door. When they entered the hall Raynie bit her lower lip to keep from uttering any of the doubts she still harbored. Hesitantly she inquired, "Mother, you're shivering! Are you okay? If you're not sure, you know we don't have to do this today? We don't have to do this ever if that's what you want."

Jackie smiled into her daughter's transparent hazel eyes as she concluded. Raynie's been wonderful about the wedding, more help than she ever dreamed she would be with its planning. Yet, through it all, there was a sense that she had to fight hard to hide her true feelings hidden. For an instant, Jackie's heart ached for her daughter's discomfort. But today was her day, and this is what she intended it to stay.

Jackie kissed her daughter's cheek and grabbed her hand and started pulling her down the hallway. While laughing, she cried, "Come on, Raynie, I'm just a nervous bride, and I'm wilting as we speak. So come on, baby, hurry! I want Dan to get the full splendor of his marvelous looking bride, while she still looks exquisite."

Standing beside her mother Raynie was as proud as any daughter could ever be. It was a challenge at first to except the fact that Dan and her mother were marrying, but she struggled to accept what she couldn't change. To this point she had succeeded, and for now her feelings were in a healthier perspective. Today she felt different about a lot of things, and with this clear new wisdom evident, she decided she was growing up.

Admittedly, Raynie liked the change she saw in herself. The transition started right after her father's unpleasant disclosure about her mother and their relationship. After that she started to really listen to her mother. In doing so, she found out that there was more to Jackie than just being her mother, that Jackie had dimensions to her personality.

Raynie smiled tenderly because she now recognized the guilelessness in her mother. Jackie had a naive side that most people neglected to recognize. She herself, had never noticed that her mother only saw the best in the people she loved. She simply overlooked any faults they had. When she mentioned this to her father, who had always known Jackie as a smart independent businesswoman, disagreed and dismissed the parable. *Even so*, decided Raynie, *I will view mother in this new light.* She smiled to herself, she liked the new feelings of amenability and guardianship that she now held towards her mother.

Raynie heard a stir and glanced across the aisle to where Mike stood, and their eyes met in a smile. She adored Mike; he was probably the nicest man she had ever known. She noted that Dan threw Mike a disgusted look while he searched in his pocket for Jackie's ring. Lately, she had become conscious of the way Dan treated Mike. This was something she had noticed before, but for some reason it never registered as wrong. Now however, it invoked a certain amount of antagonistic feelings towards Dan, and as a result, she began to see him in a less than perfect light.

She heard the Minister deliver the final part of his service, "Now I pronounce you man and wife." At once she glanced over to get a final glimpse of Dan before he kissed his bride. He was as handsome as ever, yet happier than she had ever seen him. Silently she wished them well. Nonetheless, when she followed the bride and groom down the aisle and out of the church, she did so in a misty-eyed daze and full of regret for what might have been. Yet she was happy for her mother and by the time she arrived at the reception, she had regained control over her emotions.

The chaotic bustling of the party was a diversion that Raynie was thankful for and her maid of honor duties left little time for Simon, which she tried to avoid since she feared he'd guess her feelings. She found if she blended in with the festivities or the loudest group, it was easier for her to become invisible and a safe haven.

After dinner, when the dancing began, she danced the first dance with Simon, then she let herself fade into obscurity, while she observed the happy couple from the sidelines.

Dan was his usual self, carefree and the life of the party as he danced his new bride into exhaustion. Later, when the evening progressed into late night, and before the reception was officially over, Dan swept her mother up and headed for the exit. Laughing and thanking everyone for coming, he dashed towards the door as he bellowed one last, "Thank you all for coming, but the honeymoon and the groom have waited long enough."

Dejected, Raynie watched from the other side of the room as her mother laughed and begged her to save her from this crazed man. Raynie pushed aside her feelings of remorse and laughed excitedly as she felt true happiness emerge once again for her mother and her new life. However, soon the scales tipped towards envy, and again her heart ached for Dan and what could have been.

As soon as the plane hit the ground at the Atlanta airport, their last stop before they were home, Dan was the first one out of the aircraft's door. Jackie stood in the background bewildered and clutching their overnight case as she attempted to pushed through the other passengers to catch up. From afar she observed as he rushed to the nearest phone and she assumed dialed his Director. After all the other passengers left, she stood in the background while he called every other person, he could think of who had anything at all to do with the picture. He had grumbled to Jackie, he had lost enough time, and needed to get things rolling as soon as possible.

Once they were settled in their hotel suite, he was back on the phone again. Jackie sat back on the bed observing the entire clamor. His eagerness was creating an energy that was vibrating throughout the room. She enjoyed his enthusiasm but still she felt bored and a little put off. Afterall, this was still their honeymoon! Their last night together as bride and groom and this was not what she had envisioned.

Finally, she stood up and moved closer to where Dan stood with his shoulder against the wall. He was gazing out the window while he chattered into the mouthpiece. His back was to her when she stepped up behind him and wrapped her arms around his waist. She squeezed and waited for a response. Following several attempts to get his attention with no success, she gave up. Halfheartedly she moved to the desk that was crammed with his budget papers.

Jackie was annoyed and she sulked as she gave the hotel suite the once over. This was the last night of their honeymoon and she had wanted it to be special. She had ordered the best champagne which room service already delivered, plus an excellent dinner that should be here within the hour. She wondered if it too would join the neglected champagne that sat on the table across the room. To her, it was obvious that Dan had already ended the honeymoon along with her much anticipated evening.

Feeling dejected, she reached over and pulled several of the papers off the desk. At first, she scanned them with little interest. Numbers almost always intrigued her, but tonight her mind was elsewhere. Soon a few clusters of numbers caught her attention and without realizing what she was doing, she began to calculate the digits. When the totals were tallied, she bit down on her lower lip and studied them, then recalculated the sheet. The numbers came out the same. She searched the desk to see if there was another part she hadn't seen. *"These numbers can't be correct. There has to be more. These clearly don't make sense."* She turned to look at Dan, but his back was still to her and his mind was on his conversation. He hadn't even noticed what she was doing. She set the papers back where she found them and returned to sit on the edge of the bed.

While she sat there, she considered the stats she had just read. Then decided, *I really shouldn't jump to conclusions. I'll just wait until Dan's off the phone, then I'll ask him about the movie's budget. But how does one ask their new husband if he's broke?* And that's exactly what he is if the numbers she read were correct. She supposed there might be a chance that she misread the sheet. Afterall it's been years since she'd even seen a budget sheet. *Yes, that had to be it. I simply read them wrong. He can't be broke, even if the picture hit a snag, he still has his mansion along with all his other interests which included part ownership in Dr. Carver's practice. With that interest alone he would be a wealthy man.*

Despite her self-reassurance, she suddenly felt the onset of goose pimples and soon they spread over her entire body. She recalled Mr. Little and his phone call. He said he was calling about a late car payment, although he did say he was looking for a Mrs. Dey. Then again, he also asked for Mr. Aleut before he hung up. At the time, she had taken it for granted that he had the wrong number since she always paid cash for her cars. It never occurred to her that Dan wouldn't do the same. *What if Dan owes money on the car? Should I tell him to take it back? I certainly don't need it. I only accepted the Mercedes because it was a gift. A wedding present...oh God, what about the diamond bracelet?*

Without warning Jackie felt Dan's presence. She hadn't even realized he had hung the phone up. Now he was standing over her, smiling down at her as if he hadn't a care in the world. At the immediate sight of him and his sensual masculinity, she couldn't help but smile delightedly as he reached out and pulled her to him. Soon all doubt had been pushed from her mind, and without further thought she eagerly allowed him and her own desires to embrace and control her.

Later that evening while Jackie lay sleepily in Dan's arms, she recalled the ambiguous totals. However, she immediately decided to dismiss them. For Jackie at this point had no problem believing that what she saw was all a big mistake, and Dan most likely could explain it all away if she cared enough to ask.

CHAPTER ELEVEN

The first two weeks of married life at home had been bustling yet blissful. Soon after that Jackie began to notice a difference in Dan. She pouted as she mumbled, "What is wrong with him lately? It seems he's always angry with me. I simply can't do anything to please him."

She still couldn't believe how angry he had become when she refused to add his name to her bank accounts. At the time she was surprised by his behavior, but soon she realized that there was another side to Dan, one she had never known existed. Now however, it seemed he had no problem displaying his negative qualities. *That* she thought, *became quite evident last night when she denied his second request to be added to her accounts.* He wanted, or more to the point, he demanded access to her checking accounts. His outburst frightened her far more then she would like to admit. Now, more than ever, Jackie felt the need to keep control over her own funds. Her fluid assets were never a compensation for him marrying her, only a benefit to be shared, *if,* and when she chose to do so.

Lately she had become very aware of Dan's sudden interest in her money, and this brought about a wary feeling. She knew the smartest thing to do in a predicament like this, was to be cautious, and cautious was precisely what she intended to be. Nonetheless, she did not want to be unfair. Yet the thought of giving up any kind of hold on her new husband...well, that might prove to be unwise; and not at all in her best interest. She needed some way to keep track of him and doling out a few bucks here and there was the only way she knew how to keep him in check. Especially with this new attitude of his.

Jackie considered the last night of their honeymoon, the night she discovered the budget sheets on their hotel desk. The memory made her shutter. Is *Dan in dire need of some real cash? Is that why he's behaving so strangely?* However, she really didn't believe that since his actions were as if he blamed her for his problems. *So,* she decided, *whatever it is that's bothering him, has to be something I did. Besides if he really needed money, he would surely ask me for a loan, wouldn't he? How can I find out,* she asked herself? She can't simply ask him straight out if he needed cash. Because he refuses to even discuss the movie with her. How can she even bring up the subject of a loan without first telling him that she snooped around his papers? Her discovery wasn't intentional. Nonetheless, when you read someone's papers without their consent, it's still snooping. *My God, I wonder if that's why he suggested selling the house. Maybe he thinks he can use the money for his project. Doesn't Dan realize how wealthy I am? They don't need to sell anything.* Although, she thought, *Dan never mentioned using the cash for his own purposes. His argument was only that they should move to a newer more affluent area.*

Jackie had vehemently disagreed. She loved Bel-Air and her house. She saw no reason to move. Despite this fact, Dan was adamant about moving. Jackie decided that she would try to be reasonable and so she listened to his rationale. But in the end, she explained once again that she had no intentions of ever selling her beloved Tudor. She owned the property free and clear, not to mention the hundreds of thousands she had recently spent on redecorating each and every one of the twenty-six-rooms. After her declaration, Dan's arguments grew heated. His anger that night had become so out of control that at one-point Jackie wanted to scream. She even debated whether she should inform him that he was the only one who was going to be selling something, and that is his damned inconsequential Production Company. She had decided it had to go.

Before that dreaded fight, Jackie had hinted several times that Dan should at least explore, if not consider other options. She even mentioned several people of power who she knew were interested in him. She tried to explain that with these associations he could easily be a great success and very quickly. However, her comments had made him even more angry and he rejected every one of her recommendations. Consequently, for the time being she decided to drop any further discussion of his future options or suggestions that he abandon his production company. But her mind was made up, he will have to shut down production.

"It's been close to a month, Aleut. You said you'd have my money by the end of February. Ya know you only have a couple of weeks, right? Do ya hear me, fuck-head, two weeks? We don't wanta hear no more excuses; our patience is running paper thin. You will pay up Aleut or"...., he laughed cruelly, to make his point."

This phone conversation from Javier, via Paulo, kept running through Dan's mind. Paulo scared the shit out of him, anyone could see the guy really enjoyed his job. He was a mean Portuguese who stood about five-foot-seven. Dan guessed he weighed close to two hundred pounds, which he rightly suspected was mostly muscle, not fat. "Hell," he muttered as he punched at the air, "I just don't know what to do about them or this whole damn situation. Damn you Jackie."

He had asked Mike for some more money, but all he could come up with was about seven thousand dollars. When Mike had handed him the envelope that contained the wad of cash, he asked him straight out, 'What the hell good is a measly seven thousand dollars going to do me? Mike, you have access to Louis's accounts, and you come here with seven thousand bucks? But Mike just walked away without comment. "Besides, most of that went on the back payments for Jackie's damn Mercedes," he groaned as in pain, "Jesus".

What's he going to do? He had to do something, and now. The damned picture is close to being completed so he's not about to quit. He should have never bought the fucking Mercedes. At least the seven-grand put an end to those aggravating phone calls. But what is he going to do about the loan? "Shit," he grunted. Nervously, he stood and began to pace the room while he tried to think things out. The damn interest has continued to pile up on the fucking startup money he had borrowed. It was almost impossible to stay ahead of it. "The answer is simple," he mumbled, "Pay back the first loan."

The principal wasn't due until the picture was completed. That's what was stated in the initial loan agreement. The primary note was to be paid out of the movie's profits, but these damned interest payments were to be paid weekly until then. But every time he was late, the payments doubled, then tripled if it went past ten days. He didn't remember reading that in the contract. "Damn, he should've read the fine print." He flopped himself back onto the chair as he wailed once again, "Damn it." He knew once the show hit the market the bucks would start rolling in and he wouldn't have to worry any longer. But for now, he needed a huge hunk of cash, along with a lot more time."

He thought of Jackie and muttered, "Shit." He really believed that once he married her, all his problems would be resolved. He at least figured by now, he'd be finished with those creeps and their outrageous interest. "But that bitch...that stupid little bit...."

The memory of Jackie and their last conversation made his blood start to boil. He still couldn't believe what an idiot he had been to have married that conniving little bitch. He still couldn't believe her gall. "Who does she think she *is*, not to put me on her bank accounts? We're husband and wife, I should have free access to anything she has," he grumbled. "All that fucking money just sitting in some damn bank vault begging to be used and she won't let me near it. I never realized how closefisted she was. God, worse yet, was her reaction to selling the house. You would've thought I asked her for ten pints of blood or something... what a selfish little bitch!"

He swallowed the last drop of his vodka, then stared at the empty glass as if it were a monster and the cause of all his problems. Finally, he slung the glass across the room. He immediately felt a slight tinge of release as he watched it crash against the fireplace. He laughed callously when the crystal shattered into a hundred tiny pieces and spilled across the marble floor. He swiped angrily at the sweat on his forehead, grumbling, "Shit, I bet she had this whole thing planned from the start. She probably never intended to share her damn fortune with me. It was all a game, like holding a carrot in front of a rabbit just to see how far you can get it to go. Damn her. Damn you, Jackie; go to hell!"

Dan shoved his fist in his jacket pocket and pulled the diamond bracelet out and eyed it. He hoped this will keep Paulo off his ass, at least until he figured out what to do next. Jackie sure as hell didn't deserve it; he should have never bought it for her in the first place, "Damn bitch."

Raynie held Mike close and kissed his cheek as she whispered, "Ooohhhh, Mike. I have missed you so terribly. You can't possibly have any idea how much."

"Me too, so I do have an inkling of how you feel. Good God, Raynie can you believe it's been close to two months since the wedding. Wow, it's unbelievable! By the way, I should say once again, just how beautiful you looked as a Maid of Honor." He bent his head closer and whispered, "Even prettier than the bride herself."

Raynie laughed and answered, "Thank you, Mike. But right now, that doesn't seem to be as important to me as it once was." She smiled and added, "My mother is gorgeous, and anyone can see that. I guess for the first time in my life, I can accept this truth and live contentedly under her shadow without feeling less of myself."

Mike reached a hand to his mouth as he staggered and gasped for air. While at the same time he prattled, "Oh my God, Raynie! Is that you talking? Have you gone and grown up on me? Or maybe you're only feeling sorry for yourself and playing, poor pitiful me?"

Laughing once again Raynie replied, "I'd like to think it's the first choice and I'm growing up and not that latter dispirited fable."

"Well, sit, sit young lady and please...you must tell me all. I have to hear exactly what brought about this elevated state of awareness. Oh my, I'm so proud of you."

"Only if you buy me a tall vodka tonic with double lime and *promise* to listen without making any witticisms about my new-found serenity."

"I promise. Boy scouts honor, I'll totally behave myself, and of course, mind my P's and Q's. As for your drink, it is on its way as we speak."

Over their Chinese chicken salad, Raynie briefly explained some of the factors that she attributed to her recent peace and perceptive-ness, which she reminded Mike was fortunate for everyone con-cerned, especially since it came before Dan and her mother's wedding. By the expression on Mike's face Raynie could see he was dying to interrupt.

But he squelched his desire and put aside all his remarks with a smile and a nod of agreement. He told himself he would not break his promise to listen without comment. However, when Raynie stopped to eat a few bites of her meal he did relate, "You know, Raynie, I could see a change in your self-confidence when we were standing in the reception line. You had an air of tranquility about you that I've never seen before. It was *then* and still *is* quite attrac-tive. I attributed it at the time to your new friend Simon Charles. Whom, by the way, is distressingly and an unprecedented find in your life... and if I might add, quite handsome. He seems like an ex-tremely honorable man. I hope he's in some way part of this new-found peace."

Raynie lifted her napkin and dabbed at her chin. "You know Mike, I really haven't given it much thought, but I think he is. I think he's a big part of it. You see when Simon and I talk, he really listens to me." She laughed, "No matter how ridiculous I might sound, he's patient with me. I like that he, without hesitation, calmly points out when I'm headed in the wrong direction, which, unfortunately, usually points to Dan."

"Raynie, do you think you're over that obsession you had for Dan?"

She hesitated and bit her lip while she considered the question, then asked. "Mike, when you were a child, did you ever have something that meant so much to you, that when you lost it you felt like you lost a piece of yourself?"

"Why... yes, I guess I have..., if I'm understanding you correctly. I felt that way when I lost my grandmother. She had always been a big part of my life and no one has ever come close to replacing that closeness."

"Well, that's sort of what I mean, but not quite. You see, I was thinking more of a belief or a fantasy. You know like Santa Claus or the Easter Bunny."

Seeing the uncertainty in his eyes she continued to explain by example. "See, when I was a little girl, my father would carry me outside to the patio every night and we gazed at the stars in the sky. Each time before he took me back inside for Mother to put me to bed, he always said," *Okay, baby, now let's reach. Reach up as far as you can. Up, up to the heavens above... let's see if we can snatch a star.* Then he would ask, *do you have it?* Of course, I always answered, *YES, yes, daddy, I have it.* At that moment, he would quickly add. *Okay, Ray, now let's close our eyes and keep your hands clasped tightly, we certainly don't want our star to get away. Okay, now let's make a wish. Do you have your wish? Now open your eyes, then hands and blow that star away as hard as we can. See...see there it goes, there goes your wish up, up, up to the heavens above, where all wishes come true.*

She fell silent and smiled at the memory. After a minute she continued, "See Mike, when we blew at our hands, sparkling dust flew in every direction... and Mike..., I truly believed that we had caught a star and my wish was going to come true...," She sighed before she continued, "and they always did." She played with her straw as she stared into the near empty glass and looked up solemnly into Mike's gentle eyes.

"Butttttt," prodded Mike

"But when I was six, I saw my father put a powdery substance in his hand as we passed his desk headed for the patio. I asked him about it and without dress or fluff, he told me the truth. I don't think my father realized it at the time, or even now. In that single instance, I lost something, something that meant so very much to me. So much in fact, I swear I felt my little heart break."

Raynie shook her head and laughed at the juvenile image she had conjured up, and added, "See Mike, in reality, it was nothing more than a silly illusion fabricated by a daddy for his little girl's amusement. For me, it was a real physical reality and when my balloon finally popped," she snapped her fingers for effect. "Poof, it disappeared into thin air, taking along with it something very innocent and precious." Raynie inhaled deeply and after a minute she amended. "I guess, what I'm trying to summarize here, in a roundabout way... is, that's how I felt when this sudden insight hit me. Before that point I felt like I had lost Dan. Then *poof!* I suddenly realized I never had him. It was all in my head. Nothing more. Yet I still felt as though I lost something very real and dear."

Mike didn't utter a word. Instead he reached out, took Raynie's hand and kissed it delicately then stroked it softly. Eventually he whispered, "Thank you for sharing that with me Raynie, it was beautiful. I believe most people would rather not share their cherished moments of innocence, let alone moments of self-perception. I honestly believe that it's one of the nicest things one can give another... I mean sharing one's most tender thoughts. Anyway.... Yes, I think I do understand what you mean. However, instead of feeling sad for you, I'm afraid I'm very glad. See Sweety, I've always feared that somehow you might accomplish your aim and end up with Dan. Sadly, I believe he could never be good enough for you."

"Mike, you're always saying things like that. Why? Dan's your best friend, so it seems if he's good enough for you, he should be good enough for me."

He laughed and cantered, "Touché. I'm afraid I can't argue with that logic. What's more, you're right. Dan is my best friend and I really do love him. But contra to most peoples' beliefs; I wholly see him for what he truly *is* and always has been."

"Which is?"

"Dan is and always has been a man of extremes."

"How do you mean?"

"He's a man in a mode of maximal drive. He not only wants to succeed; he must succeed. At times, his need is close to the point of absurdity and often closer to insanity. I have witnessed this very behavior countless times. Yet as much as I despise it, to some extent, I understand his obsessive intensity...and have from the very beginning. Moreover, I must sadly confess, I encouraged it by supporting him."

Raynie witnessed a slight change in Mike's tone as he spoke about Dan's past actions. It held a touch of anger and Raynie added, "Mike, you were only being a good friend."

"Yes, that's what I told myself in the beginning. But Raynie, as his desire for success grew, Dan began to change. I've seen him deliberately damage people's careers for nothing more than vindictiveness. Yet I stood by and said nothing..., all in the name of friendship. Even when he became appallingly flippant about it, I still said nothing and accepted him for whatever he was at every point of his many transformations."

"Mike, how could you say you love him in one breath, then be so critical the next?"

"Raynie my dear, it's been years since I came to grips with this startling apocalypse. At that time, I began to understand Dan, I recognized that it was inevitable that he would change as his obsession grew. I'm afraid that I was right. The man you see today is all that is left. A shell of the Dan I used to know. His appetite for success has devoured the real Dan Aleut, and all that's left is this shell, filled with self-indulgence." He sighed downheartedly before he added, "I shall always regret that I stood by and watched without a single word of caution to anyone. But, on the other hand, I am eternally grateful I will not have to do the same with you."

"Mike!" Her voice was miffed when she loudly gasped his name while the waiter turned sharply to throw a warning glance in her direction. She fought against the anger. Disbelief covered her face, and she lowered her voice to ask, "Mike, how can you say that? I mean... that's awful. He is supposed to be your best friend, plus you should keep in mind he's also married to my mother. I am sure she would have noticed such a flawed personality and would not have married such a man."

"I am sorry Raynie that you don't like what you're hearing, but Dan is the way he is. And there's nothing we can do to change that. I have stood by helplessly never saying anything as he changed more and more into a self-obsessed, self-serving human being. Whom, if I may add, has perpetually used every person who ever cared for him for his own gain." Mike recognized that Raynie's anger was deepening, so he lightened his tone. "Sweetheart relax, all I'm saying, is, I would have hated to have sat by and watched him turn you into one of those people."

"That's despicable, Mike."

"Raynie, please chill out, I'm not attacking Dan. I've said the same to his face. He knows what he is. He hides it from the world, but he knows there's no way he can hide it from me. I only meant I'm glad you didn't have to deal with it because he would've eaten you alive."

She sat there for several minutes. She could feel herself fuming one second then wanting to cry the next. "This can't be true," she argued; "Dan's not like that..., he can't be."

Mike smiled but said nothing.

After several minutes Raynie suddenly looked up, and her face held a new concern. "Mike, what about my mother? I mean if this is true, what's going to happen to her?"

"Sweetheart, Jackie can take care of herself. I know you don't really like to believe that, but it's true. I'm sure Jackie is aware of... what you called, Dan's flaws, and is willing to live with them for the time being. Raynie, your mother is extremely strong. Matter of fact, one of the strongest people I've ever met, so don't worry about her. She'll be okay."

After a long period of silence Raynie finally broke the mood with a change of subject. "Mike, why do you let Dan treat you the way he does? I've noticed lately that things in your relationship seem to be lopsided."

"Yes, you're right, it is. But then, like I said, I've always loved Dan. Although Dan has never seen us as anything except friends, he was my first love. *And* before you ask, **NO**, Raynie, we've never had an intimate relationship. I guess you could say, me giving all I could to the union, was my way of keeping him a big part of my life. I suppose it was an unhealthy relationship from the start, and I'm sure my selfish needs attributed to the creation of the Dan we see today. Yet, if truth be known, I would've done far more than prostitute myself for his success. I probably would have died for him if he had asked."

Raynie held Mike's hand to her cheek. She was hoping to comfort and relieve some of the pain she was hearing in his voice. In return he patted her hand and merrily added, "That is, until I met Louis. Now I understand the difference between love and lust. Which brings us back to where I can say confidently that you, Miss Raynie Dey, are beginning to comprehend the difference."

She smiled to show her support for Mike, but once again she had the feeling that she had lost something she really never had. Yet, she had a sense in some significant way it was going to affect her and change her life forever. *Is this a premonition, she asked herself, or a prediction?"*

However, soon after she felt this fear, she realized that what she sensed was not for herself, but for her mother. This realization made it grow infinitely worse since she was sure, that when it came to Dan, her mother was much more unsuspecting than most believed. She was sure Jackie only saw Dan through the eyes of blinded love, and if what Mike says is true, she wondered if her mother would be up for the fight.

Raynie tried to push her fears aside. She remembered what her father had told her a couple of months ago, and if what he said was factual, then Jackie can take care of herself. Mike plainly saw this strength in her, so she too. She should trust her mother's fortitude and instincts.

CHAPTER TWELVE

I t was late Sunday afternoon when Raynie met her mother for a game of tennis. She immediately grew alarmed at the strained look on her mother's face. This certainly was unprecedented. She couldn't remember ever seeing her look this upset even during her divorce. At once Raynie thought of Mike and his allegations, but quickly tried to push her trepidation aside. She didn't want to be unduly suspicious of every little thing concerning her mother and Dan. Jackie probably only needed some rest. Plenty of newlyweds wear a tired look and it was usually from a lack of sleep, not stress.

She forced a broader smile and gave her mother a peck on the cheek, and avoided any direct questions that might unfairly intrude on her new life with Dan. But after Raynie won the first and second set, then the match, she knew something was seriously wrong. There was no way she could ever beat her mother more than one set, let alone a match. Everyone knew Jackie was as close to an accomplished player, as anyone could get without being a rated professional.

"Mother let's stop for a while. I'm tired. Better yet, let's call it a day, and if you let me, I'll buy you a glass of passion tea and a lobster salad."

"Sure, honey that sounds wonderful. Let's freshen up a bit first, okay?"

When they left the locker room, they hurried towards their cars while Raynie playfully teased her mother about her game. As they rounded the corner both ladies gave a sudden yelp at the unexpected sight of Dan. He was slyly grinning while leaning nonchalantly against Jackie's Mercedes. Raynie thought his stance looked like a James Dean impersonation and she guessed planned.

"Hey.... sexy ladies, are you looking for a good time?" Her mother took his hand and laughed, so Raynie joined in, but she flinched when he wrapped his arm around her waist and jerked her closer to his side.

Jackie pretended she didn't notice and immediately asked, "What are you doing here, Dan? I thought you said you had a mountain of work to finish up at the studio."

"I completed it as expeditiously as possible, my sweet love. So here I am... hoping to convince the two most stunning women I know to have an early dinner with me." Opening his arms wide he stepped in front and took a slight bow as he declared, "Your handsome stud-master at your service."

Jackie giggled at Dan's flirtations.

Then Raynie jumped in, "I'm sorry Studly, but you're too late. I'm taking Mother to dinner."

Jackie jumped in, "Raynie, we can do the salad and tea thing next time. Why don't we take Dan up on his invitation and do something naughty? Like Steak Diane, baked potato with everything on it, followed by some delightfully fattening dessert."

Glancing from one face to the other before answering her mother, she apologetically replied, "Why don't you two go on? I have several tasks that need my attention."

Witnessing the instant disappointment spread across her mother's face, Raynie hesitated before she added to her response,

"Go on ahead and I'll meet you at Los Feliz Inn. Once I have the errand or two done, I'll be on the way. I shouldn't be too long, but don't wait on me, okay?"

Her mother immediately perked up and happily agreed. Before anyone could think of any other protest, Raynie hurried towards her car. As soon as she drove away, she decided, I really don't want to spend the evening in the company of Dan Aleut.

Ever since Mike had informed her about the other side of Dan's personality, Raynie felt uncomfortable at the prospect of spending time around him. Lately, she caught herself going over past events and often questioned if Dan had a hidden agenda in everything he did. Without thought, Raynie turned her car in the opposite direction and drove rapidly away from Dan and the Los Feliz Inn. She would call her mother later with some excuse. She was absolutely sure once she apologized, her mother would forgive her for not making the date. At this time, Raynie became conscious of an underlying disappointment, "Damn," she muttered, "I really wanted to talk with my mother alone, away from Dan's influence. Something's not quite right and I need to find out what's going on." Picturing her mother's-tired face she asked, "What has Dan done to you, Mother? Is he mistreating you?"

Her first instinct was to call her father and inform him of the situation but decided against it since she knew he and Pam usually went to their Palm Springs condo for the weekend. Most of the time they stayed until Monday morning so they would miss the heavy Sunday night traffic.

Raynie spent the next three hours driving around the freeways before finally turning her car in the direction of home. She felt her tensions ease as soon as she pulled into her driveway. After putting the top down, she sat there enjoying the soft music on the radio. The stars were bright and with the radio so low she could hear all the night's rhythmic sounds.

She inhaled the smells of the magnolia bush that was in an early spring bloom. In wonder she asked, "Why can't life always be this tranquil? Why does it have to be so complicated? This is a time in my life when everything is supposed to be easy. Afterall, I'm young and some say beautiful. I have a great job I love, and the show is doing well. Not to mention, I have more money than I can ever use. Plus, I'm free and unattached, so why in the name of hell; do I feel life is so complicated? Am I the one who makes it so?"

A twinkling star caught her eye and for an instant she felt a twinge of loneliness. She missed the simpler times in life, the un-complicated past, when the only man in her life was her daddy. She sighed, "Sometimes, I long to be that little girl of years past."

For a mere second, she felt a tinge of warmth, and the strong feeling of her father's arms around her. "Daddy, I wish I could go back in time, even if for only a minute. I'd choose our time together and make one last wish." She was thoughtful, then asked, "I wonder what I would wish?"

She smiled and leaned her head against the headrest to make herself more comfortable. After a minute, her mind began to drift. Soon she found herself at her Mother's wedding and immediately she thought of that old cliché', *Always a bridesmaid, never a bride.*

Jackie stood at the altar tall and proud, her beauty glowed in her elegant gown. Raynie fought the sudden surge of envy. When she succeeded in quashing that emotion, it was simultaneously replaced by a shot of panic. She was deftly aware that she shouldn't be going where her mind was headed. She thought, *"I was doing so well and here I am once again, dreaming impossible dreams."* Her mind's eye shifted to where Dan stood beside Jackie. His back was to her and the chapel was full of people. Raynie could hear the, *I do,* and her heart did a flip flop. Now it was she who was standing where her mother was supposed to have been.

At that moment, her heart began to beat faster and faster as he lifted each layer of lace away from her tear-stained face. Suddenly it felt like her heart stopped completely, and she was amazed and elated when she gazed into the smiling gray-blue eyes of Simon Charles. She immediately felt a rush of relief, it was Simon, not Dan, she was dreaming about. Happiness spread through every inch of her body and she smiled softly. Yes, she had to admit, at least to herself, that she was missing Simon terribly.

"I hope that smile is for me?"

Startled, Raynie jumped as she reached for her purse and searched inside for the can of mace that she always carried there. But before she could pull it out from the handbag's side pocket the door swung open and there in the light, stood Dan.

She jumped out of the car and yelled, "What the fuck are you up to Dan? You scared the stinking shit out of me."

"I'm sorry baby, but when I saw you sitting there so full of sweet thoughts and smiling, I didn't want to disturb you, then I couldn't resist it. You looked so damned sweet and beautiful in the moonlight."

She backed away and asked, "What are you doing here Dan? Aren't you supposed to be having dinner with your wife?"

"I know, but Jackie had a headache and when you didn't show up, she decided to call it an evening. She said she needed to go home and catch up on some needed rest." He smiled a suggestive grin and slurred, "She hasn't been able to get much sleep lately..., if you get my drift."

About this time Raynie realized that he'd been drinking, and from the sound of his voice, a lot. She backed even further away from him towards her house. While something in her head was screaming danger. She wavered, but she didn't know what to do. She didn't want to overreact. Maybe she was being stupid. After all this was Dan and he wouldn't hurt her. But on the other hand, he was acting strange and the look he was giving her made her feel extremely awkward. It was as if he was expecting something from her.

Raynie's carriage became defiant as she threw her shoulders back and stood tall to demonstrate a strength she didn't feel. She asked again harshly, "So, why are you here, Dan?"

"Your sweet little old Mommy wanted me to check in on you, she got worried when you didn't show up and you didn't answer your phone. As far as I can see, you're suuure lookin good to me.

So, baby...do you want a share some of those sweet thoughts you were thinkin about?"

Ignoring his questions and the lust she was seeing in his eyes she nervously asserted, "That's why we have phones, Dan. You should've kept calling and saved yourself a trip."

"Like I said, we tried, but no one answered. So that's when the old Mother hen got concerned and decided that I should go out and look for you. She's at home sitting by the phone in case you call. She said she didn't want to miss it." He hesitated and steadied himself, then looked her up and down again before he finally repeated his implied slurs, "She said she was worried about her baby girl. She just wanted to make sure you were okay. She thought I should find you and make sure you're fine. Well, from where I'm standing, I'd say you're sure looking pretty damn fine to me."

Dan stared at her as if he were waiting for something. The look in his eyes made Raynie feel nervous and she took another step towards the porch before he continued to stagger towards her again. He mumbled drunkenly, "I guess you could say, I found what I was looking for." He smiled stupidly at her and sneered, "Yes, I absolutely found what I'm looking for."

She didn't like what he was inferring and even more how he was referring to her mother, but she ignored his impertinence and decided it was best to keep her dialogue short and to the point. She started to back away while she mumbled, "Well, as you can see, I'm fine. So, thanks for checking. If you will... ahh, can you please tell Mother I'll call her in the morning...okay, thanks again, bye Dan?"

Dan stood there leering at her, but he said nothing. Hoping he'd get the hint and leave she added, "Good night, Dan."

In haste Raynie turned and headed for the porch. But when she reached the front door, she had trouble with the lock again. She jiggled the key back and forth, then pushed the door with her shoulder. However, before she could unlock it and get inside Dan was there between the screen and by her side. She really wanted to draw back when he put his hand on hers and asked, "Raynie, you're not gonna just leave me out here, are you? I just want to spend some time with you."

Instead of withdrawing she shivered inside but stood fast to show confidence. "Dan, it's getting late and I'm waiting for a call. So, if you don't mind, I'd like you to leave."

His only answer was an angry shove at the door. Before she could react, he pulled her into the room and yelled, "No damn fucken way...baby. You're not playing any more of your stupid games. You've been begging for this since I met you and you're one damn Dey woman, that's not gonna cheat me out of what she promised."

Raynie was more frightened than she'd ever been in her entire life. She tried to push him away as he attempted to force her against the wall and tried to kiss her. His slobbering advances made her want to vomit. She screamed, "Dan, stop, I never promised you anything. I don't know what you're talking about... please, Dan, don't. Dan, please go! Please, don't, don't do this; just go away. Dan, you're scaring me. Dan, please stop this insanity." She caught herself in a half sob as she realized she was begging. Then she asked timidly, "Why are you acting like this? Are you drunk, Dan? Can't you just go home to Mother, please?"

By this time, she could feel herself moving closer to hysterics and she reached out and fought with all her might. Yet Dan didn't seem to notice her efforts and continued his assault. At one-point, Raynie felt her fist make contact and Dan incoherently slurred, "No you don't. Stop fighting, Raynie! Dammit Raynie, I'm not going anywhere. So, stop pretending you don't want this, bitch."

"I don't Dan. Please go away. I don't want anything from you."

"Don't give me that shit. You've been after me since I met you. Always flirting and throwing yourself at me every damn chance you got. Hell, I should know. I had to listen to your damn fucken mother accusing me of flirting back. Well now here's your chance baby. I'm here to give you exactly what you've been asking for. I'm yours for the taking."

Dan staggered then caught himself as he added, "Come on Raynie, don't play hard to get, I've had a rough day." Suddenly Dan lurched frontward and grabbed her again. He was so close; she was stuck between him and the wall and couldn't move. Her growing fear gave her greater strength, and she fought back by kicking, slapping, and screaming with all her might. But she was no match for his intoxicated passion. She felt sickened as his hands probed her body and once again, she pushed and shoved, but he was all over her.

With each blow she threw that made contact, he threw one back. Her eyes were blinded with tears and she heard her own screams and they seemed so far away. When he pulled her blouse away and off her shoulders, she choked on her sobs. From far away she heard the ripping tears of her clothes and for a minute her mind went blank as she tried to close herself off from what was happening.

Suddenly Raynie heard a loud noise and Dan's grip slackened, then released her. She pushed and scooted as fast and as far away from him as she could get. Every inch of her body was shaking. As hard as she tried, she couldn't focus or see who was standing over her. She felt a touch and she wrenched. Feeling the softness of a warm hand she immediately knew who it was. Instantly Raynie threw herself forward and plunged her battered body into Shannon's arms.

Shannon held her close and rocked her back and forth for several minutes before she lifted Raynie's head upward and urged, "Raynie, can you hear me honey? We gotta get out of here before he wakes up. He's gonna be damn mad when he comes out of his stupor and realizes I hit him over the head with that damn brass figure. Come on, honey, get up. Let's walk. You can do that, can't you? Come on. You're okay, Raynie. He didn't do what he intended. We need to get to my place so we can call the police."

Her voice changed from the tender cooing to disgust as they started to pass over the slumped torso of Dan. Shannon swiftly brought her leg back and gave him one swift kick as she muttered, "Damned asshole, I hope you burn in hell."

Staggering and stumbling they made it to Shannon's house before they heard the car start and take off. Once they were inside, both exhaled a sigh of relief. Shannon hurriedly checked to make sure every door and window was locked. Finally trusting they were safe; she went over to where Raynie sat silently on the couch. Raynie appeared to be in a trance, but as soon as Shannon touched her, she dropped her head on her friend's lap and began to weep.

Shannon attempted to console her without success. After a while she gave up and let Raynie cry until she finally fell asleep. It was only a short period before she woke with a start. It took the frightened Raynie a minute to realize where she was. Once, she did, she began to remember the offensive assault. Her heart began to race wildly as the entire episode came crashing in on her. She reached out to pull Shannon close to her once more then asked, "How did you know?"

"I heard the noise when I pulled into the driveway. At first, I thought maybe you were just havin a good time. But then I heard a loud commotion, and I could hear your voice and the panic in it. Then you screamed. I didn't know if I should call the police or go in and help you myself. Only I was afraid the police would take too long, so I grabbed the first heavy thing I came across and ran to your rescue. Shit...Raynie, I was scared out of my wits."

Raynie hugged her firmly and whispered, "Oh God, Shannon I owe you. Thank you so much."

When Raynie pulled away and sat back, Shannon caught the first full glimpse of her face, "Oh, Raynie your face. What did he do to you? Did you know that creep? I couldn't see his face, so I didn't recognize him. Raynie, we need to call the police."

Raynie wiped at her tear stained face and hiccupped a whimpered, "ye..yes, I know him."

"Whooo? Was he your date?"

"No! No, he wasn't my date. It was Dan."

"Shannon looked sideways at her friend as she attempted to put things in some kind of perspective. After a minute she asked skeptically, "You don't mean your Mamma's Dan? Not the guy you wanted for your own. The one you said you loved."

"Oh God, Shannon that sounds so awful, but it's true; Dan was right I was asking for it."

"No! Raynie, no. That jerk had no right to lay a hand on you. It wasn't your fault, do you hear me? He had no right to touch you."

Raynie nodded her head in agreement, but Shannon could see she was still in a state of confusion. She could also see Raynie wasn't sure if she agreed with her or not. Shannon sat quietly while Raynie searched her face then asked, "What am I going to do Shannon? What? I can't call the police; I can't tell anyone. Everyone knows that I've been acting like a tramp. I mean it had to be obvious to everyone that I wanted Dan." Almost immediately new panic covered her face and she deemed, "Oh, God. Everyone will think I deserved this. But I swear..." Once more she fell back in Shannon's arms and burst into a mournful wail. Between sobs she sniffled, "Nobody's gonna believe me... nobody, and I deserve it."

"No, Raynie, you are wrong honey. You're not the one who's done anything wrong. It's Dan. He's the one to blame. The guy's an asshole, and out and out scum of the earth."

Shannon comforted the distraught Raynie as she cried late into the night. Afterwards, when she fell into a restless sleep Shannon stayed awake on alert with a watchful eye. She felt so unbelievably bad for her friend. With Raynie's head laying restlessly on her lap she now and then stroked her friend's battered cheek. She listened to each breath Raynie drew then released. As time ticked away and the quiet of night filled the house, Shannon began to weigh the only details she knew. Finally, she shrugged. The only experience she had with something like this was with her cousin Deedra and even the police treated her badly. Maybe Raynie's right and it's best if she says nothing at all.

CHAPTER THIRTEEN

The next morning Raynie stood in front of the mirror. She was trying to decide how to conceal the puffiness along with the dark bruises that covered one side of her face. Unexpectedly she was startled by a knock at the door. She stood rooted as panic flooded her veins. She couldn't decide whether to run for the back door or pretend she wasn't home. Her only conscious thought was: *What if it's Dan and he's back to finish what he started. I have to get out of here.* Yet her feet wouldn't move.

All of a sudden, she heard a more determined knock, and Mike's voice called her name softly. "Raynie, Raynie, are you okay?" She stood still, not a muscle moved or a breath exhaled as she waited in a silent transfixed state of turmoil. For the first time since the start of the assault, she began to consciously feel the wild raw fear that raged within her. Minutes ago, when Shannon left her standing in her living room, Raynie assured her that she was okay, but now she knew she wasn't. She didn't want to see Mike; she didn't want to see anyone. Her only wish was to be invisible. She knew eventually that she'd have to face people, but at her own chosen time, not now. She wasn't ready, not yet.

Once again, she heard Mike's voice; he was talking softly, not more than a loud whisper, "Come on, Raynie, I know you're in there. Your car is still in the driveway. Please let me in. I really want to help." He began to stammer, and his voice sounded close to a sniffle when he added, "Raynie..., I... I know wh... what happened last night. I'm here for you, Raynie. You know I wouldn't hurt you, don't you? I just want to see for myself that you're all right." He waited and when she didn't answer he said, "Raynie, I'll stay out here all day if I have to. I am not leaving until I see you." He said nothing more. He just leaned his tall slim frame against the door and waited quietly for Raynie to decide what she wanted to do. After about ten minutes or so he heard the chain on the door being removed. The lock twisted then slowly it opened.

Raynie stood behind the open door with only her swollen eyes peeking around the walnut structure and said, "Okay, you've seen me, now go away."

"Raynie pleaseee, I know you must hate all men right now. But Raynie, this is me, Mike, I'm your best friend. You know I would never hurt you. Somewhere deep within yourself you know that. I know you do. Please, won't you let me in?"

Raynie waited a minute, then cautiously stepped back, and opened the door all the way. Once inside, what Mike saw almost broke his heart. He stepped closer and took Raynie in his arms and a tear rolled down his face when she wrenched. She seemed so fragile and child-like, and he couldn't think of a single word to say.

A few minutes later she pulled away and asked coolly. "Did Dan send you?"

He noted her voice was full of repugnance.

"No Sweety, he doesn't even know I'm here." He took a deep breath and exhaled before he continued, "I'm sorry baby. I knew he was having problems and drinking a lot. Still...still..., Raynie, I never dreamed he was capable of something like this. I'm so sorry. This is hideous behavior."

Raynie felt the sensation of nausea and realized she hadn't eaten since yesterday morning. The thought of food made her feel queasy and her stomach lurched. She threw her hand to her mouth and ran to the bathroom. Mike could hear the sounds of retching as the door was slamming shut behind her.

When Raynie came out about fifteen minutes later, Mike had a pot of coffee and toast sitting on the table. Raynie's face was white behind the purple marks left by Dan's blows. He wanted to cry for the pain she was enduring, but nevertheless he only encouraged, "Come on baby, sit down and at least nibble at it."

Once Raynie began eating and sipping the coffee, she could feel her stomach's discomfort ease up, and soon it felt much better. After she finished two pieces of toast and three cups of coffee, she pushed herself up. She stood and walked over to the window. Looking out with her back to Mike she asked, "What did he tell you?"

"Raynie, he was drunk. He said he doesn't remember everything or how far it went. Only that he hurt you." Mike walked over to where Raynie stood and turned her around so he could see her face. He touched it softly and avowed, "Raynie, he's really beside himself. He wouldn't want to hurt you for anything. He just wasn't himself last night." Mike wavered and then went on, "Dan's worried that you're going to tell Jackie. He said he loves her and wouldn't want to lose her for...for...He's so sor..."

Raynie felt her body tremble as all the fear and pain came together and changed into one big ball of hatred. When it finally exploded, it was full blown out of control rage. She ripped herself away from Mike's grasp and cut him off in the middle of his sentence. Her shriek was loud and uncontrolled, "Love! Love! Dammit, Mike. He's using you to ask me, not to tell his wife that he tried to rape me! You're no fucking better than he is!" Her anger grew and she screamed, "You're no friend of mine! You're just the same as always. Dan's little puppet! Doing whatever he tells you to do to cover up his mess and protect him! You are as loathsome as he is, and your evaluation of him last week was nothing more than a simple mask to hide your true self, along with that despicable depraved love you carry for him!" She laughed a disgusted growl as she taunted, "Remember Mike, you said it. You said you'd do anything for him, even die. Well right now, I wish both of you were fucking dead! Now, get the hell out of my damn house...Go back to Dan and your sick exploited relationship! As for my mother...!"

She stopped short and hesitated, she felt unsure of what to say next because she didn't want to hurt her mother in any way. Finally, full of frustrated anger, she cried. "You tell Dan if he ever hurts my mother, I'll kill him myself! Now get the fuck out of my house, Mike."

"But Raynie, that's not wh..."

She ran over to the door and slung it wide open and yelled, "GET OUT! GET THE HELL OUT, NOW!" She slammed the door behind him and marched straight over to the phone and dialed. After several rings, she heard the comfort of her mother's soft voice. Immediately she asked, "Mother..., are you okay?"

"Why, of course dear, why wouldn't I be? But from what I hear, Dan said you're a bit under the weather. He said you thought it was the flu."

Raynie gnawed on her lower lip before she answered, "I'm much better today." She paused as she fought back her distaste for Dan and his lies, then asked, "Mother...can we have lunch Wednesday?" She paused and waited for her answer, but quickly added, "Alone."

"Why, of course honey. Are you sure you're, all right? I can come over and take care of you. You know, like the chicken soup thing."

Raynie smiled at the thought of her mother attempting to play nursemaid. "No, Mother, I'm fine. I'll just see you on Wednesday at our usual time and place. I love you. Bye." Quickly she sat the phone back in its cradle as she thought, *I'm going to do whatever I have to do to protect her.*

After Raynie hung up she realized what time it was and grabbed the phone again and dialed the studio. As soon as Marsh heard her voice he yelled, "Raynie, where the fuck are you? We're about to start shooting!"

"Actually, Marsh, I was calling to let Derrick know, I'm not coming in today."

"What! No, Raynie, I need you."

"Marsh, you'll be fine. Just stay cool."

"Are you sick?"

"Well, in a way. I fell off my porch yesterday and I'm pretty sore and bruised up. I just need a couple of days to soak it off. I'll be in on Wednesday."

Raynie drew herself a hot bath and filled the tub with bubbles and added a bath salt that indicated it would ease sore muscles. As soon as she laid her head back against the tub, she began to relax in the sweet-smelling water. It didn't take long before she could feel her body going limp from the water's warmth. Several times her mind drifted back to the night before, and she fought back an urge to cry. Ultimately, she decided to face the inevitable and let her mind travel back over the past fifteen hours.

Dan was drunk. That she was sure of. However, that didn't excuse him or his actions. What did he mean when he said...*You're one Dey woman who's not going to refuse to give me what she promised? Did her mother promise him something and reneged on her word? What did Mike mean when he said Dan is having a lot of problems and drinking heavily?*

Raynie tried to recall if Dan ever drank a lot in the past. She didn't think so. Although, as Mike recently pointed out, there was a lot she didn't know about Dan Aleut.

"Was Dan having problems with his Production Company? Maybe the movie's going over budget or something," she muttered out loud." *Except that's almost expected now a days. Most films go over budget, she concluded thoughtfully.*

Raynie sank fully beneath the bubbles and made a mental note to look into Dan's financial situation. She also decided that she would ask her mother if she had any of the answers to these questions. She hoped so because a few answers are what she needed to ease this feeling of impending doom.

Raynie wondered if this was a sixth sense or merely a side effect to her recent cataclysm. After giving it some thought, she decided it really didn't matter. She had an urge to circle the wagons and keep her loved ones safe. This is exactly what she intended to do.

CHAPTER FOURTEEN

"What! What do you mean, you don't know if she's going to tell Jackie? God dammit Mike! Everything I have is on the line here. Everything I've ever worked for is about to go up in smoke and you sit there like you haven't a worry in the world. Christ, can't you get it through your fucken head that I need you now more than ever before. Mike, you've got to help me. Tell me what to do because I don't know anymore. If Raynie goes to Jackie, I'm finished, I'll lose everything."

"Dan, you are your absolute worst enemy. You're the one who keeps doing one stupid thing after another. Why do you have to keep dragging me in the middle of it all? Right now, I think you deserve anything and everything you get."

"God dammit, Mike, I asked for your help, not another one of your Goddamn sermons. I don't need anyone to tell me what I'm doing wrong. Hell, if I want to hear that, I can go home and listen to Jackie."

"Dammit Dan, until you acknowledge that what you did and what you're doing right now is wrong, then we're not going to be able to fix it. Nobody can."

"That's bullshit."

Mike stared angrily at the man he once knew as well as he knew himself. Now he wasn't quite sure where that person was. This man was a virtual stranger, an utterly awful person who cared for no one other than himself. Frustrated, Mike angrily bellowed at the hard-hearted man that stood impassively in front of him. "As far as I can see, Dan, if you don't straighten up your act you're going straight to hell in a handbag and justly so!" He turned to leave and when he grabbed the doorknob, he suddenly stopped. He decided to give it one more attempt before he gave up entirely. He turned to face Dan and his voice softened while his tone grew close to a plea, "Dan, I remember that you once told me that Jackie is always talking about helping you. She wants to help you become the success you've always yearned for. So pleaseee, please let her. Why can't you simply accept her help and be done with it? You know as well as I do, that she not only knows everybody, she knows the right people. I know she would be happy to help if you will only ask."

"To hell with you Mike! All I want or ever wanted from Jackie was her damn fucken money. I don't want *her* or any of her pompous ass friends telling me how to run my Goddamn business."

Mike was completely frustrated but took another stab at it, "But you're in trouble Dan, and they can help you."

"More likely, they'll run my ass and my company into the ground. You know damned well the whole lot was unhappy when I started this project. Most thought I should stay working for the big studios. They acted like I stepped over the line, and that I should've known my place, which is under the thumbs of jackoffs like them. That, my damn friend, is exactly what Jackie thinks too. She wants me to be their puppet so she can control my every move. Like I told you before, all I want from that bitch is for her to just shut up and back me. Instead, all I hear is how she wants me to go back to work for the fucken big shots. In her words, 'Dan, you may have been impetuous by starting your company too soon.' Jesus, can you believe that? She even had the nerve to say, 'We can do this little thing later when we're more prepared.' Hell, first of all, where the fuck does she get-off telling me what I can or can't do. Secondly, where the hell did, she get this, *WE*? As for her calling Aleut Productions, a little thing. Well she can go to hell. The Damn Bitch!"

"Dan, I'm sure you're taking it all wrong. She didn't mean it like that."

"The hell she didn't. She wants me under her control, and as far as she's concerned, me going down, will put me right where she wants me."

"Dan, if you don't ask her for the money, those thugs are going to hurt you. They may even kill you. Dan, you have to tell Jackie the truth. You don't have any other choice."

"I'm not telling Jackie anything, and you better make sure Raynie keeps her mouth shut too or I'm damn sure not going to get any money out of the bitch. And without her money she's no damn use to me at all."

Dan stopped his gait in midstream and turned to face the distressed Mike. He raised his finger to almost touch the tip of his nose and shook it at Mike vigorously and violently threatened, "But, I can tell you this, I'm at the end of my rope, and I don't intend to stand by and let Jackie, together with her friends, ruin me. You can mark my words, Mike. I'll get that damn money if I have to kill her for it. She's not keeping it away from me any longer."

"Dammit, Dan, stop talking stupid. What are you planning now?" Suddenly his eyes lit up and he asked, "Dan, you're not thinking of embezzling it, are you?"

"I don't have to steal what's rightfully mine. The law says if we're married, I own fifty percent of everything, and I intend to use my share to make me even richer."

"But all that money is Jackie's, Dan. When she finds out you took it, you'll go to jail. Even worse yet, she'll tell everyone she knows, and you'll never work in this industry again. Have you gone crazy, Dan? This is your life you're talking about; please don't do something you'll seriously regret."

"You are exactly right, Mike. It is my life, and I intend to take control of it from this point on. Jackie's only my wife, not some matriarch who can give me charitable gifts here and there in an attempt to make me happy. I own half of everything she has, and I want my share, and I want it now!"

When Jackie saw Raynie seated at the table they had reserved, she felt her heart sink. Something was terribly wrong. Jackie, without hesitation, rushed over to Raynie's side and pulled her chair closer to hers as she sat down. She at once grabbed her daughter's hands and begged, "Raynie, what is it? What has happened? Tell me! Please tell me?"

"I'm fine Mother." She forced a laugh and kidded, "Mother, don't be a drama queen, I've had the flu that's all."

"That's all! You look awful. Why didn't you call me and let me take care of you? Why is your face swollen? It almost looks bruised. Were you in a car accident?"

"Mother, I fell off my steps and bruised myself. It's no big deal, I'm fine and I'm not here to discuss my health. I only have an hour for lunch so let's talk about you."

"Me? Why do you want to talk about me?"

"Well, not you exactly, but you and Dan."

Immediately Raynie recognized the look that crossed her mother's face. She could read from her expression that she thought she was after Dan again. Suddenly, Raynie was sure she had made the right choice, by not telling anyone about Dan and what he tried to do.

Reaching out and patting her mother's hand to reassure her, she bent forward to kiss her on the cheek. Then smiling a difficult, but nevertheless cheery grin she said, "*Mootherr*, I just want to know how married life is? Are you happy? Is Dan treating you well? Is it everything you hoped it would be?"

She saw the happiness flicker across her mother's face and relief filled her smile. Laughing, Jackie said, "Oh sweetheart, yes. Married life is definitely good, and Dan treats me very well. Besides, you know me well enough to know that I wouldn't take anything from anyone and that includes Dan. Sure he's moodier than I realized, but it's nothing I can't handle."

"Yes, I guess I knew that Mother, but I think I just needed to hear it all from you."

Raynie sipped at her iced-tea and continued to chitchat until their order was placed in front of them. The waiter asked again if he could bring them anything else and then retreated to whereabouts unknown.

Preoccupied Raynie fell silent and watched the couple seated at the next table. She pretended to scrutinize the server as he poured the couple's wine into their glasses. She used this time to put her thoughts in order for her next question. Once she felt she was ready, she moved her gaze to face her mother's wary stare. Yet, before Raynie could ask her question, her mother began to speak in a low troubled tone.

"Raynie...Raynie, I hope I'm not overreacting, but I think Dan's having money problems." Jackie thought about what she said then hurriedly continued. "You see Sweety, when we were coming home from our honeymoon, I noticed some papers on the desk in our hotel suite. I want you to know, I wasn't intending to snoop, I just started to shuffle the papers around mostly from boredom. Then I noticed that they were budget sheets...and well. Anyway, you know me with numbers, and before I knew it, I was unconsciously adding them. Raynie the numbers were...well way off. I know you may think this is none of your business Raynie, but Dan won't talk with me about it, so I can't find out what's going on. Anyway, I was hoping that since you're on the inside, maybe you can ask around and find a few answers. I would do it myself, but I don't want to call attention to him or the situation, which I know would happen if I asked the people I know. I just wish he would talk to me, but...he..." Jackie shrugged her shoulders and fell silent for a few minutes before she completed her misgivings in a fretful tone. "I do want to help him, Raynie. I even tried to suggest in a roundabout way that he go back to work for one of the big studios. Only Dan doesn't want to hear it. He won't even discuss it."

Raynie sat quietly and picked at her salad. Their patio seat was next to the sidewalk, and she watched several people stroll pass while she weighed her mother's words. As she evaluated what her mother had asked her to do, she realized it was exactly the information she had hoped to get from her mother. She had wanted to find out if Dan was in financial ruin and what he meant about the Dey women not giving him what they had promised.

Raynie assessed the worried look in Jackie's eyes and realized that this request was difficult for her to ask. This realization only added to her animosity for Dan, and instantly she was again forced to battle with her anger. She realized she now needed answers not only for herself, but for her mother as well. At that moment she could almost taste the hatred she harbored towards Dan. She choked back the urge to cry when she suddenly recalled Sunday night's horror. She trembled then guardedly avowed, "Mother, on Sunday afternoon when we played tennis, I could see something was wrong. You were more than just a little worried about Dan's possible money problems. Your mind was elsewhere throughout the entire game. To tell you the truth, I can't remember ever seeing you so distracted or distressed."

She paused and took one more sip of her iced tea before she hurriedly moved on, "Consequently, that was one of the reasons I wanted to see you today. I wanted to ask if there was anything I can do. I am deeply concerned about you and your welfare... Mother." She wavered, then rushed on, "Mother, I hope you won't be angry with me, but I already started to check around. I apologize if I overstepped my boundaries, but I took it upon myself and asked several people I know who work on Dan's set. They say there are no major shooting problems with the movie. Nothing more than what's normally expected. You know, stars and their attitudes, etc., except another source said he heard a rumor that there may be a few minor problems with Dan's backers. However, he reminded me that it was only a rumor; he didn't have anything concrete. Although, after a few additional inquiries, I got a different perspective. Now I have a hunch, it's far more than just a little financial problem…well, I guess what I'm saying Mother, is your suspicions are warranted. Dan has a big problem with his finances. I don't know if it's the backers who are giving him the headache or not. All I know, is the money is close to being gone." With due precaution Raynie pushed on, "Mother, I hope you're not angry with me for assuming your problem was with Dan? But that was the only thing I could think of that would have you that upset."

"No, honey, I'm not angry with you. Besides, I can't say that I wouldn't have done the same thing if I were in your shoes. In all honesty, I'm glad you have some information for me. It may not be much, but at least it's enough to answer a few of my unanswered questions."

Raynie waited as she watched her mother's eyes dart back and forth as she cogitated what she had just learned. Suddenly Jackie's expression changed, and Raynie knew she'd come to some conclusion. Eagerly, but composed, she waited until Jackie was ready to divulge her revelation. After some thought, Jackie decided there was no nice way to say what she was about to say without sounding dubious, so she professed. "Honey, like I said, I want to help Dan, but I don't want to give him a free reign over my money, which seems to be what he wants. He's asked me several times to sign him onto my checking account. He also asked to be added to my savings and investments accounts. His reasoning is that this would save him and me a lot of wasted time since it would eliminate the transferring of funds. But, as you see, I'm not convinced. I have an uneasy feeling about doing this. I simply don't think it would be a wise move for me. What do you think, Raynie, am I wrong?" By the time Jackie concluded her disclosure she was close to tears. It was easy enough to hear her uncertainty and again she asked, "Raynie, is that being unfair to him? I don't want to be unsympathetic. I do want to be a good wife, but." She shook her head in dismay.

"No, no! Mother, you're not wrong. Please don't let Dan make you feel at fault. You don't owe him anything, and he shouldn't expect your financial backing just because you're married to him."

"I do want to help him become successful, sweetheart. Yet, on the other hand, if it isn't a smart investment...I don't know, Raynie...,I guess what I'm trying to make clear in my own mind, is whether or not it is a prudent venture to be involved in. I definitely have no intention of throwing good money after bad and with Dan acting so irrational...well damn..., Raynie, he won't tell me anything about the project, so I have nothing to weigh against my intuition. As it stands, I certainly can't make any decision other than the one I've made, and this, my dear, is what was on my mind Sunday afternoon. You see Dan and I had this very discussion earlier that day, and he was livid when he slammed out of the house that morning. In all honesty, he was so angry, I wasn't sure if I would ever see him again."

Raynie held her mother's hand and whispered, "Oh Mother...." Yet she couldn't think of what to say.

Jackie squeezed Raynie's hand to let her know she understood and then went on, "Raynie, I really do love that man. I've never loved anyone like I love Dan, and I would do just about anything not to lose him, but instinctively, I think the biggest mistake I could make is to give him money right now."

Once again, Raynie had an uncontrollable desire to protect her mother. She reached out and hugged her close asking, "Mother, are you ever afraid of Dan? I mean... has he ever hurt you or threaten to hurt you?"

Her mother pulled away surprised and in an appalled manner, replied, "My goodness, Raynie, of course not. That's not something Dan would do. Never, ever. It's just not in his nature; he's too gentle and kindhearted."

Raynie knew better than this but still she chose to stay silent. She loved her mother and didn't want to be the one to break her heart, so she smiled and agreed, "Yes, I'm sure you're right, Mother." Immediately she moved to lighten the tone of their conversation and joked, "I don't know what's wrong with me lately. I guess when I stayed home with the flu, I watched too many of those miserable talk shows. You know the ones, where people actually beat one another up and everybody hates everyone. Maybe that's why I'm sounding so cynical." Shaking her head, she laughingly suggested, "Maybe I better start watching more reruns of, La Verne and Shirley."

Raynie felt better when she saw her mother's tenseness disintegrate and she joined her in her laughter. Immediately Raynie raised her hand for the waiter, "Let's celebrate me being over the flu. How about some yummy creamy dessert? I don't have to leave yet...," glancing at her watch she declared, "I still have at least fifteen minutes before I'm really late."

Jackie released another relieved chuckle and confirmed, "Raynie, you are forever late. To tell you the truth, I can't remember a time when you weren't. Matter of fact, I think you set the pace long ago when you were born two and a half weeks late, and if I recall correctly, you threw your father's and my long-awaited vacation to Paris into chaos. Maybe that's why you turned out to be such a Daddy's girl."

"Now Mother; come on, how would that make me a Daddy's girl?"

"Well, I would have to say, he was forever grateful to you for saving him from what he described as, *Three weeks in purgatory!*" Laughing at Raynie's expression, she added, "And yes, I'd love some cheesecake and coffee."

On the drive back to the studio Raynie attempted to put into perspective what her mother had confessed to her at lunch. She considered Dan and his request for money. The idea that he had gotten angry when Jackie refused his request didn't surprise her. It seemed that Dan always expected to get his way. Considering his circumstances...he must be feeling desperate. But to think he had thrown a tantrum when he didn't get what he wanted infuriated her. However, she also needed to take into account what harsh facts she had newly learned from her colleagues earlier this morning. Dan's production company is in debt. Far more than she let her mother believe. He wasn't just close to being broke as she had indicated to her mother; he was overdrawn on most of his accounts. She can only guess, but she thinks the company is close to folding.

Regardless of all the facts, from what she's heard, Dan refuses to accept his imminent failure. He has gone about business as if nothing were amiss. She also learned that some of the key cast members are close to jumping ship. She sighed, "Maybe with all this overwhelming uncertainty and ruin looking him in the face...." She shook her head in disbelief. "Maybe Dan's near the breaking point and that's why he's been acting so crazy." She was surprised by a sudden emotional surge of reprisal and smiled with satisfaction. Somehow his impending doom gave her joy. She cursed, "Dammit Raynie, you should be ashamed of yourself." Nonetheless the concept still made her feel glad and she savored his pain and approaching adversity with unadulterated gratification.

Raynie wondered if she should speak with someone about her mother's concerns. With all these unanswered questions, a new distrust for Dan and his motives had begun to surface. Plus, she felt a strong need to warn someone, but whom? Who can he hurt besides Mother and warning her is out of the question?

She toyed with the idea for several minutes before she asked herself, "Who can I turn to with these suspicions? Who can I trust to help protect Mother?" Better yet, she wondered, who is going to believe me, especially after the way I've been behaving these past months?"

She wanted to cry when she recalled all those months when she'd thrown herself at Dan. Now everything was different, she despised him. She was frightened of him, especially what he was capable of. One thing she was certain of, is he couldn't be trusted. She wished she could turn to her mother for comfort, yet it was her mother who needed comforting right now. She felt overwhelmed with uncertainty then decided, "No, Raynie let's not panic, get a hold of yourself. Think girl, think."

Calmly she thought, *If, or when, my mother learns the truth, she will leave Dan and she'll need a strong shoulder to lean on, in any which case I, intend to be that shoulder. So, the less I have to do with*

Dan's undoing, the easier it will be for mother to come to me for comfort.

"God," she uttered anxiously, "I hope I'm wrong about Dan and his unscrupulous intentions; but no matter how I look at it, it seems Mother's in trouble." Deplorably, it appears that Dan has always been after more than marital bliss; it seems, he was far more interested in the enormous fortune her mother has; than her mother herself.

CHAPTER FIFTEEN

"**D**amn, I'm running late again." Raynie searched for the phone that she knew was buried somewhere beneath the pile of scripts, breakdown sheets and shooting-schedules. Her desk was a mess, yet she didn't have time to worry about it now. It would have to wait until tomorrow along with the laundry piled on her bed. "One quick call to Father and I'm out the door, but where's my phone? Move kitty?"

Midway through her hunt she stopped and smiled when she recalled what her mother had said about her always being late. She picked the phone up but set the headset back in its holder immediately after. Grabbing her purse, she headed for the door. There was no need to call her father, he wouldn't expect her to be on time any more than her mother would. He would have his cocktail and socialize with the other patrons, many who were longtime friends and business associates.

Yes, her father had never been short of companions. Rarely did he sit alone for any length of time before someone felt inclined to join him. This had always been a sore spot for her and now for the first time she realized why, *I truly dislike sharing him,* she thought.

She pondered their times together then determining, *in all honesty, I rarely win my father's full attention.*

She shook her head sadly before resolving, *come to think of it the only time he'd ever been fully hers, was years ago when they shared those moments beneath the stars. Then and only then, was she his complete focal point.* Her body almost wrenched with surprise and she stopped and stood still as she felt her heart sink. "At long last I understand." It wasn't the wish-game she lost years ago; it was the private moments alone with her father. It wasn't the fantasy or the wishes that came true, but the simple innocence of a shared moments that was irrevocably lost forever. It was around that same time that her father's practice grew to what it is today, and in that ensuing period, he had less and less time for her. Clearly, she had never gotten over this loss. It seemed like most of her life, she had continued to search endlessly for that same undivided attention. This revelation frightened her but nonetheless she realized it was true. Wearily she sighed and headed for her car, "Oh Daddy, I guess my need for you never dwindled and shamefully, I simply substituted you with a sundry of unworthy young men. The more inaccessible you were to me, the needier I became."

Raynie walked pass Jimmy and waved as he blew her a kiss and pointed in the direction of her father's table.

Although the restaurant was crowded, she could see her father. He was seated with an old business acquaintance and she slowed her pace so she could observe them as they happily carried on their conversation. When she was close enough to see his face, she thought, *Daddy, are you the reason I always want what I can't have? Can it really be that simple? The little girl inside me, never satisfied her need for her father's attention. Wow, if this is true...'* but she had little doubt that it was right on. She smiled slightly as she thought, *Simon would be proud of me.*

Her father stood up immediately and announced, "Here's my beautiful daughter." He kissed her cheek as he asked, "Honey, you remember Ralph Nader, don't you? We haven't seen much of him these past few years, but I'm sure you remember him."

She smiled warmly while she said her most gracious hello. She had always liked Ralph and what he stood for. Ralph shook her hand and mumbled sincerely how glad he was to see her again, and immediately excused himself.

Ray kissed his daughter and pulled a chair out for her to be seated, at the same time he declared, "Honey, you'll have to excuse Ralph. His mind is elsewhere. He's rallying supporters for a new campaign. He can't stay idle in any one place for very long."

She gave a soft laugh and said, "Thank you Daddy; but no need to explain. I fully understand, as a matter of fact if Ralph didn't have his mind on one cause or another, I would think it was out of character."

She smiled as the waiter welcomed her with a glass of white wine. As he set it down in front of her, he asked, "Can I bring you your usual shrimp cocktail, Miss Dey?"

Raynie nodded and smiled another thank you before she took her first sip. Ray watched her for several seconds before he finally asked, "Sweetheart, what's bothering you? Are you okay? Are you still feeling ill from that bout with the flu?"

"Nothing's wrong Daddy. Everything's fine. I'm fine, Daddy."

"Honey, I think I know you pretty damn well and I wouldn't hesitate to wager that I can tell when something is wrong, especially when you repeatedly call me, Daddy."

Before she could answer she heard the unexpected resonance of Simon's voice as he walked eagerly towards them. He went directly to her father's side of the dinner table and excitedly pumped his hand up and down in what resembled a friendly handshake. The surprised look on her father's face was unique and one she saw little of. Yet she had to admit she utterly enjoyed the noteworthy scene. It was clear that her father really liked Simon and she was glad.

Simon then turned directly back to face Raynie and at once, placed a gentle kiss on her lips. Afterward he whispered a tender, "I have missed you far more then I can say, Miss Dey." Raynie wanted to laugh out loud at her father's expression of obvious befuddlement.

She giggled happily and mouthed almost silently, "Me too, Simon." Immediately she glanced up to where her father still stood, rattled, and stunned. She could see he was struggling to get his wits about him, which was a rare scene, and she was enjoying it immensely. She bit her lip so not to laugh as she noted the change when he desperately struggled for something to say to hide his awkwardness. Once again Raynie giggled with pleasure, since she rarely saw her father lacking or having difficulty with words. Ray realized his foolish actions and stopped in the midst of a puzzled smile as he stumbled, "Ahh...Simon, so nice to see you again...ahh, yes, yes indeed. Very, ah... nice to see you. He coughed then asked, "You will join us, won't you?" Clumsily, he sat down and fell back into his natural stability. "Simon, please excuse my bad manners. I am simply surprised to see you. I thought I heard you were out of the country. Please, do join us for dinner?" Simon turned back to face Ray for only an instant as he voiced a delighted, "Yes, yes! Of course! I most certainly will."

Alternating back towards Raynie he added, "If you and your lovely daughter will allow me a minute or two, I have to say goodbye to a couple of associates. Then I will be delighted to join you." Simon winked at Raynie and excused himself with a, "I will be right back, my love." Thereupon he disappeared into the room full of waiters, customers, and tables.

Ray's flustered gaze moved to where Raynie sat and immediately muttered, "You little scamp, you never once even hinted at your involvement with Simon Charles. Not even when I lectured you about fabricating just such. Not one hint, nor a mention of his name after that day, you little devil, you."

Turning her eyes away from the departing Simon, Raynie smugly faced her father and playfully teased, "A girl *don't* tell her daddy everything, ya know."

For an instant Ray witnessed the same flicker of pain he'd seen earlier. Her beautiful, but guarded hazel eyes, held a secret. He knew there was something wrong, but she was not going to share it with him.

Ray's instinct was to question her about it, but he knew it would be useless to ask about her personal life. She was too much like him and would want to deal with her problems on her own. Her message was quite clear, just as she intended it to be. Furthermore, she was right, little girls rarely tell their daddy everything.

Ray stretched back and comforted himself while he observed Raynie. She had turned to search for Simon. Meanwhile he crossed his arms and made no effort to suppress his satisfied grin. It was easy to see that Simon was in no way Raynie's problem.

The evening was warm, and the orange blossoms smelled fresh and fragrant on the drive to Simon's place. Raynie had laid her head back against the soft leather of the seat; she felt contented. Dinner with her father and Simon had been far more than just pleasant and she was happy that the evening would be continuing instead of drawing to an end. She felt the car's movement as it turned to the right and she lifted her head. Simon had pulled off the 210 freeway and headed towards the Pasadena hills. She asked, "Simon, do you live near here or up further in the hills? I've always loved this area."

"In the hills, my sweet. I was lucky enough to find one of those grand and beautiful old villas that rarely come available."

Eventually they pulled through a huge iron gate. Beyond the entrance there was a line of enormous palm trees that completely blanketed the driveway. They stretched from the front entrance all the way to the house which Raynie estimated had to be at least a block. As they drove, she gasped at its beauty. "Oh Simon, you truly are one of the fortunate, I know people who would sell their souls for such a place."

"Well then, I would have to conclude that their priorities are befuddled, my dear, for these are only worldly goods and not nearly as precious as one's soul."

She smiled pleasantly pleased by this simple, but true dogma. She loved to hear his discriminating views on life. Though, at times it still surprised her that this extremely auspicious and complicated man could come up with such simplistic ideas. Lucky for her his success had not polluted or diluted his basic nature. His success was only a part of him and not the whole man. In her world this was incredibly unique.

When they pulled up and stopped in front of the magnificent structure that Simon called home, Raynie at once became enamored with the warm glow that surrounded the estate. The gentle radiance immediately gave her a feeling of warmth as it projected an earnest welcome.

Simon opened the large embellished Spanish doors, then stood aside for Raynie to enter as he said, "Welcome to my humble abode."

At once she felt like she stepped back in history. The setting was richly extravagant. The large roomy foyer was connected directly to a long hallway which looked directly into the open doors of a grand ole library. This was the kind of room that she'd only seen in old movies. It had gigantic ladders that hung from the top of the bookcases to the floor and slid from one side of the room to the other. In the center of the chamber sat a huge cherry-wood desk that was as large as her dining room table. The décor and its furniture she could see was meant for the comfort of a man. Its hues all boasted warm variations of brilliant earth tones. The tones, she guessed, was what gave the room its gentle radiance of friendliness regardless of its enormous size. Raynie liked it at once.

Simon started to remove Raynie's coat when suddenly out of nowhere appeared this elderly woman. The woman looked to be totally at ease with her surroundings and with Simon. She swiftly approached them and commenced to slap at Simon's hands, as she muttered, "That's me job, now. And I won't have ya goin about tryin to ease me burdens young man. Me may be old, but me not be put under as of yet."

He laughed at her spunkiness while he told Raynie, "I would like to introduce you to my very first love, and of course the mistress of the house, my dear sweet overseer, Yula Barrett. Yula has been with my family since she came to us as my nanny over thirty-seven years ago. As you can see, I no longer require the need of a nanny, but Yula has taken it upon herself to be my guarding angel. Rarely does she let me out of her sigh. So, where I go, Yula goes."

"It's so nice to meet you, Ms. Barrett."

Yula grinned lovingly at Simon then moved her jolly smile towards Raynie. She spoke in what Raynie determined was a broken Irish accent, "Now don't ya go payin a mind ta him and whet he's sayin. He's just pullin me leg. It's his way of gettin me back cause I make hum behave and keep a mind to his manners. Especially when he's wit somp yung pretty thing, like yourself. That's the only over seeon I do, and Simon knows it."

Raynie laughed good naturedly, she really liked their friendly banter and it continued throughout the time Yula helped her with her coat and hung it in the hall closet. Then she heartily excused herself and hurried off to continue her duties.

Simon whispered into Raynie's ear, "I truly love that woman." At the same time, he reached out and took Raynie by the hand and led her into the living room. It, too, was opulent and even lovelier than she could have imagined. It was completely opposite of the library, although in size the room ceiling was the same immense height, in size it was twice as big. However, it was decorated in softer sallower colors that made you at once feel at ease. The outer terrazzo floors glistened around the soft colors of the Persian rugs intricate floral designs and she caught her breath when she saw that one side of the room was completely a wall of windows. The panorama twinkled with lights from the evening stars and its view of the city was breathtaking. Raynie moved forward slowly in awe of its beauty and asked, "Is there... a terrace out there."

Simon walked over to the wall on the other side of the room while he answered, "Yes there certainly is. First, let me pour you a brandy; then I'll give you a tour of the garden." Simon opened a cabinet and pushed a couple of buttons. At first lights flickered softly then brighter. Soon the night became alive outside the wall of windows. There it displayed a garden that exhibited a radiant bounty, along with a magnificent pool and deck that was fit for royalty.

After Simon closed the doors behind them and Raynie stepped several feet forward, she could see that most of the yard was full of the most exquisite flowers. Her mother who was an avid gardener, *would adore this Eden*, she thought. The landscape was lovely. On one side of the yard stood a gazebo facing a flowing waterfall and beyond that a vista of lights shone from the city below. They twinkled like a crystal chandelier gleaming in the night. The beautiful view stretched the complete three hundred and sixty degrees and Raynie thought, *this must be what fireworks looks like to a child.*

Simon watched and appraised her appreciation. He was happy that she was enjoying the beauty. When he saw her eyes glisten, he murmured quietly his agreement, "Yes, its beauty can make you want to cry."

Raynie smiled but remained speechless. The view itself could easily make one overwhelmed. Suddenly a surprising cool wind softly blew without obstruction across her face and Simon's arms immediately encircled her waist to help protect her from the cool air. At this moment she knew she could, with little effort, stay here with him viewing this sight forever.

After a time, Simon kissed her neck and felt her tremble. Concerned he asked, "Are you cold? Do you want to go back inside?"

"No, Simon. Please.... Not just yet. I'll be fine with your arms around me."

They stood quietly nestled close together for several minutes when Simon broke the silence by leading her to the gazebo while murmuring, "Come, come, you'll be warmer in here."

Grateful, Raynie sat back in the comfortable swing and leaned her head on Simon's shoulder. As the swing swayed slowly back and forth, they sipped warmth from their brandy and together they appreciated the beauty that surrounded them.

When Simon felt Raynie relax her head on his shoulder he heedfully asked, "Raynie, when are you going to tell me what's wrong?" He said nothing more. The silence that followed his question enveloped them and closed off every other sound. Even the far away chirps of the crickets that Raynie had been listening to, seemed to have halted their healthy tone. Finally, she touched his hand and smiled fondly into his eyes. She liked that he said, *when*, instead of, *will* you, tell me. She felt safe and cared for when she was in his presence; and this gave her tranquility. This was all so new for her, yet it fit. In Simon's arms she was more satisfied than she ever dreamed was possible. Yes, somehow, he was exactly right, and this made her feel complete. She reached over and kissed him lightly before she began to speak. "Simon, you know that old cliché, that life is not a bed of roses?"

He nodded yes, and she went on, "But, mine always seemed so close to being just that. Now I ... She stopped in mid-sentence and laid her head once again on his shoulder. Without constraint she began to tell him all about Dan and that terrible night. When she whispered her last, "I felt so ashamed, Simon."

Simon was holding her so gently that for an instant Raynie thought he was afraid she would break. But soon she could feel his arms tighten and he held her closer. This time it was she who felt him tremble, and she opened her arms and moved closer to embrace him. "Come here, Simon, I'll warm you," Raynie urged gently. She had no idea that Simon's quiver was not from the nip of the night's cool air, but from his newfound abomination for Dan.

Simon was afraid to say anything for a long time. Raynie's confession brought forth an enormous amount of rage and he was fighting for control. Once he felt he achieved restraint, he promised himself that Dan would pay and with far more than a minor slap on the wrist. He would pay where it hurt the most. He will find that one most important thing in Dan's life, and destroy it painfully slow.

Suddenly Simon drew Raynie away from his shoulder and kissed away her tears. "Raynie, you are safe now and nothing will ever hurt you again. As for *shame*, it is not allowed. It is Dan who should be cowering in shame, not you. Except I suspect a man like him; would not know the meaning of the word. Raynie; I promise he will get his in the end. Men like that always do."

Simon moved back closer to Raynie and she snuggled into the crook of his arm. This is how they stayed while they talked far into the night. At last when the night moved to meet the brink of daybreak and the cold was no longer bearable, they moved to the warmth of Simon's splendid living room.

Chapter Sixteen

Jackie sipped her iced tea and gave a distasteful glare at her salad. "Come on, Raynie I don't want to hear any more excuses. You know it's not going to be the same if you're not there. Besides, this is our first big party as man and wife. You have to come."

Raynie saw the glimmer in her mother's eyes as a new thought came to her. Excitedly she bantered, "Oh, and sweetheart, this will be a perfect time for you to show off that wonderful dreamboat of yours. Simon will come, won't he?" Not giving Raynie any time to answer, Jackie hurried on, "and of course your father and Pam are coming. Come on, Raynie, say you'll come. You can also bring your sweet little friend Shannon and her date. Besides, I haven't seen her in months. She didn't even make it to our wedding. Oh, and before I forget, Mike said he'll be there, and he even talked Louis into coming. So, see dear, you have to come. Otherwise you'll be the only one who doesn't."

Suddenly, Jackie stopped her chatter. She could see her pleas were not getting through to her daughter, so she kicked it up a notch. Reaching out she grabbed Raynie's hand and held it theatrically to her heart. "Oh, my dear pleaseeee come, pleaseeee! If you don't, I can just see the gossip columns now. It'll be horrid; it'll be all over the morning local news stations? On second thought, our names will be in every gossip column from here to New York..., and...and possibly even beyond. It'll be full of torrid innuendoes. I can just imagine what they'll say. Oh, and your dear father, oh my.... I mean, he will be so upset when he reads the garbage they'll print. Raynie, I can see it all as clear as day, '**Mrs. Jackie Dey Aleut and her only daughter, Raymeana May Dey, whom her mother has always been totally devoted to, refused to attend her mother's and new husband Dan Aleut's first big bash. *IS* there a *rift* between the two *beautiful* and *rich* Dey women? More to follow on the evening news.**"

Jackie inhaled a huge breath of air, and begin her appeal once again, "Please Raynie, please say you'll come. I couldn't bear to read such trash written about us. Please say you'll come. You and Simon can see a play anytime, you can't miss our party."

Laughing at her mother's depiction Raynie begged, "Mother, do you always have to be so overly melodramatic? I mean, even if it were true, who would really care if the Dey women were having a problem in their relationship or not? *Buttt,* let's just say by some re-mote chance, there is one miserable busybody out there that's des-perate enough to be interested in our life, the media, local or otherwise; certainly, wouldn't be interested enough to put it in print."

"All right, so maybe I am putting it on a little thick, but if it helps me make it clear to you how important your presence is to me, then my embarrassingly sad performance is more than worth it."

Raynie glared into her mother's optimistic eyes and felt herself sway slightly. She fluffed her hair with both hands before she rubbed her chin several times and finally gave in to her mother's pitiful pleas. "Okay, Mother, you win. I will try, *but* I can't promise you anything yet. First, I need to see what Simon thinks about it. I'll call you tomorrow and let you know one way or the other. Now, can we please change the subject Eat up. I have an appointment in less than twenty minutes, and I have to get out of here."

All of a sudden Jackie was pleased with herself as she began to eagerly munch at her salad. Raynie recognized her mother's self-satisfaction and smiled in spite of her feelings of dread. Her mother had probably been sure from the very start that she would get what she wanted since she usually did.

After Raynie left the restaurant she started to feel uncertain about her decision to go to the party. Even the thought of facing Dan made her feel sick to her stomach. Up to this point, she'd been successful in her efforts to avoid him. In fact, she hadn't seen him since that loathsome night. But she knew it was only a matter of time before she would run into him; that was inevitable. In reality she knew there was no way she could avoid her mother's husband forever. Nonetheless she still felt a heave of panic and within minutes of its onset, her fear had swollen and festered until it gripped her whole being. She shivered when she thought, *I'll, be spending the entire evening in the same house with that man. A man who if it hadn't been for Shannon would've been my rapist.*

The house was lit up like Disneyland during its last explosive celebration each night at closing time. Raynie held Simon's hand close to her side during the long walk from the car to the front entry. All the while Simon kept trying to reassure her by continually whispering his support, "Raynie it will be all right. You will see, this will not be as bad as you think. Please try to relax, and remember, keep calm. Remember what you said to convince me to come. You are doing this for your mother. You are not going to help Dan hurt your mother by avoiding her. Keep these thoughts in mind and you will be okay. Most of all, keep in mind I am here for you, and I will not let anyone hurt you."

The smile Raynie gave Simon was a half-hearted effort of reassurance. She wanted to do better, but her state of mind wasn't in it. She kept getting these dreadful panic attacks, and for the umpteenth time she wished Shannon could have come. She would have really liked her friend nearby and she was sure Simon could have used the support. She would have felt better if he didn't have to carry this burden all alone. Unfortunately, Shannon, was still in Europe and wouldn't be back for three more weeks.

Without warning Raynie halted her stride. They were about to enter the house and she felt timid and a thought to turn and run away overwhelmed her. Quickly she glanced in Simon's direction and a surge of well-being emerged and dissipated her others urges. "Thank you," she said, as an amazing emotion filled her heart. This was something new, a feeling she never experienced before, or at least for any man other than her father. Which wasn't absolutely the same; but awfully close. Raynie wondered; *Could this be love?*

Simon felt her gaze and smiled his reassurance as he patted her hand to comfort her. Raynie smiled and inhaled a deep breath and released it as quickly, as she walked through the entrance, at which point she stole one more glimpse of Simon's profile for comfort. "*I know he'll take care of me. I know it. So why do I have this urge to run and hide?*"

She took one more deep breath and released it as slowly as she could while she scolded herself, O*kay, Raynie, grow up. Just stay close to Simon's side and you'll do fine.* At that moment, she knew she was right. Everything was going to be okay. This, after all, had been her home her entire life. This was her safe haven, and nothing could hurt her here.

Jackie greeted Raynie with open arms, and when she turned to welcome Simon, she flashed her approval at Raynie. Simon laughed at Jackie when she asked, "Oh, Simon, where were you before I tied the knot?"

His response was just what Raynie needed and it meant more to her than the many gifts he'd already given her thus far. "Mrs. Aleut, I must confess, I have been out and about in search of my one true love." He bowed towards Raynie and continued, "As you can see, I have, at long last, found the lovely lass. After that moment on I realized why I possessed such an ardent obsession in my search, for it turns out she is the very essence of my soul." At that moment Simon bowed his head, kissed Jackie's hand, and added, "It is truly wonderful to see you again, Jackie."

This delighted Jackie who beamed with pleasure. Smiling broadly, he turned to face Raynie and after a quick wink he asked; "can I bring you a glass of white wine?" She nodded her head and smiled modestly as he excused himself.

Jackie watched Simon's departure as he headed toward the open bar on the north side of the room. Once he was out of hearing range, she grabbed her heart and uttered a breathless, "My God Raynie; he is a dream come true." Then she immediately turned and snatched her daughter's hand as she said, "Come on Raynie, let's go say hello to Dan before you start mingling and forget." Without a seconds' hesitation Raynie searched the room for Simon. He stood at the bar with his back to her while he waited for his order. At the same time her mother continued to pull her towards the study where Dan stood with Mike and several other guests. She closed her eyes and fought the panic that flowed throughout her body. By the time she opened them her mother stopped and cried, "Hey, look who's here?"

Her search for strength had been successful enough that she had her shoulders set and had garnished a strained smile for the encounter. Bravely she peered into the group. Everyone moved to encircle her while they noisily welcomed her with kisses on the cheeks and swift hugs. Quickly she relaxed and her smile grew when she saw that Dan was nowhere in sight. Apparently, he had left the area before they had reached the cluster. Raynie scanned the faces in the group and stopped on Mike's. She could see that he was pleased to see her, but when he reached out to kiss her cheek, she saw his slight hesitation. He wasn't quite sure how his salutation would be excepted, or worse, what Raynie's reaction would be.

Graciously Raynie smiled and gave him a look that read, *I'm sorry I beat you up, Mike.* Almost immediately he sensed her message and grinned his relief. His voice was full of cheerfulness when he said, "It's so good to see you my sweet lady. Your loyal subject has missed you terribly." After everyone had added their own greetings, Raynie began to feel like her old self again. That is, until her mother said, "I'll be right back dear, I'm going to find Dan. I'm sure he's somewhere nearby," and she hurried off to find him.

Raynie only waited a minute after her mother left and turned to make her escape. She wanted to find Simon and her safety net. Unfortunately, she only made it halfway to her sanctuary before she walked straight into the one person, she had hoped she wouldn't see.

Dan stood unwaveringly with a smug grin pasted on his face. Raynie could see he was full of self-confidence as he scornfully said, "Well. Hello, *R-a-y*. It's really good to see you. I must say you certainly look terrific tonight."

Raynie froze and said nothing. Her silence only encouraged him, and he continued, "I was happy to hear that you would make it tonight. We really do want to see more of you around here." He looked her up and down then added, "Yes, you sure do look good tonight."

Raynie gulped a loud gasp when he stepped closer, and instantly she could smell that he had already been drinking. She tried to stay calm and think of something harsh to say, but her mind went blank with fear. Suddenly she felt the warmth of an arm around her shoulders, as Simon curtly declared. "Well, at least we know he is perceptive, if not the sharpest knife in the drawer."

Dan staggered a bit when he moved sideways to face Simon. His glare was pompous and defiant. He immediately stepped closer to Raynie to show disregard for her safeguarding angel. Yet, halfway into the stride Dan came to a sudden halt. For an instant, his foot stood frozen in mid-air and his face held fear. Simon had moved in the direction enough to blocked Dan's aggressive move, but this in-itself; was not what stopped Dan's approach. It was the malevolence pouring from Simon's steel-gray eyes. Simon's hate shot through Dan like a bullet. Dan cursed under his breath when he felt the burning stab of Simon's stare. In that instant, he recognized Simon knew all and hated him for it.

Raynie enjoyed the alarmed expression she saw wash over Dan's, now ashen face. He was thoroughly unnerved, and in a panic, he looked for any avenue of escape. When his eyes fell on

Jackie, he hurriedly excused himself and rushed her way. When Dan was out of sight, Simon grinned and whispered. "Raynie, my dear, I don't think you will have to worry about him for the rest of the evening. I'm sure he will find some remote corner where he can safely lick his wounds in private."

Louis stood alone leaning against the fireplace while observing Dan and his retreat. He recognized how disturbed he was, and he couldn't imagine what it was all about. He wished he could've been a fly on the wall and heard the conversation. It was evident that Raynie and her new gentleman friend had severely put Dan in his place. Louis grinned inwardly as he determined, yes, the scene was truly something pleasurable to witness. His interest soon heightened as he studied Raynie who was still vigilant while she thanked her rescuer. This was unlike Raynie she is always unruffled. For this reason, Louis decided to investigate. He enthusiastically pushed himself forward then moved his body laggardly towards the center of the room to where Raynie stood with her emancipator. But before he made it to where they stood the two had moved to the sofa where Mike and a few other guests were involved in some lively conversation. Without delay he changed his direction so he too could join the group as well, yet promptly after his decision he was intercepted by Dan himself.

Louis smiled distastefully and muttered, "Good evening, Dan. If you will excuse me, I am on my way to join Mike and Raynie."

Obstinately Dan remarked, "Matter of fact, I do mind Louis. If you have a minute or two, I need to talk with you. Alone."

Louis grinned while he replied, "Other than what is expected of any courteous guest, I do not see a thing we have to talk about. So, again Dan, if you will excuse me...I..."

Dan grabbed Louis by the arm and hissed, "Come on, now. You at least owe it to me, to hear me out."

Louis could smell the heavy scent of liquor on Dan's breath and stepped back so he could breathe more comfortably. He remembered that Mike had told him that Dan had been drinking pretty heavily lately. Regardless, as far as he himself was concerned, it had nothing to do with him. If Dan drank himself to death, there'd be no tears from this side of the conversation.

Cautiously Louis removed the hold Dan held on his arm and remarked, "However, it would be quite interesting to hear how in the hell you come up with me owing you *anything.*"

Dan turned and said, "Let's go out to the courtyard so we can talk without being interrupted."

Louis quickly cast a look over to where Mike was sitting with the others then moved to followed Dan out the French doors.

When Dan was far enough away from the house where he felt comfortably sure that no one would wander out and disturb them, he turned and avowed, "Louis, I know you don't care for me and I'm certainly not fond of you, but we do have a shared bond. Appallingly and with great regret, right now I'm afraid I need you. Things aren't going well for me at this time and I sincerely need your help. Your support could help immensely."

Louis instantly turned to leave, but again Dan grabbed his arm and pleaded, "Louis, please, I'm begging you. I have nowhere else to turn. The least you could do is hear me out."

This ignoble behavior was unlike Dan, it had to be the drink, decided Louis. Even so, he had no desire to be part of this conversation. "Dan, we went through this once before, and my answer is still the same. I have no intention of ever helping you or your problematic career. So, as far as I can see, we have nothing to say to one another."

Dan's fury immediately became evident when his face turned a bright red under his dark California tan, as he stuttered and spat his words, "You-you-you obnoxious pompous ass. I...I have never done anything to deserve your disrespect. Anything at all. And all I've ever gotten from you is opprobrious defilement. All I'm asking from you is a little financial help, which I know wouldn't put you out in any way. I would think that's the least you could do for your lover's best friend!"

"Best friend!" Louis screeched. "Dan, you have never been a friend to anyone in your entire life. You've abused Mike's naiveté while you used him for your own financial gain. Now you have the nerve to stand here in front of me, the man who actually loves Mike, and label your abuse of him as friendship? Well you, sadly, are even more of an idiot then I thought."

Dan stepped closer and growled, "The only fucking idiot I know is standing here in front of me. As far as love goes, the only person Mike's ever loved is me, and you've always been too stupid to see that."

Louis gnawed at the inside of his cheek and clenched his fist tight as he snapped, "Dan, you're drunk. Get the hell out of my face before I remove you myself." When Dan didn't move, Louis started to walk away from him and was jerked back and around to face another spew of Dan's anger. Dan's eyes almost bulged with uncontrolled rage as he spat outward, "And you're a damned fool, because you won't face that Mike still loves me. Whenever I want him, he's mine. Whenever I need him, he'll be there"

Louis almost choked on his hatred for this despicable man. He had an almost wild desire to smash his arrogant face into a mass of oleaginous blubber. Instead, without another word he turned and marched back to the party to find his defamed lover.

Louis felt certain that Dan's detestable implication was a lie. But if any of what he insinuated was true than Mike and he were finished. Mike had always known that as far as their relationship went, the one essential element...was trust. Mike had always sworn that he and Dan had never been lovers which *is* exactly what Dan was now implying.

Chapter Seventeen

Raynie was glad today was the last shoot and that they'd be on a hiatus. These past few months had been long and laborious, and she was ready for some down time to herself.

Marsh hurried over to sit next to Raynie before anyone else had a chance to take the seat, "Hi boss-lady."

"Marsh, I'm not your boss. I'm an associate."

"If you say so, boss."

"I say so, okay."

"Okay. But, if that's true, can I ask why you're always telling me what to do?"

She laughed, "Okay, so I'm a bossy associate."

Without further comment, Raynie went back to reading her afternoon shooting schedule, while she and Marsh sat in silence munching on their commissary lunches.

Eventually Marsh asked cautiously, "Raynie, how's your mother?"

Raynie stopped nibbling and looked up at him questioningly. "She's fine. Why? I mean, why do you ask? You never asked before and besides, you barely know her, so why the sudden interest?"

"So much for being circuitous," he muttered.

"Marsh, it's not in your nature to be indirect, so spill; what's going on and why the concern?"

"I'm sorry Raynie. I don't want you to think I'm trying to cause trouble or anything, but it just doesn't seem right not to say anything if you know something. Wouldn't it be callous of me not to? Say something, I mean."

"Dammit Marsh, stop beating around the bush and tell me what's bothering you."

He stumbled around in his mind for the right words, then finally gave up and mumbled, "I saw Dan the other night."

"So."

"He was at a club and he was all over this blond bombshell. You know the kind that looks like she belongs in a club. Anyway, later that evening they left together. Dan looked like he was pretty-well gone, but she didn't seem to mind. I'm sorry Raynie, but I don't like to think of someone making a fool out of your mother and in turn, hurting you."

Raynie stayed speechless for some time and Marsh couldn't tell if she was angry with him or not. At last she put her hand on his, "Thanks Marsh. I know it's hard to be the messenger of unpleasant news; it can make you feel pretty uncomfortable. Yet, I guess in reality your news isn't really all that bad."

Marsh shot Raynie a doubtful look and started to ask what she meant. Then he recalled some things he'd heard through the industry grapevine and decided it was best to drop it. Instead he just nodded in agreement and went back to his lunch in silence.

Raynie sat there eating slowly while contemplating what Marsh had told her. She wasn't sure what to do with the information. She knew it'd be stupid to confront Dan, yet she couldn't go directly to her mother either. Simon was out of the country again so she wasn't sure whom she could turn to for advice. Certainly not Mike. He hadn't been himself lately, not since her mother's party. She still couldn't figure out what that was all about.

A couple of days after the party she and Mike played tennis, it was at that time she noticed the difference in him and his attitude towards Dan. Something definitely had changed between the two because this was the first time that she knew of that Mike and Dan were not speaking. She asked him about it and he reluctantly muttered something about some loathsome lie and that Louis had been right all along. Dan was nothing more than a user and a wretched egotistical opportunist, whose first priority *is* and always *has* been, himself. He ended his attack on a note that surprised her more than his anger, "And hopefully, one day someone will be strong enough to put him out of his misery."

She couldn't guess why, at this point, he had come to his new judicious reasoning, but nevertheless, she was glad that he finally came to grips with the real Dan. She sighed silently... in any case trying to talk with him about Dan was out of the question, thus leaving her with one choice, as always, her *father.* Maybe it's time to open up and tell him everything. The whole damned truth. About the attempted rape, the money problems Dan's having on his production, along with what Marsh had just told her, other women.

Raynie stayed silent as she mulled over these thoughts. Suddenly she jumped up and started to search for her car keys, while at the same time asked, "Marsh, will you do me a favor?" "Sure, anything."

"Will you tell Derrick that during lunch I got deathly ill and went home early? I just don't think I can face another wrap party."

Marsh gave her a dismal look. He could tell she had been contemplating the news he had bestowed upon her minutes ago. He hoped she wasn't going to do anything she'd later regret.

To Raynie it was plain to see he was unhappy with her request, she hoped it was only because she wasn't going to the party. She attempted a smiled when she saw his effort to alter his mood to show his support.

"Hey girlfriend, don't give it a seconds' thought. I'm sure Derrick will understand." He laughed and added, "after all we are eating commissary food. It's a miracle we've all made it this long." He had hoped his quip would ease her troubled look and when he saw it didn't, he became serious, "Honey, you go on and do what you have

to do. Don't worry about Derrick or the show. I'll take care of closing down production. You just take care...and Raynie, will you call
me next week?"

"Thanks Marsh, and yes I promise I will call." She automatically
brushed a kiss across his cheek and hurried away.

When she charged through the entryway to her father's suite,
she saw that Kelsey was busily locking the door to his office. Raynie
could see by the personal items laying on her desk, that she too was
about to leave for the weekend. A sudden rush of disappointment
shot to its peak; she really wanted to talk to her father. He was the
only person she could count on to ease her concerns. She smiled,
but it didn't cover the disappointment that was still clearly visible
on her face. "Hi Kelsey." She asked, but already knew the answer,
"Did I miss him, is he gone for the weekend?"

"I'm afraid so, dear. He left unusually early today. He and Pam
are probably near Barstow by now. They decided to go to Vegas for
the weekend. It was one of their spur of the moment trips."

"Damn."

"Is everything all right, Raynie? Can I help with something?"

Raynie sighed, "No. Thanks anyway."

Kelsey watched as the disheartened girl turned to leave. Raynie
really looked upset and this concerned her. She wanted to ask her
what was wrong, but she didn't want to impose. It wasn't her nature to be overly friendly. Instead she suggested, "If you really need
to speak with him, Raynie, they'll be at Caesar's as usual." She hurried towards her desk while she offered, "I'll get you the number.
They should be there in about two to three hours. Why don't you
call him then? I'm sure he wouldn't mind."

"Thank you, Kelsey, but no. It's okay. It can wait till Monday.
Raynie headed for the door and remembered her father's busy
schedule. She turned back and questioned, "Is he free on Monday?
Maybe I better get a time when he won't be busy. I much rather talk
with him when we won't be disturbed."

"I think he's free for lunch, but let me check to make sure he didn't pencil something in. Sometimes he forgets to tell me when he does and more than once, we've had conflicting schedules."

Raynie waited expectantly, while Kelsey pulled his appointment book from her desk drawer and breezed through it. Smiling, she tapped the book and declared, "Well it looks like he's all yours from twelve-thirty until two. Should I pencil you in?"

"That'll be great. Thank you, Kelsey. Will you also let him know that I'll bring lunch from Po Po's Deli, so we can eat here?

"Sure, he'll appreciate that. I think he gets tired of going out. Occasionally he does enjoy a sandwich at his desk."

"Thanks again, Kelsey, I'll see you Monday." Raynie was almost out the door before she remembered her manners. "Oh, and Kelsey, you have a great weekend too."

Raynie ran down the stairs instead of using the elevator. She didn't know where she was going, but she had this urgent need to get there fast. Again, she thought about calling her mother, but she didn't know what to say. She then decided, *if I just drop by for a quick visit, I can check things out. Besides, I'll feel better if I know she's okay. I wonder if mother has any idea at all as to what Dan's been up to.* Her mother wasn't a fool, so she suspected Dan wasn't going to be able to keep the wool pulled over her eyes for long. Then if she already knows, she may need someone to.... She stopped her deduction and muttered, "Oh, dear lord no; I'm starting to sound like Thomas's character on *Detective Alley.*"

She shook her head as she pictured Thomas Herrington, who played the lead detective on the show. He was usually serious in nature, but even more so in his gumshoe roll, Detective Alley Krimmer. She cried out laughingly, "No, Lord, please save me, I can't stand it." Then scrambled into her Beamer and sped off in the direction of her mother's house.

Throughout the entire trip, she kept repeating the same prayer, "Please God, don't let Dan be anywhere in sight."

After ringing the doorbell once she cautiously let herself in. She hesitated momentarily and peeked around the door. When she was satisfied that Dan was nowhere around, she immediately quickened her steps and entered the foyer. She threw her purse and keys on her mother's favorite antique. An old, but charming 1820 English Satinwood escritoire, that has sat in the entryway for as long as she can remember. Immediately she began yelling, "Mother! Mother, where are you? Mother, are you here?" She was about to give up when Jessie walked up behind her and said, "Excuus me, Miss Raynie." Raynie felt her body jump, and fear shoot instantly through her, before her mind registered that it was her mother's maid who had spoken. Jesse continued, "You Mamma she not in here. She in da gardon, outback."

"Oh! That's great. Thanks, Jessie." Raynie changed her direction and headed directly towards the backyard as she gave a grateful, "Thanks Lord." Reassured, she hurried her pace since she knew that her mother would be alone, because if Dan were anywhere nearby, Jackie certainly wouldn't be in the garden puttering.

Raynie smiled lovingly at the first sight of her mother. She moved quickly and quietly to the shaded area under the huge willow tree. She stood soundlessly, concealed by its cover while she watched her mothers' comical attempt to dig up an overgrown gardenia bush. Her mother's large sunbonnet flopped up and down every time she thumped her foot against the shovel. "This is hilarious," Raynie muttered to herself. She shook her head and made a mental note to buy her mother something a little more attractive for her gardening excursions. Those worn jeans and checkered shirt were ready for the Salvation Army bag.

Her thoughts refocused as she watched her mother's concentrated effort on the task at hand. She looked much too delicate and fragile to attempt such a feat. Yet, the bush that appeared to be as big as she was and just as threatening, was giving in to her continued labors.

Her mother always loved her garden and handled as many of its chores as she thought capable of and her schedule would allow. She especially liked to work in it when she was worried or upset and needed time to think through a difficult decision. From what Raynie could see of Jackie and her thumping foot, she would guess that this was one of those times.

Suddenly Jackie felt her presence and glanced up. A startled look followed by a surprised expression crossed her lovely but strained face. She smiled her welcome and hurriedly set her tools aside. "Hello dear. I didn't expect to see you today. Why aren't you at your wrap party? Isn't today the end of your season?"

"Yes Mother, but I had a headache and didn't feel like staying."

"Oh, I'm sorry to hear that. Can I get you something for it? How about some herb tea or something to eat? Sometimes that helps."

"No, thank you Mother. I feel much better now. But..., if you're not too busy, I would like to spend some time with you."

"Honey you know I'm always free for you. Come, let's go sit by the pool and I'll have Carmen bring us some ice-cold lemonade. How does that sound?"

Raynie sat playing with the chocolate chip cookie that Carmen said was fresh baked only minutes before. She wanted to talk with her mother candidly but didn't know where to start. Or... even if she should be saying anything at all. Yet she felt compelled to help *if* her mother needed her. She loathed the thought of Dan mistreating her mother in any way. After a minute or so Raynie looked up when she sensed her mother's penetrating stare. Their eyes met and instantly Jackie saw the confusion in her daughter's eyes. She was worried about something; that was evident. Yet it seemed she didn't know how to bring it into the conversation, and that was uncharacteristic since Raynie was usually pretty much straight forward and had no trouble speaking her mind. Jackie remained silent and waited. She knew Raynie would tell her when she was ready. She smiled her encouragement in hopes to ease her discomfort and loosen her tongue.

Raynie smiled back and swallowed the bittersweet chocolate she'd just bitten from a cookie. Finally, she asked, "Mother; will you please talk to me? You see, I've noticed that lately you've been upset, and I would like to help if I can. I know it may be none of my business, but the other day you mentioned that you were worried about Dan and his situation. Is that it, or is there more?"

Jackie moved to pick up the tray of cookies and reached out to offer Raynie another. Her eyes suddenly filled with a hint of uncontrolled tears. Hurriedly she set the tray aside while she pretended to ignore the one tear that escaped and rolled down her cheek. After she composed herself, she whispered, "Honey I think you might have been right about me and Dan. I'm afraid... well, I think I may have rushed into marriage. Maybe I should have listened to you when you said I wasn't thinking straight. Maybe, I just had a fool-hardy need to feel desired, I don't know; all I know *is* I'm in trouble now."

Raynie didn't know how her mother found out about Dan's little liaison, which is what she assumed she was talking about. But she was immediately relieved that she wasn't the one to break her mother's heart with the foul news. However, when her mother began to explain what was wrong, Raynie was astonished that it was something completely different than what she had expected. It wasn't at all about another woman, or any affair; it was far worse!

"Sweetheart, I believe Dan's been stealing money from my accounts. God; Raynie I've been such a silly fool. I can't even imagine why I haven't noticed any of his idiosyncrasies before now. I mean he's consumed with this desire to own his own production company and it appears at any cost. Worse yet, from what I gather his company is doing far below par. Plainly it's not doing well at all."

She shook her head in disgust before she moved on. "Raynie, lately Dan's been really pushing me to give him money. He doesn't say it's for the picture, but I know it is. Like I told you before, I don't think it would be a wise investment; the whole damned thing is too risky. Anyhow my steadfast answer is *no,* and this has angered him beyond control. Now he's blaming me for all his life's failures especially his problems with the production company. But... Raynie it was failing before we married, so why can't he see that? Why is he being so thick-headed? Why can't he see it's not me, but that whole damn project was a mistake from the get-go?"

Raynie figured her mother's questions were meant to be rhetorical, since she exhaled then quickly moved on with her next disclosure. "Honey, in the beginning I did intend to support Dan and his endeavors, but after seeing his predicament, I decided he needed to be more diverse or change his direction completely. There are plenty of other opportunities that *I* can easily help him obtain, yet he still refuses to discuss them with me."

Full of frustrated questions Raynie finally cut in and asked, "M o t h e r, wait. Did I understand you correctly? Did you say that Dan was stealing from you? What do you mean and how do you know this?"

Jackie stood up and walked over to the edge of the pool. After a minute she turned to face her daughter and quietly declared, "I found several checks that were written for a lot of money and they had my signature." She hesitated then finished her accusation; "And Raynie I know I never signed them. It may look like my signature, but it isn't, and worse, when I asked Dan if he knew anything about them, he tried to convince me that I was just forgetful. He said that I was the one who had written the checks for cash, probably for some charity and just forgot."

She stopped and leaned closer to Raynie's face and asked in a mournful voice, "Tell me, Raynie, how in the hell does a person write a check for over three hundred and thirty thousand dollars and forget?"

Raynie gasp, "Wa...what! Mother did you say..."

But before she had the entire question out of her mouth her mother interrupted, "Yes, that's exactly what I said. Dammit Raynie, what am I going do? It's not so much the money as it is, he lied. How can I trust him now? What else has he done that I don't know about? God, I just don't trust him anymore."

Raynie bit her tongue because she had no intention of mentioning the things she had come here to reveal. Her mother continued, "Jesus Raynie, I don't know. I guess I just don't know what to think." As soon as her declaration was out, a new idea hit Jackie and she yelped, "Ooh! Oh, My God, Raynie, do you think he married me for my money?" She answered her own question before Raynie could once again open her mouth. "No, no, I don't believe it. I can't. I know he loves me, he's simply desperate, that's all."

Raynie saw the look on her mother's face and she could see that she was not at all convinced of what she'd just tried to tell herself. She realized that she may have just hit on the truth. Dan didn't really love her after all and never did; he only cared for her money.

Raynie stood and walked over to join her mother by the edge of the pool. Jackie looked so confused and unsure of herself. Raynie felt so bad for her which once again deepened her hatred towards Dan. Her mother was suffering all because of him and his voracious appetite. She reached out and tried to comfort her mother. Jackie instantly welcomed the refuge as she cried softly in her daughter's arms.

After a time Raynie gently asked, "Mother what are you going to do? You can't let this continue."

"Sweety, I really don't know right now. I guess I need some time for it to sink in, but don't worry baby. I won't let my pride or silly embarrassment get in my way. Nothing's going to stop me from making the right decisions." Jackie's voice shifted and sounded more like a moan, and when she continued it was as if she were alone. "I really have to keep in mind; I am an intelligent business-woman. This complete mess has been nothing more than temporary insanity. Sure, I've made some unsound decisions, but that doesn't mean I'm going to continue to do so. It's time I start thinking with my head again instead of my heart."

Suddenly Jackie remembered she was not alone. Her manner changed back to, Jackie, the woman in charge. "But, for now my dear, I think you better go. Dan's going to be here anytime now, and I don't want him to guess I know the truth. I'm sure if he sees that look of animosity in your eyes, he will easily guess the cat is out of the bag. However, for now, that's something I'm not ready to deal with, not just yet anyway. I certainly don't want to make any more reckless decisions. First, I have to sort things out. Then I'll set my plans in order. I am not about to be Dan Aleut's patsy any longer."

Jackie reached out and stroked Raynie's cheek, then spoke in a gentler warmer manner. "Raynie..., baby, please, please don't waste your time hating Dan. I see the glare in your eyes, and I don't want you wearing it for me. Now wipe that anger off your face and give me a smile. That's better." She kissed her daughter's cheek and patted her hand and added, "much, much better, sweetheart. Now off with you."

The look Jackie was witnessing was far more than Raynie's immediate animosity for her mother's current situation. It was accompanied by a large fraction of disgust which stemmed from Dan's infringement on her life as well. Yet she said nothing; she had no intention of ever revealing the truth to Jackie or anyone else. Dan's behavior has already hurt her mother and she had no desire to add to her pain.

Raynie was very mindful that her mother was trying hard to be brave, but the strain on her face was all too apparent. Dan's insidious actions were breaking Jackie's heart and when Raynie started to leave, she felt like she was abandoning her mother in her time of need. Jackie continued pushing Raynie in the direction of her car as she pleaded, "Raynie my dear please, don't worry about me, I'll be fine.

Vacillating between uncertainty and concern, she backed slowly out of the driveway. She fought her need to go back and support her mother when she confronted Dan. In the end, she started to cave in, but instead gave a quick glance in the rearview mirror and stepped on the accelerator and she sped away. After a few blocks she stopped at an intersection and growled out loud, "Dammit. Damn you, Dan Aleut, you are an asshole, and somebody needs to put you in your place. I really hope Simon's right and men like you, do end up paying in the end."

CHAPTER EIGHTEEN

Jackie felt so alone as she watched Raynie's car pull away. Despite her overwhelming need for camaraderie, she knew she needed to deal with her thoughts on her own. She turned to head back to the garden and her earlier project, but when she started to pass the brick bench that sat next to the walkway; she unconsciously seated herself. The long bench was primarily for guests waiting for their cars to be brought to the front of the house. For Jackie, the rose garden encompassing the seat, had always been a tranquilizing effect after a hectic day. She often sat there while reflecting on life's woes and wonders.

She looked around despondently until she spotted a bird perched on a branch in a nearby tree. It was one of her favorites, a robin. It glanced in her direction and flew away as a sparrow hovered then rested to watch her. Wistfully she pleaded, "What am I going to do little sparrow? How am I going to handle this? I don't want to look foolish. I hate to think I'm just another older woman who's been taken for a ride by a much younger man. I hope no one ever finds out. I'll just die if they do. Little bird..., can you tell me why I didn't see any of this coming? I've always prided myself on being so levelheaded. The smart girl behind the pretty face. So why did it change with Dan?" She took a deep breath and smelled the sweetness of the roses as she wondered, *I know I have a strong sexual attraction to him, but that's no excuse. That could have easily been quenched without marriage. Was I so blinded by love that I became a simpleton? Although in the beginning Dan was different..., maybe the two together...?*

Jackie sighed and fought another urge to weep. She missed the Dan she used to know. Back then he was devoted and always so attentive. He, without fail made her feel exhaustively desirable. Now he is nothing like the man she fell in love with. Was it all an act, because he has completely changed? Recently, he even stopped all intimate relations with her, and worse, he seemed to find fault in everything she did. At first, she attributed his behavior and lack of sexual interest to stress. Unfortunately, the other day she heard rumors that would utterly discount her latter theory.

Suddenly Jackie realized she wasn't alone, Dan stood over her while he waited for an answer to a question he had asked. She had not heard his words, so she remained silent while he repeated a disgusted, "Again I ask why in the hell are you sitting out here in that god-awful getup."

Jackie started to answer but before she could express her excuse, he accused, "Jesus Christ Jackie, you don't even have any makeup on? Have you lost your mind?"

Conscious of the way she looked, Jackie half smiled as she once again tasted rejection, for now he had not only drawn her attention to her inelegant attire, but without makeup her youthful beauty was in question. As she painfully faced how she must look in his eyes, her first instinct was to offer an apology. Instead she chose not to acknowledge his distaste and asked, "What are you doing home so early? I didn't expect you for at least another hour or so?"

Dan reluctantly bent over and kissed her cheek. She could smell the liquor on his breath. This too was something she had never noticed before they were married.

Abruptly Dan turned and headed for the door as he threw back a quick account, "Just came home to shower and change clothes. I'll be going back to the office to work late. Don't bother to wait up for me."

After Dan entered the house, Jackie sat there and speculated, 'How stupid does he think I am? If he was working late at the office, why did he need a change of clothes?' "Well," she muttered, "soon he'll be changing a lot more than just his clothes, especially if all goes as she had earlier arranged."

Jackie realized that Dan was going to be inflamed when he learned that she changed all her accounts over to a trust for Raynie. Still and all, she hadn't settled on that decision yet. She still felt unsure whether to go through with it or not. Right now, everything was on hold until she gave her final say so. Although... the thought of Dan's life immediately changing to a less extravagant lifestyle was quite tempting, and if she does initiate the GRAT Trust Fund, that certainly will become a fact. Since the trust would only bestow an adequate, but compared to now, a scant annual allowance for him to live on. Jackie snickered into her hand as she glanced around to make sure Dan wasn't anywhere nearby. She thought, '*it'll be simply delicious. I'm sure he'll make a mad dash to lavish me with all kinds of affection in hopes of salvaging his losses. The move will surely change that wretched attitude of his, plus... hopefully curtail that obnoxious behavior he's developed these past few months.*"

Jackie smiled to herself as she decided, no matter what *Dan's* ardor was in the beginning, it was not going to work on her any longer. She was not going to let him make a fool of her anymore and the *trust* would insure that.

Of course, he was going be incensed and she was positive he would fight it, but if she chooses to go forth and put this plan into action, he may not find out about it until it's too late. Sadly, for my young money-starved husband, once the, GRAT Trust Fund is initiated, it is unconditionally irreversible. "Yes, my sweet, soon your cornucopia will draw to an end and there is not a damned thing you'll be able do about it."

Amused by her strategy she wanted to laugh but held it back. Sure, there's a slight deviousness to her plan, but that's what makes it all the sweeter. Even better, her life itself will not change in the least, due to the substantial nest-egg she has hidden from all except her dear and trusted *ex.*

Another smirk crossed her face and she crooned, "Jackie, you dirty dog." She sucked in an enormous breath of fresh air and threw back her shoulders. She was now beginning to feel more like her old self as her confidence began to regenerate and replenish every part of her inner being. "Jacqueline Dey Aleut is nobody's fool and never will be...again." She openly declared, "and regrettably for you Dan you will soon learn this lesson, but unfortunately not soon enough. Sorry Dan, I'm afraid you are the only one who will pay for your matrimonial faux pas."

Jackie turned to head for the side gate and back to her earlier garden chores. As she came upon a window that looked straight into the den, she halted her step to watched Dan as his handsome frame moved around the room. Afterward she shrugged, "Well my darling, as much as I desire your masculinity, I can also do without it, not to mention your difficult nature." *Still for now,* she thought, *it will benefit me far more to play the wounded party. At least until I complete my protective stronghold on my vast holdings. Afterall, money is the all-important and I am not about to lose a single cent of it to you, Dan Aleut."*

Jackie glanced at her watch and decided her garden projects would have to wait for another day. She needed a bath and makeover before her dinner engagement. She and Louis Carver were meeting for an early dinner and she intended to look her absolute best. The fact that Louis is a notable plastic surgeon always made her feel nervous. She worried that he may evaluate her appearance and she would come up short. She shuddered at the thought of corrective surgery and mumbled to herself, "Tell me why, why I couldn't just stay young and beautiful...why?"

While Jackie spent the next two hours pampering herself, she became aware of various stages of optimistic hope of restoring her youthful beauty. Yet, at other times she caught herself dreading the prospect of spending the evening in the presence of a man who eliminates crow's feet for a living. Finally, she realized her mood was primarily because she didn't really feel like company tonight. But Louis was persistent he said it was consequential that he spoke with her, and the sooner the better. She couldn't imagine what was so important. Since Mike and Louis were both more Raynie's friends than hers; she couldn't understand his insistence. For an instant, she considered canceling but remembered how covert Louis had sounded on the phone. Immediately she changed her mind. His behavior wasn't at all like the Louis she knew. He sounded so peculiar and mysterious when he called. This was why she accepted the invitation in the first place. Now, once again her interest began to peak, and she moved to hurry her task. Following all the pampering and hypothesis', Jackie at last gazed into the mirror. Unquestionably she was finally ready to face Doctor Carver, along with anything he had to say.

Jackie's face was as white as the napkin that lay across her lap. She could not believe what Louis was telling her. However, it did explain Raynie's peculiar behavior lately. A bitter distaste filled her mouth and she realized that she was close to the point of retching. She grabbed for her wineglass and ignored the funny little sounds that escaped her lips when she gulped a large mouth full of the acrid red wine.

Louis watched but said nothing more as Jackie struggled for self-control. He could tell that she was close to choking on the wine's pungent flavor, yet he sat calm and did not impose.

Her eyes watered from its bite and they darted around Louis's face while they looked for any hint of prevarication. Finally, she choked and coughed into her napkin. Frantically Jackie's mind fought to grasp and discern what Louis was trying to say. Maybe she misunderstood, but with all his effort in trying to be delicate; he wasn't being clear. But no, his insinuation was utterly clear, and she had not mistaken its proposed message. Terror began to fill her as she asked through clenched teeth, "Louis are... are you trying to tell me...tell me... that Dan raped Raynie?"

"No, no Jackie not raped, attempted rape. But he would have if he hadn't been interrupted by her friend, Shannon Hicks."

Jackie gaped at him as if he were a monster from another planet, before she repulsively replied, "You've never liked Dan. For some reason you've always been against him and this is a despicable way to get back at someone."

"Jackie, I am not a monster, and I don't gossip, and you know that. This is not an incident that I would have generated about any person, no matter how much I despised them. I don't know what Dan has told you about me, but I can confidently be sure that most of it was iniquitous. And..., I hope you will keep in mind, one-sided."

Jackie paused as she evaluated the attempted rape verses an actual rape, then asked in an obviously shaken voice, "If this is true; how...how do you know about it? Dan certainly wouldn't have told you."

"That's very true, but the one person Dan always runs to when he has any problem...; would."

"Mike," she stated.

"Yes, Mike. I would have come to you sooner, but he only recently told me and up till now, I've been unsure of how I should handle the information. At first, I considered not saying anything at all since I really didn't want to be the bearer of bad news. Nor, did I want to hurt you."

Louis hesitated, then decided to go on, "Jackie, I am sure you are aware of most of Dan's heedless behavior, and I think you will agree, he appears to be getting worse. I, for one, am convinced he is close to losing control. It seems he no longer cares who he harms or to what extent. So that is why I thought it best you know all. I figured it might be much better for you to be aware Jackie since you are smack dab in the line of fire."

Jackie sipped her wine while she gazed straight into the enigmatic blue eyes of her pernicious adversary. After recognizing nothing more than compassion, she knew all that he had said was true. With this acuity she felt a sharp stab of realty, it shot through her entire body as she came face to face with the agonizing truth. The lash of what Dan had done stung. Yet, this anguish was nothing like the hurt that followed, when she finally grasped what wretchedness her sweet little Raynie, must have endured..., alone. It was deplorable, and since Jackie knew her daughter, she knew she would have done anything to keep the news from her. In Raynie's mind, suffering alone for her mother's well-being was not a high price to pay. She had always had this need to protect and shield her fragile mother. *Oh, Raynie, why did I let you believe I was so helpless and needed your protection? It's my fault that you couldn't turn to me. I choose to play the meek person you've always known. Jackie the victim, but this was never meant to hurt you, but to keep you away from the truth.* Jackie's friable mien was adapted years ago for what she liked to call the upper-hand advantage. People were less guarded when they thought of you as weak; unconsciously she carried the deception over to her daughter. Raynie never saw the strong ruthless person, the true Jackie.

Surprisingly for the first time in Jackie's life she felt an unselfish desire to be the mother her daughter needed. With this urge brought an unfamiliar need to protect her child, and God help anyone who hurt her, including Dan. Angrily she thought, *he should have never attempted to hurt Raynie. He can steal, cheat and lie to me, but violating Raynie is unforgivable, and now his price will be exceptionally high.*

Jackie stood up and turned to leave without so much as a thank you for dinner, let alone the information. Her sense of sanity was at its turning point and all she could see was Dan hurting her daughter. She took several steps before she slowly turned back to face Louis and indecisively asked, "I... think. I... think, it'd...I would appreciate; if this conversation stays between us, alone. I need time...

Louis stood to face her cold gaze, lifted his hand, and nodded his head slightly in agreement. "You need not say more," he said.

Her vision focused momentarily, and their eyes met and held, but neither said anything else. Across the table where Louis stood, he could feel and see her pain. He had no desire to add further grief to her distress. There was no need for her to know that he had his own reasons for keeping quiet. The threat of losing Mike, if he ever found out he had betrayed his confidence, was very real. Although he felt bad for her heartache, in his mind his potential losses outweighed hers greatly.

CHAPTER NINETEEN

Raynie sat patiently watching her father enjoy his eggplant sandwich from Po Po's Deli. She couldn't imagine even liking the vegetable sandwich, let alone craving it as he so often professes to do. At last she saw him pop the last bite into his mouth and his smile grew close to rhapsody. Thereupon she decided, now was the time to turn the sparse dialogue in the direction she wanted it to move.

"Daddy, I never realized before, or should I say before I met Simon, how life's direction can change so suddenly. Totally without warning, love or I imagine even hate, can enter one's life in an instant. Love is such a strange thing; it seems to come if you're ready or not."

Raynie stopped and gave her father an absent-minded grin, and he in return gave her a questioning gaze. She wavered but moved on without further delay. "Daddy I'm astonished how quickly love can knock you off your feet when you're not expecting it. It's almost breathtaking." She caught herself and added, "In a matter of speaking of course, and I am only guessing; but I can imagine a person encounters a strange range of emotions. From what I've witnessed it seems to muddle one's mind. I mean a person can easily lose any sense of intelligent judgment. I guess because they choose to relinquish all sensibility by surrendering all guards...ah, sort of like Mother with Dan."

Ray stared skeptically into what appeared to be a concerned Raynie's somber expression. For the longest time he evaluated her and her references. Then coughed uncomfortably before he expressed in a troubled tone, "Honey, Simon's been extremely good for you. I've seen such a positive change in you lately and it warms my very being to see you so happy."

He paused while he searched for the right words and considered how far he should push this. Finally, he began to reword his thoughts, "Sweetheart, I can see that you're concerned about your mother and her current circumstances. But...I'm not sure if you should be involved in this." He faltered, before he added gently, "Considering your past feelings for Dan."

Stunned by what he was saying she burst forth, "But Daddy. Daddy my past feelings have nothing to do with this; I'm really worried about mother. Daddy you just...." Raynie abandoned her plea when she realized her voice had begun to rise.

She calmed herself, then tried again, "Daddy, I believe this may be a lot worse than you know. I'm quite sure Mother has tried to hide it from you, but with the divorce and her situation, she's feeling rather hopeless. I believe even if she was the one who initiated the divorce in the first place, it still devastated her, and her ego."

Dubious Raynie waited for her father to respond, and when he said nothing she added, "I've been keeping an eye on Mother lately. She's in a very delicate state of mind and it all stems back to Dan and his recent conduct." She recognized her father's sober look had jumped from seriousness to holding back a laugh. "Daddy please listen to me. I'm not being dramatic here. I'm truly worried about mother and what she might do."

"Honey, your mother is an extraordinarily strong woman, and she will survive. In fact, I'll take bets that she will be the one who comes out of this mess smelling like a rose."

Raynie lowered her voice as if someone might overhear what she was about to say. "But... Daddy, there's more.... I was recently told that Dan's been out with other women. Furthermore, his production company is in terrible financial trouble. As a matter of fact, his employees are already looking for other positions elsewhere. Of course, Dan is in denial and from what I understand, he's also been drinking way too much. I'm afraid he might be out of control."

Bleakly Ray nodded his head and revealed, "I've heard the same."

She could see that he still wasn't convinced that Jackie was in trouble, so Raynie quickly moved to the facts that her mother had confided in her last week. She truly had hoped she would not have to use this information, but at this point her mother's well-being is all that was important to her. "Daddy, I don't know if I should be asking you this or not... nevertheless, I'm too worried about mother to hold anything back...has Mother mentioned anything to you about the checks?"

Immediately Ray raised his brow, and a new interest touched his eyes. When he began to speak, his voice held a notable change, "What checks? What are you talking about, Raynie?"

Raynie hesitated but she remembered the downtrodden look on her mother's face. At that second she also recalled, her mother didn't tell her not to say anything to her father, or anyone else for that matter. With this rationale, she continued. "I'm surprised you don't know. Mother usually tells you everything and something this momentous, I would have thought you'd be the first she'd turn...."

"Dammit Raynie, stop beating around the bush. Tell me what checks you're talking about."

While he waited for her answer, she watched her father's expression change from doubt to anxiety. Once again, she felt the fear she's felt for days. "Daddy, what's going on? You're scaring me. I can tell by your face that you know a lot more then you're letting on. You do, don't you?"

His stern expression never changed and again he firmly demanded, "Tell me about the checks, *RAYNIE, NOW.*"

"Okay, but you also have to tell me what you know." She took a deep gulp of air and waited for her father to agree. Once he nodded his agreement. She proceeded, "Mother said she found several separate checks over the last three months. They were all written against her personal checking account and each for the exorbitant amount of three hundred and thirty thousand dollars. Mother said she didn't write them although her signature was on them. Dan tried to convince her that she had just forgotten she had written them... Raynie crossed her arms and said, "Now Daddy, we both know that that would be near impossible, knowing Mother as we do?"

"Yes, I would have to say that your mother has always been well aware of her financial state of affairs. I can't see her not remembering she wrote a thirty-dollar check, let alone a three hundred and thirty-thousand-dollar draft. And three times you say? That's just inconceivable!"

Ray rubbed the afternoon stubble on his chin and when he spoke his undertone was scarcely audible; "But this does explain quite a bit."

"What do you mean, Daddy? And why aren't you surprised by this news?"

"Well, to tell you the truth baby, I unfortunately heard some rumors. Right after I heard those heinous implications, I asked an old acquaintance to do me a favor and check around. After I received his report, I decided it would be wise to do a deeper investigation on my own. I soon found that Dan and his financial predicament are quite different from what we were led to believe. He wavered while he weighed the situation and settled. "Appallingly, I discovered that he is hard up for cash. Not only that, but he has been living close to the bone for years. I also learned that he is not, nor has he ever been, a partner in Carver's Surgical Practice. Neither did he own the house he and Mike lived in. From what I understand it was Mike's. A gift from Louis. I can go on and on... etc.... etc....

"Are you sure about all this, Daddy?"

"I'm afraid so dear. There's no doubt about it. Yet, as bad as that sounds it gets worse. I've also heard he's been playing around with some pretty hard money and most of the time he's been seriously behind on his payments. From what I've been told, this habit recently brought talk of a contract being put on his head." His voice softened and he said, "You see, sweetheart, he owes a lot of money to these individuals and these guys don't fool around. They can get damn ugly, especially if they see any kind of threat of losing their investment. Most of the time they do whatever it takes not to lose face."

Raynie was appalled and her first instinct was to ask, "How can we help him? We can't just let somebody kill him Daddy."

Ray could see the horror on Raynie's face at the thought of such a possibility. It was immediately replaced by panic then moving close to hysteria. Quickly, he attempted to bring an end to the image his news must have presented, and he vigorously reassured her, "Stop... stop... baby. It's okay. It was only talk of a hit. It was called off almost as soon as it was on the table."

"Why? How? I mean I thought once a person was mixed up with something like that it was over; there's no changing it. How do they call back a... hit?"

"Well, from what I could gather from one of the guys I talked with. The contract never hit the streets since Dan came up with the cash in time to rectify the situation. Everyone was happy for the time being. My contact also informed me that Dan bragged to the moneyman that there was a lot more cash where that came from. So, they decided that he was worth a lot more alive than dead. Well, now we at least know where he used your Mother's money."

Raynie's look was uncertain and her father tried to simplify what he said, "To pay the interest on his back debts, Raynie. With these types of loans, you pay interest through the nose and if you're late it becomes almost impossible to keep up."

She stood and nervously fidgeted with her hands as she walked from one side of the large office to the other and back again. She was trying desperately to work through all the new facts she had just learned: Dan being penniless and thugs out to get him. All this kind of talk was new to her and she wasn't sure how to process it. Suddenly she paused and turned sharply to face her father. Once they were face to face, he could clearly see her fear before she spoke it.

"How, my God Daddy, how in God's name do you know people like that? People like the ones you're talking about, they don't tell just anyone things like they told you. What do you have to do with them? How do you know these people?"

Ray smiled at his daughter's innocence and answered, "Sweetheart, I've been in this industry an awfully long time. I will venture a guess that I probably know every type of person there is to know."

Feeling foolish at her obvious ignorance she gaped at her father and re-analyzed his implication. When it finally sunk into her befuddled mind, she asked, "You know these men well enough that they trust you? They will talk to you and give you information?"

When he didn't answer, she decided to wait. But when he didn't go on, she realized he wasn't going to give her any more information. In the end, she asked, "Daddy, what do we do about Dan? He could be in real trouble. Shouldn't we help?" She wavered before she went on, "As well as it may be deserved, the thought of something happening like *that*...well it's horrifying. I mean they could kill him. . . right?"

He studied her overwhelmed expression for a long time. Eventually he came to the conclusion that there was no way he was going to lie to her and get away with it. Anyway, she was bound to find out sooner or later, and given the circumstances as they stood today, *probably sooner*. "Honey, Dan's been playing this game a long time and a person can only go so long without running into a brick wall. That's just the name of the game and I'm sure far smarter men than Dan have attempted to outwit these guys and failed. Unfortunately, when they realize the money has come to an end and they will soon enough.... Dan will pay in another way."

Chapter Twenty

When Simon pulled up to the front of his house, he was delighted to see Raynie. She was perched on the hood of her car, legs crisscrossed and reading a magazine. It was obvious that she had been waiting for his arrival for some time since her cheeks were red from the sun. Simon smiled at her beauty and jerked his car to a stop next to her BMW. Without a second's hesitation he jumped out of his car and sprinted in her direction. Before she could look and re-act, he promptly scooped her up in his arms, and Raynie did little to resist. He was blown away with surprise and was deeply moved when she didn't argue. Instead she wrapped her arms around his neck and kissed his face from side to side. After several kisses, she withdrew and began to playfully object, "Simon, Simon. Put me down. I'm going to hurt your back. Simon I'm much too heavy to be picked up."

Laughing at her ridiculous statement, he refused her demands and carried her up the stairs to the front door declaring at the same time; "Raynie you are as light as a feather and I am sure you are quite aware of this so stop chasing compliments."

She was laughing and screeching. "Simon Charles! You're a scoundrel, a charlatan, a, a ...let me down, you, masher! Do you hear me? Let me down or I'll have to...to...!"

He kissed her open mouth and halted her last protests. Still in his arms they entered the morning room. He tenderly sat her feet to the softness of the rug and kissed her once again. Raynie shivered at the touch of his lips. His kiss was as soft and weightless as if it were a light wisp of summer breeze and it tickled as it brushed gently across her lips. Yet, almost instantly his kiss moved to a more ardent passion. He whispered her name, and she felt her heart leap as she recognized and thought, *this is exactly where I want to be.* Simon was holding her closer than she'd ever felt him before and soon she sensed the warmth of his physical desire as it grew close to explosion. Simon paused embarrassed by his indisputable hunger and he pushed himself away as he immediately started to voice his uncertainty. Concurrently Raynie covered his mouth with her kiss and pulled him back into her arms while hastily moving closer to his passion.

Again, he pulled his lips away and looked into her eyes. In a flash she recognized his obvious question. Without uncertainty, she forced his lips to hers and kissed away his doubt. At last Simon gathered her into his arms and carried her up the stairs to his master suite.

Dan sat at his desk reflecting on Jackie and her behavior the last few days. He couldn't figure out what was going on in that head of hers. She seemed so distant and obviously preoccupied. He was completely surprised and was caught off guard when she refused the first sexual overtures that he had shown her in weeks. 'Maybe I better pay more attention to her, at least until I get what I want. Yes, that has to be the best way to go until I can implement my plan.

He had made the decision earlier to get rid of Jackie although he intended to keep a large portion of her money and assets. "Shit, marrying her was a big mistake." *But at the time what choice did he have.* "God, I'm sick of putting up with her shit. Damn her and her mood swings. She's a major pai...."

Suddenly his tit-for-tat with him-self was interrupted when Cassy pushed the door wide open and entered the room. Slowly she flaunted suggestively as she walked across the floor. Her walk remarkably revealed what little she was hiding under her skimpy outfit. Once she was positioned in what he guessed she thought was a sexy pose, she smiled and murmured, "We're ready for ya, baby. Everyone's in the conference room. Should I bring in some coffee and donuts?"

Dan muttered, "Don't bother. It'll be a short meeting." When he passed her on the way to the conference room, he patted the softness of the lace bra she wore under the see-through blouse and felt the firmness of her well-endowed silicon breast. Smiling as he pushed pass her, he blew her a kiss. Cassy at once attempted to block his exit as she winked and asked, "Should I wait in here for ya, boss?" Dan reached back and tweaked her bottom but didn't answer her question. Instead he left her standing by the door with a huge grin pasted across her lips. As soon as he was out of hearing range, he mumbled to himself, "You'd think I just presented her with an Academy Award for best performer. God I'm sick of her, along with all these other half-witted, no talented want-a-be actresses."

No sooner had the meeting been called to order when the door flew open with a loud bang. Suddenly in walked the obnoxious Russian playboy, Patrick Garrett. His Romeo smile was plastered ear to ear, and he exhibited an intolerable impertinence as he headed straight for Dan. When he stopped in front of where he sat, Dan almost swallowed his tongue. His mind went wild with questions then blank while he tried to figure out why Patrick was here. He didn't invite him, and besides, he was a behind the scenes guy. And above all, he wasn't behind on his loan; he still had three weeks before he needed to worry about that. In light of this, Dan began to feel braver and stood up to greet his intruder. Yet before a word could escape his lips in protest of the interruption, Patrick good-naturedly voiced boisterously, "Gooot morning staff. I'm very hoppy you are all heere to velcome me like this. It shows a greaat deal of suppoort."

The look on everyone's face including Dan's was disbelief and confusion. Patrick stopped and stood next to Dan at the head of the table, while at the same time, he slapped a loud clap on Dan's back. After the smack, he wrapped his arm around Dan's shoulders and jerked him close to his side as he proclaimed in his Russian brogue, "Vell gang; let me introduuce myself again...I am Patrick Garrett." His smile grew even larger and he added, "Your nuew boss." Grinning like an old-time grade-B movie star, his eyes began to scrutinize his audience. He looked from face to face as he proclaimed, "I am suure we are all gonna be gettin aloong jest fine. Uuh?" Beaming even greater he nodded his head up and down; and asked, "You do agree, don't chyou. Aah, yess, I see we do agreee?"

No one disagreed and Patrick confidently continued, "But... if yyou haave a dooubt or sooom concerns, please, please feeel free to see me about it later. Yoou see, I belieeve in an oopen-door policy. If my staff is noot haappy; then I too, am noot haappy. Now I vealize that some a yoou might noot be suure about staaying vith the company, but I suure hope yoou vill reconsider yoour ooptions and deecide to staay." Again, he deliberately glanced around the room and a new threat filled his voice, "Yoou knoow, I heear todaay's job markets can be murdder... besides I amm suure yoou vill find thaat vit us, things vill be a lot less vorrisome than out there."

Dan was stunned, he dithered before he started to sit down then immediately stood up straight. His face was a purple red, and he gulped loudly for a breath of air. It was plain for everyone to see he was close to suffocating on his anger. Aggressively Patrick pushed him back into his chair. All the while his handsome smile stayed pasted on his lips and his menacing eyes immediately moved towards the door as he muttered as quietly as possible, "I vouldn't if I vere yoou, Aleut."

Dan's eyes automatically followed Patrick's gaze to the door and saw that Javier and Paulo were perched on each side of the jambs.

He swallowed more air and his face turned from the purplish red to completely white as he fell back against his seat. He said nothing more throughout the rest of the meeting.

A half hour later everyone was dismissed. When they were about to leave the room, Patrick announced in a passionate voice, "please, can yoou all pleease vaat a minuute. Yoou must be poliiet and say your gooud viddance to yoour old chum here; Mr. Aleut...," Again, he flashed his big Hollywood grin and added, "He's gooing to be leavin us now and he's noot coomin back. Is thaat noot vight, Mr. Aleut?"

Everyone nervously looked over at Dan as they uncomfortably mumbled their unsympathetic goodbyes. It was plain to see they were not unhappy about the change. They avoided eye contact and immediately shuffled towards the door.

It was obvious to Dan that no one was sad to see him go. When the department heads hurried to exit the room, most as soon as they cleared the doorway, seemed to become giddy with laughter. Dan had caught their taunting glances throughout the meeting, and this increased his anger. He saw that they had no loyalty, they openly detested him. His resentment continued to grow until it now felt like it was strangling the breath from his lungs.

Patrick had also studied the staff as they left the room and smiled a satisfied smirk. He could feel the first tinges of their enthusiasm and this gave him a feeling of power. Yes, he was pleased with himself and once he announced that lunch from Angelino's was going to be served in the atrium, everyone applauded and thanked him. He swelled with pleasure. He could tell this takeover was going to be a cinch. No one was going to give them a problem, no one at all. *Yes,* he thought, *a little treat now and then and everyone will be happy.*

Finally, after the last person had left the room, he looked at Dan and muttered, "vhat a bunch of simple saps"

At the same time the last person had shuffled out of the room Dan's fears momentarily dissipated and he turned to Patrick and stammered in unchecked fury. "You ruined me. I'm ruined. You fucken bastard, all my dreams are destroyed. My life is over, you moron. I'll never be anything in this town again. How could you do this? I told you, you'd get your fucken money. How could you ruin me like this? I'm not behind, so why the take over?"

Patrick said nothing only smiled broader than before. At that time, Paulo stepped forward and grunted as he grabbed for Dan's arm, "Come on let's get packin, jerk-off," Dan snatched his arm away before Paulo could get a grip on it and yelled, "It's bad enough being escorted from the room, I certainly don't need to be led out by some big ape."

With this Patrick laughed and shouted loud enough so people in the hall could hear, "Oh, by the vaay, Aleut. Yoour old laady, she said to be suure to tell yoou not to voorry..." his laughter rang an octave higher as he added, "cause she vill take care of you, veeal gooud...."

Dan was furious. What the fuck is Jackie up to? What kind of game is she playing now? She must've figured out he took the money and now she's going to make him grovel. Why else would she ruin him? "The fucken bitch, she'll be sorry. She's the one who's gonna, pay not me."

Dan moved around the room, grabbing a few items off the wall then from his desk. He figured he'd be back as soon as he straightened this out with those stupid goons and that damn bitch. He grumbled under his breath, "Once I'm back, every last one of these traitors will be fired."

Finally, he gave Patrick a filthy look and stomped out of the room. He was furious and he shoved several people aside when he hurried through the halls and out to his car.

Patrick observed him from the window of his new office and decided, "Yes, Dan is pissed off. There's no dooubt about it. Vhat a pleasure it is tooo vitness?"

Dan revved up the car motor and sped from his parking space, squealing his tires as soon as the car hit the street. Patrick continued to watch as Dan went through a red light. He turned and picked up the phone. He waited patiently until she answered, and said only four words, "He's on his vaay,"

Jackie again assured Jessie and Carmen that she would be fine. She said she was going to have a quiet lunch alone while she read one of her favorite old books. "Anyway," she said, "Dan's most likely going to be late again, so I'll probably just go out this evening. Maybe I'll do a little shopping than some dinner at a cafe. Either way, there is no reason you two should stay. Now be on your way. Go."

Jesse stammered, "But, Mrs....., ya might need something."

Again, Jackie reminded them, that all their work was done and as for her the only thing she needed was some solitude. She repeated one more time, "I am not going to take no for an answer. No more arguments." She stood fast with her hands on her hips and insisted, "So go, get out, go...take the afternoon off. Enjoy some sun. Like I said, I'm fine."

This was not entirely uncommon. Jackie had always been generous with them so reluctantly they agreed. Relieved Jackie quickly said her goodbyes and told them she'd see them tomorrow. She turned and headed straight for the library. She wanted to make sure all was in place. Her intent was to get everything on tape without Dan being wise to her objectives. She figured that if he were ignorant of the camera, she'd be able to get a complete confession out of him. There was no way she was going to let him get his hands on *her* money and this videotape was going to ensure that.

She glanced around the room. Satisfied, she smiled and said, "okay action." At once Jackie was startled by the sudden loud bang of the door, she turned and braced herself. She was ready to face Dan and his incontrovertible rage. As soon as he crashed through the library door, she recognized the extent of his anger, even before he opened his mouth to scream at her, "You damn fucken bitch! What the hell did you think you were up to? This is probably the stupidest thing you could've ever done. Now you're really gonna pay! I mean, I'm gonna own you, bitch. You are a stupid, stupid little tramp. I got witnesses and everything. Yes Jackie, I would say you really blew it this time. There's not a court in the land that's gonna let you ruin a man's livelihood and get away with it."

Chuckling as she stepped forward Jackie stood her ground and shouted, "A man no, but a despicable moron, yes! You're no better than a mangy ole alley cat! You only married me for my money, so no court's going to reward you for your deceitful actions by giving it to you. Not only that, but you've also blatantly cheated on me with any little want to be starlet that would have you. And *I*, have witnesses all over town who will testify to **that**! Mr. Hollywood Producer."

"So, big fucken deal, everybody cheats on their damn wife. That's no big deal." Dan threw a disgusted look in her direction then began laughing, "Especially if she's an old has-been like you. Who's gonna blame me? Huh? Who Jackie, tell me? Why don't ya tell me that, bitch? You seem to think you have all the fucken answers, so WHO?"

She could see he grew more confident when he saw her flinch, and her startled expression gave him the fuel he needed to continue his barrage. "Yes, that's right. You know damn well I'm right, don't ya, bitch? No, not one person's gonna blame me for cheating on a woman that's fifteen years older than me." He sniggered then muttered, especially when other guys are cheating on wives who are half their age."

Jackie bite her lower lip so hard she could taste the iron-like-flavor of blood and this angered her more than what Dan had just spewed. Furious that she had let his words get to her. She took another angry step forward and almost spat in his face with her bloody venom when she spouted back, "Maybe some of what you say is true, Dan. But I'll bet those guys aren't stupid enough to openly steal from their older, much wiser, and *richer* wife!"

Dan took a step closer to match hers and when he was face to face, he screamed, "You don't have one bit of evidence. You can't prove I ever took a damn cent from you. Jackie, you're nothing more than a senile old lady. You are so forgetful; you can't even remember when you write a check. Which, I imagine, can only strengthen my case. I may even be able to have you institutionalized."

"God, Dan you're pathetic. You don't even have balls enough to tell me the truth face to face. But, but that's okay, because the courts will be able to see that that's not my signature on those checks. And you can mark my words, there's *NO* chance in hell that you will be able to put me away or ever get control over my money. Not even over my dead body."

Jackie paused, but only for an instant before she shot, "Still and all...if I think about it, I probably won't need a confession from you after all, for I'm sure once I inform the police or better yet, alert the newspapers, that you tried to *RAPE my daughter! You* won't get a damn penny of *my money."* Jubilantly she added, *"You...* won't even be able to show your fucking face in this town. Appeased, when she saw the blood drain from Dan's face, she smugly turned to walk away.

Suddenly Dan grabbed her by the arm and swung her back to face him and more of his onslaught. "I don't know what you're taking about you filthy little bitch. You would say anything to ruin me wouldn't you!"

"Dan, we're not all as petty as you. Despicable, as it may be, it's not only true. But I have all the fucking proof *I need*!"

"What! Who?"

"Raynie, Raynie herself!"

Dan's face went chalky white before his cheeks colored a bright crimson. He realized that Jackie had the upper hand, and this intensified his anger. Instantly he stepped one foot closer and snapped, "Raynie's nothing but a slut. A filthy little whore just like her mother. There's not a single person in this town that would ever blame me. Why, everyone knows that she's been throwing herself at me for months. Yes, sir, she's nothing but a pig, just like you Jackie."

Jackie's anger finally got the best of her and she growled. "You... you're nothing but a foul mouth excuse of a man! You make me sick, to think I ever thought I loved you. You've done nothing but lie to me since the day I met you. You came into this marriage for money and money only, and when I wouldn't give it to you, you stole it. You've cheated on me countless times and worst of all, *y o u* attempted to rape my daughter, and you have the *n e r v e*...to call *meeee* a pig!"

She never saw it coming, but Jackie could feel the burning sting at the same time she heard the loud sound of the smack. Falling backward she hit her head hard against the desk. Dazed she fought to sit upward and collapsed back onto the floor. The room was spinning, and she could barely make out his figure as he continued to move towards her. She once again fought to sit up, but the sharp pain hastened her attempts. Despite her efforts she could feel his hands as they grabbed her tightly as she slipped deeper and deeper into darkness...

Chapter Twenty-one

Raynie opened the envelope; surprised that the return address was her mother's. However, the note was even more surprising. The brief scribbled words were to inform her that her mother had left town for a few days. It read, 'that she didn't know when she'd be back. That she needed time to think about her relationship with Dan. She had to make some decisions on what to do about her precarious situation.'

To her surprise Raynie felt her knees go weak and she fell back against the loveseat. She was worried about her mother and leaving town like this was absolutely strange behavior for her. Jackie always called her if she was going away. Raynie couldn't imagine her just taking off especially without leaving an address or at least a phone number where she could reach her. Yet, she did have to admit that lately Jackie had been under a great deal of strain. Maybe she's right she needed some time to be alone so she can get her head on straight. Again, Raynie dubiously studied the note. The writing was messy. It looked like her mother had written it in a hurry. In any event there wasn't anything to hint where she intended to go. Laying the letter aside she whispered, "Unfortunately

Mother, I guess I have no choice. I'll just have to wait until you call me to find out what's going on." *Jesus,* she wondered, *what has Dan done to her now?*

Raynie recalled how troubled her mother looked the last time she saw her. The memory made her feel uneasy and she immediately reached for the phone to call her father.

"Your father's been out of town since the evening you two had lunch together," Kelsey reported. "I'm not expecting him back for at least two more days. You know how conventions go.

"Do you know if my mother called or if she left a number for him where she could be reached?" Raynie asked without comment on Kelsey's last remark.

"No," answered Kelsey. "I haven't heard from Jackie and as far as I know neither has your father before he left town. Come to think of it," she added, "it's been at least a week before that, that she talked with him and that was on some legal matters." Kelsey hesitated than went on, "Raynie, I'm going through my messages and I don't see anything from the service that Jackie called and left a number for Ray. But if she does call, I'll be sure to give you a ring with the information."

Raynie laid the phone back in its cradle and once again read the note. She wanted to help her mother deal with this awful dilemma, but it looked as though Jackie wanted to handle it on her own. At this time Raynie heard the horn honk from the driveway and she ran to open the door for Simon. This had been a whirl wind week and now they were jetting off to spend a glorious day and night in San Francisco. From there they planned to spend a couple days at her favorite cliff side resort at Pebble Beach. Simon also mentioned a night in Aspen at the Hotel Jerome. She smiled when she remembered Simon's expression when he told her what he heard about the hotel. He loved historic hotels, and someone mentioned he might want to check this one out. Not at all fancy, but interesting they said.

She heard Simon's steps on the stone and grabbed her suitcase and ran out the door leaving her mother's note and her concerns behind.

Dan was beside himself with frustration. He'd tried to reach Raynie at home more times than he could count, but she was never there. He had left countless messages. Thus far she had not returned his call. He also called to talk with Mike, but the maid said he was out. *Dammit*, he thought. Up to now he'd left about fifteen different messages with Mike's staff, and so far, he still hadn't returned his calls.

He downed the last of the vodka in his glass and headed for the liquor cabinet. He poured himself one more drink and looked at his watch. It was barely eleven o'clock in the morning. "God dammit," he shouted! "I've had enough of this bullshit, I'm going over there to talk with Mike, and if Louis has a problem with it so be it."

Dan rang the doorbell several times and after a minute or two he heard footsteps. Automatically he braced his stance in case he had to encounter an attack from Louis. He felt relief wash over him when the maid opened the door. From where he stood Dan could see the suitcases in the hallway. Without waiting for an invitation, he pushed the door and barged into the foyer.

The startled maid jumped back and let out a startled screech. At once, Dan began shouting, "Okay, where in the hell is, he. Where's Mike? Mike, I need to talk with you dammit, and now!

The maid was obviously frightened and started to stammer and never uttered an intelligible word until Mike entered the hallway and rushed to her side. Mike, who was also flustered by the commotion, but more concerned for his staff-member, bellowed, "My Lord, Vera; what's the matter? Are you okay? What's going on?"

When he saw why she was startled, his voice immediately changed, and it was easy for Dan to hear his displeasure, "Oh... I see. It's you, Dan." He turned back to Vera and sympathetically said, "It's okay Vera, you can go my dear, I'll handle this."

Vera backed slowly out of the room. When she moved passed Mike he added, "Why don't you take a little break sweety; you look pale from your scare. A nice cup of tea may help."

Vera smiled her thank you at Mike then quickened her steps. It was obvious that she was still frightened by Dan, and his intrusive manner, and while exiting she made sure she left a wide girth between her and her aggressor.

Dan didn't wait for the girl to fully leave the entranceway before he asked Mike in a sarcastic tone, "Are you going somewhere? Maybe you were trying to avoid me, is that it, Mike?"

Before Mike could speak, Dan burst out loudly, "So, Mike, now that you move up town, you think you don't need your old friends anymore, is that it? That's it, isn't it? Now that you have your, Dr. Perfect, you don't need your old buddy Dan no more. All your needs are being taken care of by Dr. Perfect."

Mike tightened his shoulders and held his head high as he returned the same sarcastic grin and answered, "One day, Dan, you're going to realized that the world does not revolve around you."

Mike turned and walked over to the telephone, and picked up the pad that lay next to it then went on, "Even though it is none of your business, Louis and I have been away for the past several days. We just returned minutes ago. Judging by the number of messages you left, I would have thought you would have guessed that by now."

Ignoring Mike's contemptuous manner, Dan shot, "So, Dr. Carver's in, is he? Well, all the bett..."

Mike cut in before Dan could add more derogatory remarks about Louis and retorted, "Again, it's none of your business, but Louis is not here. He dropped me off before he went to the office for a short while. If I may, can I emphasis, *a short while*, in hopes that you will get my drift. Anyway, what the hell do you want, Dan?"

Mike turned to move from the foyer and Dan followed him into the living room and instantly began to denounce, "You fuck ass. Don't you walk away from me, I've always been your friend, even when we were kids and everybody else treated you like shit. Who stood up for you? Huh, Mike..., who? Me, that's who. Me! And now suddenly you chose to forget that fact. I just can't believe you Mike. You've turned your back on me. What kind of man would turn his back on his best buddy when he needs him most? The one friend who had always been there for him; no matter what the need. I have always been there for you, Mike. Always."

Spinning around and facing the accusation and the madman who's been impersonating Dan lately, Mike stated. "Dan, what the hell are you talking about? As for the kind of man I am, I'm afraid you wouldn't recognize it. It's called decent and guiltless or in this case blameless. So, if you're here to yell at me for something I didn't do, don't waste your time. Because I still haven't got a clue of what the hell you're talking about."

"Don't give me that shit, Mike. You told Jackie what happened with Raynie. You're the only person that knew. It had to be you."

"I didn't tell anybody, anything. I wouldn't hurt Jackie like that and if you were thinking straight, you would know that."

"Then tell me who did. I know Raynie didn't."

"How in the hell do I know who told her Dan? And how do you know it wasn't Raynie herself? Jesus, Dan, you're losing it. You know how close they are. I'm surprised she hadn't told her before now. Furthermore, as far as I'm concerned, if she had decided to tell her mother I really couldn't blame her. She has every right to talk with her about something so horrid. Come to think of it, she also has an obligation to let her mother know what kind of monster she is married to."

"Oh, now I'm a monster, now that you feel you don't need me anymore. Now that you have the illustrious Dr. Louis Carver to take care of you, I'm a monster. Well I'll tel...."

"No, Dan, I'll tell you. You *are* a monster because you have no conscience. You never give a damn who you hurt. You are everything a human should not be. Now if you don't mind, I'd like you to leave."

"No Mike, I'm not going anywhere. Not until you hear me out."

"Dan, I've asked you nicely to leave this house. If you don', I'm calling the police and reporting an intruder."

"Mike, I need your help, you can't throw me out, I need you."

"Sorry, Dan, but I'm terribly busy with my unpacking and I can't wait to get into a tub full of hot water and bubbles. So, sorry, I just don't have any more time to stand around here and discuss your miserable life."

"Mike, what has Louis done to you? Mike...can't you see he's turned you against me? He has, hasn't he, why can't you see that?"

"Why, Dan? Because I'm no longer that little puppet you used for years? No, Dan, it wasn't Louis who did anything to me. It was you. You and your greedy obsessions that did this to me. For years, you kept me blind with your so-called loyalty and friendship tunes. But Louis saved me. He has helped me realize who and what you are. Alas, now that I can finally see the real Dan..., I'm sad to admit this, but it sickens me."

Dan shouted, "Mike, forget that bullshit and listen!"

"No, Dan, for once you're going to hear me out. As usual, you decided to take what you wanted. You...you selfishly attempted to keep me in your clutches by taking everything away from me. It didn't matter if my life would be destroyed as long as you got what you wanted, and that was to keep me emotional dependent on you. Well, this time when you told Louis things that weren't true about us, you went too far. When you told him that big fat lie, that you and I were lovers, you destroyed any friendship we ever had. Mike spun around and almost ran up the staircase as he screamed, "Now get the hell out of my house, and don't you ever come back!"

Chapter Twenty-two

A s soon as Simon pulled the car to a stop, Raynie jumped out and ran up the steps and bolted through the door. Once inside she continued the race until she stood in front of her desk. The answering machine was blinking away. Hurriedly she pushed the rewind button and leafed through the mail while she waited. She was dying to see if her mother had left her a message or sent her another note. She listened eagerly to the first few seconds of each message before she pushed the skip button to go to the next. After listening to all nine messages and noting a tenth and eleventh was a hang up, she thought, "*maybe... that was her? No, Mother would've left a message.*" Again, she searched through the mail she still held in her hand.

Simon shoved through the doorway carrying two pieces of luggage along with five shopping bags full of new clothes and souvenirs. When he saw the disappointment that had replaced the smile Raynie had worn only minutes before. He at once dropped everything and rushed to her side.

The happy expression she had worn earlier was now strained with worry. Raynie sat herself down firmly into the chair next to the table that held the phone. She stared at the device as if it were a liar. Simon caressed her shoulder for reassurance. Raynie looked up and attempted a smile as she started to shove her body back against the seat. Halfway back she realized that she'd forgotten to look for Nikkei. Immediately Nikkei gave a disgruntled screech and skittered off the chair.

Simon ignored the startled cat and kept his attention fixed on Raynie and her obvious disappointment. He knew the answer before he asked the question. but he asked it anyway, "Nothing?"

Raynie glanced up to meet his question and noticed his gorgeous eyes held concern. Sadly, she shook her head. "Simon, I'm really scared. What if she's had an accident on her way to... to ... I don't even know where. Simon, this just isn't like my mother! I mean, to simply take off to places unknown, especially without at least notifying me or...or my father first. It...it doesn't make sense."

Raynie stood and started to pace back and forth as she began mumbling to herself, "Something's not right here. We should have heard from Mother by now. I don't even know where to start looking. Yes, I'm sure something has to be wrong, but what? I just don't know. It's not like her, Simon. As of this morning Daddy hasn't heard anything. And yesterday when I called her staff, they said they hadn't heard from her either. Something's clearly wrong. It's been days and no one's heard a word."

"Raynie, please, will you please slow down? We can start checking. We can start with my staff calling all the hospitals in a two-hundred-mile radius. We can even call the police if that will help ease your mind a bit. Though I believe it may be a little too early for so much concern and such a move...."

"But, Simon, I can't just sit here and do nothing."

"Raynie listen to me. You said you received a note the day we left, right?"

"Yes, but it didn't really say anything."

"Could she have gone away with Dan?"

"No! That's why she said she was leaving, so she could think about their relationship. Besides, Mike left a message on the answering machine, telling me to beware. Dan's acting crazy again and he's looking for me. Dan also left several messages that he needed to talk with me ASAP."

No sooner than the words were out Simons expression showed his anger and said, "Raynie that guy's asking for it, I mean it. If he even gets near you, I will kill the bastard with my own two hands."

"Simon! Oh my God. Please Simon, please don't ever talk like that."

Simon was going to add more to his threat but noticed the panic had grown in Raynie's eyes. Concerned he quickly moved to take her in to his arms, "Sweetheart, I'm sorry. Please forgive me. I really do not mean to add to your dismay. I just...Well, I can't help it. The thought of anyone ever hurting you...I don't know, I guess a thought like that makes me crazy with anger." Simon pushed her blond hair behind her ears and kissed her fingertips one by one, after which he murmured in a stifled tone, "Raynie, I truly care for you. And sweetheart, I will truly do anything to protect you. If Dan harms, you in any way...I swear..."

Raynie touched his lips with the tips of her fingers he had just kissed and whispered "Shisssh," before softly answering, "Simon, I adore you, and I'm sure everything will be fine. Please don't worry about me." She tenderly pushed him away and once again started her stride, back and forth as she cried out in frustration, "Oh, God, Simon, right now, all I want is to find my Mother. And... and... if the only way to find her or find information on where she is means going to Dan then I'll do it."

Simon watched her restless actions as she moved about the room. It was obvious she was highly distraught. He fell silent while searching her face and recognized that there was a lot more fear in her than he had first recognized. With this realization, his hostility against Dan shifted to concern for her. He could see she was struggling with her angst and his heart went out to her. He wanted to protect her and ease her burden, but would she be willingly to let him? From what he had seen these past months, she was extremely strong minded and independent. She didn't easily give in to what she called, coddling. However, for right now he could see she needed his support and he intended to give it to her in any form she would accept. Without further delay, he softened his voice but authoritatively said, "I will give you everything you need, my staff will assist your search. We will use every means available to us to find your mother. But we play by my rules. First thing, you can not stay here. I certainly don't want Dan surprising you with one of his impromptu visits. Furthermore, I believe you should not confront him by yourself either. So why not throw Nikkei along with these things back into the car and you can come and stay with me until we find Jackie. Agreed?"

He waited for her answer as she listed several reasons in her mind why she should stay here in her own home; one reason being that her mother would be able to contact her easier.

Finally, Simon added, "It is either that, Raynie, or I am dogging you."

Raynie couldn't help but laugh at his phraseology and she returned to his arms and placed several kisses on his lips. Relinquishing herself to his protection, she whispered between each smack, "Okay you win. You have a deal, Mr. Protector. You can be my knight in shining armor as long as you promise, *not to dog me*."

Once Raynie was settled in at Simon's, she called her father. She wanted to let him know where she would be and to check if he heard anything from her mother. Ray hadn't heard a word from Jackie, but he filled his daughter in on what had been going down since she left town with Simon.

It seemed that Dan had reluctantly been hoisted out of his seat as head of Aleut Productions. The company was taken over by a gentleman named, Patrick Garrett, a well-known front man for the local underworld. Ray also said he didn't know for sure, but rumor had it that Jackie had something to do with the upset. As her father talked Raynie couldn't help but notice that his voice never wavered; neither did it carry any indication of surprise about the rumored speculation. Raynie wanted to comment but held her tongue and continued to listen tentatively without interruption. When her father paused, she asked him about his easy acceptance. Ray hesitated only a second and decided it was time to open Raynie's eyes completely to what her mother really was. She needed to know the truth so she could more easily put things into perspective. "Sweety, you remember I told you how I knew an assortment of various types of individuals?"

"Well yes, of course I do. I'm still reeling from the information."

"Well, here's something else for you to ponder, my sweet." She heard her father suck in a deep breath as he continued, "Raynie, your Mother is the person who acquainted me with these effectual people. You see, sweetheart, your mother is a powerhouse in her own right, and I don't think Dan was smart enough to see this. Or maybe he did see it but was just plain stupid enough to challenge it. I don't know which, but I do know that his ego wouldn't let him benefit from it."

Raynie was aghast and had to make the effort to keep the panic from escaping her lips, yet it was evident when she finally voiced, "My God, Daddy, Mother's not like that. She can't be."

She waited for further clarification and when none came, she uttered a dismayed, "Sweet Jesus, I think I've lived my whole life blindfolded. I've never seen a single clue of any of this. Daddy, I'm close to twenty-nine years old and I never guessed or saw anything that indicated we were anything except a normal family."

"Ray gave a soft laugh before promising, "Sweetheart, we are normal as far as industry people go. Furthermore, as far as your Mother goes, she's nothing more than a wonderful wife, mother and an extremely intelligent businesswoman, and I repeat, nothing more."

There was complete silence for a full minute while a new fear entered Raynie's mind. She pictured the indignant face of Dan. In a panic she asked, "Daddy, do you think that maybe Mother's hiding from Dan? You said she might have been behind him losing his company and you know his temper and how much that company meant to him?"

"Yes, Raynie, I do know his temper and from what I've recently learned, *so do you.*" Again, silence filled the air and Raynie clenched her teeth as a panicky sensation tickled her stomach and trickled down her spine. She didn't ask her father what he was talking about because she feared she already knew.

Ultimately, Ray broke the silence, "Don't worry baby. We'll find your mother and no, I don't believe she's hiding. It's not her style. I'll call you if I hear from her and you do the same for me, okay?" She could hear the quiet rhythm of his breathing. Once again there was an awkward silence that lingered before Ray added, "I love you, baby. Take care."

Raynie whispered, "I love you too, Daddy. Bye."

After hanging up Raynie sat there for over an hour staring at the waterfall through the enormous windows. Her memory labored strenuously to think back over the years. She wanted to recall everything in her life. What was she missing? There must've been something that indicated her mother had some kind of power. Jackie had always had her own investments and periodically, she even advised her father on his business issues. It was also a well-known fact that her mother knew an awful lot of people throughout the industry. Yet, she had always attributed that to the fact that she had grown up in it. Matter of fact, Jackie was part of what she and several of her friends liked to refer to themselves as the original rat pack. Not the known bunch of movie stars, but the pack behind the scenes. The decision makers. Even though Jackie never held any kind of office or position she was largely in the thick of things. Which she, herself, always attributed purely because of her friendships with the many individuals who were. She sighed and thought, other than that, there was nothing else that stood out. Jackie was simply her Mother, and Daddy's wife.

Once Raynie finished breaking her life down into parts she could easily study in detail, she realized that there was nothing there for her to see. There were no buried secrets to be uncovered. They were, as her father had assured her, nothing more than a normal industry family.

Immediately after her last thought she re-examined what her father had told her to see if she might have misunderstood his implications. But when she finally stood up to leave the generous comfort of the enormous sofa, she still couldn't see her mother in any other light, except, as she had grown to know her, all these years. In her eyes, Jackie was fragile and somebody that needed to be taken care of... and that's exactly what she intended to do, starting right now.

CHAPTER TWENTY-THREE

Without further speculation Raynie went to the closet and grabbed a windbreaker and her purse. Haphazardly she stuffed her blond hair through the rear of a baseball cap and scurried out the front door.

She started in the direction of her car then remembering what Simon had said to her before he left for his appointment that morning, she changed her direction to move towards one of his vehicles instead. As promised Simon had left the keys in the ignition of the Ferrari. He had said in case she wanted to use it, so she decided to take it instead. *Using Simon's car is a lot smarter,* she thought, *Dan will certainly recognize the BMW.*

If she happens to have a chance encounter with him, she would much rather that he be caught off guard. She deduced that surprise was the only way she was going to have the upper hand.

The fear Raynie felt for Dan from their past encounter was still very real. Yet her own anxiety had now changed to fear for her mother's safety. This feeling of dread was stronger than any concern she held for herself. Determinedly she jerked the car into reverse and grumbled, "I hope you won't be angry with me Simon for not following your advice and staying away from Dan."

Simon had been clear when he had asked her to stay as far away from Dan as possible. But this was something she had to do...for her mother. She had a hunch that answers could be found at her mother's residence and she intended to find them.

As soon as Raynie pulled the Ferrari to a stop behind Jackie's house, she noticed Dan's car was not in the driveway. However, she was optimistically surprised to see her mother's car parked off to one side of the large garage. "Maybe she's returned home."

Eagerly she got out and headed inside the garage. She wanted to make sure she wasn't mistaking Dan's Mercedes for her mother's. As soon as she confirmed that it was indeed her mother's, she considered, 'If she's not home, I'm curious why she didn't drive her favorite car. I wonder which one she took?'

She looked around and all the other vehicles were parked inside the garage, all except Dan's. "Maybe Mother flew. I could check the airlines, but first let's check to see if she's home."

As she turned to move towards the door, she noticed Kenny. Kenny was her mother's all-round mechanic and handyman. He was headed in her direction with an arm load of cleaning materials. As he was moving closer, she could see that the products he carried were for detailing the car's interior.

Kenny lifted his head and surprise crossed his face when he realized he was no longer alone in the garage. He smiled a warm friendly "hello," and added, "Whata nice surprise, Miss Raynie. I didn't expect to see you round here today, not with your Mamma bein out of town and all."

"Oh, so she's not back. I thought since her car was here, tha..." Overwhelmed with disappointment she stopped. After he sat the cleaning materials next to her mother's car, Raynie deduced, "You look like you're pretty busy Kenny. With my mother gone, I would think you'd take it easy."

"Ya, but Mr. Aleut wants me ta clean all your Mamma's cars real good inside and out. I guess so when she comes back, they'll all be clean and ready for her to use."

"Oh, were they especially dirty?"

"Naaa, he just wanted them cleaner, I guess."

Raynie stood to the side and watched Kenny work for several minutes before she asked, "Kenny, have you seen anything peculiar lately? I mean with the way Mr. Aleut's been acting."

"Nope, can't say that I have, Miss Raynie; but I'm not paid to see things only taa work." He moved to sit inside the Mercedes, and after giving her one last grin he began to vigorously polish the steering wheel.

Raynie had known this big friendly man most of her life, and she would've been stunned, if he had said anything different than what he just said. He wasn't a gossipy person like most of the other staff. Kenny usually stayed to himself and kept his comments the same way. It was obvious that there was nothing here to be found, so she turned to leave. But before she rounded the corner she yelled over her shoulder, "Thanks, Kenny, if you need anything just let Jesse know and she'll make sure you get it, okay?"

He lifted his polish rag upward and waved it in the air to let her know he heard what she had said, and he knew what to do. Raynie lengthened her stride toward the house so she could continue her investigation. The house is where she knew she would get more information. Jessie and Carmen were always eager to oblige when it came to gossip.

Raynie entered through the backdoor and was not taken aback to see both servants sitting at the kitchen table, each sipping a glass of iced tea. When they heard her footsteps, they both jumped and looked up startled. As soon as the ladies realized who it was, they immediately relaxed. Hey, Missy. How you? You Mamma, she still no here? Sorry, we got scared. We think you was, Mr. Aleut. He no like us to take breaks. He say we no get paid to sit."

"Don't worry Jessie. Your secret's safe with me." Raynie moved to sit down next to Carmen while Jessie poured her a glass of tea.

She stirred the tea several times before she looked up to face two sets of extremely concerned dark eyes staring at her. Both of them seem to look as concerned as she herself was, so she decided not to hold back. "Did my mother give any hint as to where she was headed for when she left?"

Carmen looked frightened and glanced over to Jessie for support. Jessie finally spoke for the both of them, "Na, Miss Raynie. She no tell us she go som place."

"You mean you didn't see her go?"

Shaking her head sadly she answered, "Na, Miss, we no be here. She tell me and Carmen ta go, take off. Take off day. Go, she say go. So, we go. When we come back next day, she gone."

"Are you sure she never said anything the last time you talked with her? I mean, say anything about any trip."

"Na, she say she gonna hav lounch in da liberry and with her good book. She say, Mr. Aleut gonna be late so maybe she go shop, maybe eat out later."

"Then what?"

"She go to liberry and we go off. But she be wrong, cause Mr. Aleut, he no be late. He come home, and oh, oh, oh, he be very, very maddd."

"What happened?"

"We not know, we go."

"So, the last time you saw my mother, she was in the library?" After Raynie asked the question, she realized the inquiry sounded as if she were involved in a game of clue.Yet this was far more serious than any game she'd ever participated in before.

Jesse hesitated and thought about the question then started nodding her head as she continued her answer, "yas, Miss, dat is right, she be in da liberry. I not see where Mr. Aluet go."

Raynie stood up and headed for the other side of the house and the library. Maybe there is some kind of hint there; a reservation for a hotel, airline itinerary or a note, anything.

Cautiously she opened the double doors. After she entered a few steps she stood and observed the entire room for several seconds.

She noticed there was an open book on the desk with a bookmark stuck between the open pages. The room held a hint of uneasiness. The chamber smelled stale, and the air held a heavy musky odor. She glanced around the dark space before she moved further inside. The dreariness of the room was something she never noticed before. Her mother's energy always seemed to brighten up the place. Raynie hesitated; then she slowly moved inward. When she reached the desk, she picked up the book and peered at the page. Yet her mind refused to work, so she couldn't comprehend what the words read or what they meant. At last she shoved the book aside and began to shuffle hurriedly through the papers that were stacked in little piles all over the desk. Her mother must have been doing some financial work.

Out of the corner of her eye she noticed a video camera. It was on its side at the edge of the desk. '*Huh, that seems like an odd place to keep a camera,*' she thought! Especially for her mother who usually stirred clear of anything *she would consider mechanical.*

Raynie reached for it but before she could pick it up, she noticed something strange on the edge of the desk. It looked like a tiny mass of blond hair with a dark color at the end of it. It appeared to be attached to the desk. She touched the dark mass, and it felt crisp like dry blood. She caught her breath and called out, "Jessie... Jessie!

Hearing the panic in Raynie's voice Jessie instantly came running into the room holding her hand to her chest. Her eyes were wide with fear as she screamed, "What? Miss, what!"

"Jessie, when was the last time you cleaned this room?"

"Ah, ya scared da life from me, Miss."

"The room, Jessie the room; when was it last cleaned?

"Ahhh, let me see maybe two weeks, maybe more. We no come in here. Mrs. say no, it be off limits. We clean only when Mrs. say. She say this room very private, ta ever body. We no come in."

Raynie stared at the hair. Her thoughts were running wild. She looked over at the book and remembered the video camera. She reached for it and hit the rewind then the play button.

She couldn't believe what appeared on the tiny view screen. The scream caught in her throat and she began to choke on it. Jessie seeing the fear and panic on Raynie's face, ran from the room screaming for Carmen who immediately began to panic herself. Raynie pushed both ladies aside as she ran from the room and out the door to her car. Without conscious thought she threw the video camera on the seat and sped out of the driveway onto the street without seeing anything except her calling. She was headed downtown for the police station and her resolve was all that mattered. On the way she ran one stop sign and two red lights before she pulled up to the Beverly Hills Police Department. She almost hit a passing car while turning into the parking lot. She slammed to a stop and parked haphazardly across two spaces. Jumping out of the car with the camera clutched close to her chest, she frantically ran into the building. Immediately she began shrieking hysterically at the first uniformed officer she saw. "He killed her! He killed her! He killed my mother! God help me, he killed her!"

Several policemen halted in the middle of their tasks and ran to help their fellow officers, who, by this time, were having a difficult time restraining the hysterical woman. The woman was striking madly out at anyone attempting to control her. Finally, two of the larger officers were able to restrain her by wrestling her to the floor and pinning her arms behind her back. Raynie fell limp, after that she broke down and began sobbing noisily. The sounds that were coming from her slight frame were pitiful agonizing whimpers. Sergeant Goodman, who walked in immediately after the ruckus ended, at first thought it was a suffering animal moaning. He was surprised when he saw the slumped girl on the floor. His heart went out to her when she gasped several more, "He killed her! Oh, God, he killed her!" After that she fell into an exhausted silence.

A few minutes later a couple of officers helped her to her feet and led her into the interrogation room. Raynie sat in the stark room unaware while several wary officers kept an eye on her. Unconsciously they all held their hands on their guns. Raynie was still half-dazed by their earlier encounter and her head throbbed with pain. Yet, far worse was her inability to comprehend what had happened to her mother. She was feeling a variety of emotions soaring within and soon they seem to encompass her very being.

As the officers stood their vigil, Raynie began to fall into a trance like state. She could almost feel her mind trying to shut itself down, striving desperately to close off all her pain, while at the same time she was consciously battling for control. She wanted to face reality and what happened to her mother. She wanted to hurt Dan. She wanted to kill him. The realization of her discovery was suffocating her down to the core and for an instant, she wished she could crawl back into herself for protection.

Sergeant Goodman coughed lightly. He hoped this would break the hypnotic stare the girl held as she concentrated on her own hands. When she didn't move, he asked politely. "Miss, can I get your name?"

Raynie looked up and stared at the older man, but he could see that she didn't understand the question. He wasn't at all sure she even saw him standing there. In his judgment, this woman was in dire need of some medical attention. She was very near the breaking point, but instead of summoning medical help, he asked the question a second time. "Can you please tell me your name, Miss? We can't help you if you don't talk to us."

Her eyes slowly focused and her voice was barely discernible when she whispered dryly, "Raaynie...Dey."

He looked at her questioningly for a full minute before he asked, "What? What did you say?" He wondered if he had misjudged her. Instead of being in shock as he assumed, she was on some drug and was hallucinating because he thought she said, *rainy day.* Patiently he asked the question again, "Can you tell us your name, Miss?"

Still in shock, Raynie was having trouble understanding his question. *"What, what does he mean? What, is he looking for? I told him what he wanted."* She studied his face and realized the confusion. "Oh. Oh, sor..ry," she mumbled so quietly he could barely hear her words. "My name's Raynie, R a y n i e, Dey, D e y," she spelled each letter out for them. Then stopped abruptly. Her eyes darted back and forth between the officer and the stenographer, who was sitting quietly in the corner of the small room. After a minute, another officer walked into the room and handed her a cup of hot coffee. He asked gently, "Is black okay?" She nodded her head and everyone in the room watched speechlessly as she sipped several swallows of the bitter dark nectar.

Sharply Raynie looked up and asked in a voice full of panic, "Where's my camera?" Without hesitation she accused, "You took my camera. Where's my camera? Where is it? You can't take it. It's mine! I need it...." Her last words where again engulfed in a loud ragged sob as she splashed her coffee over the top of the cup. She watched it seeped down her leg. She stared down at the puddle as it settled on the floor by her foot. There had been no reaction to the hot substance that had soiled her jeans. She simply gazed at the puddle next to her feet as if it held the answers, she was seeking.

The man who handed her the coffee moved quickly to stand next to her. It was as though he was attempting to protectively shield her from the others in the room. A short chunky guy moved to stand in front of her and handed her a paper towel as he asked in almost a deadpan voice. "Miss Dey, where'd you get the camera that you carried in here?"

Hysteria instantly became visible in Raynie's eyes and she screeched, "It's my mother's! She had it sitting on her desk in the library. She must have had it running." Her panic was intensifying, and it filled her voice with each word she spurted. Her eyes once again began to dart around the room as she cried out, "Ooh... my God. He killed her. I saw it on the tape. I saw it. He killed her."

"Miss Dey, can we call someone for you?"

Crying she choked out an intense, "Yes, yes please. Please, call my father. I want my daddy. He'll know what to do. He's an attorney." Sobbing and moaning she repeated, "He'll know what to do."

At that moment, her voice hardened, and she screamed, "Hurry, dammit! We have to do something; Dan killed my mother."

She heard someone ask, "Who's Dan?" But before they could ask the question, they could see she was starting to shut them out again, so they quickly asked her if she had a number where they could reach her father. She looked unsure before she spoke then rattled off a number. The officer turned and rushed from the room to make the call. With a sniffle she asked, "Can someone call Simon? Please…, please, tell Simon. Tell him I need him."

"Who"

"Simon…Simon Charles," she whimpered.

The Sergeant's caring smile was full of concern when he said, "Sure, sure no problem, Miss Dey." He glanced over at another officer who stood by the door and ordered, "Ricky get the number. Then get the hell on it; get that Simon guy in here STAT."

Sergeant Goodman continued to observe Raynie as she stumbled and had to repeat the number, two, three then four times before she got it right. The Sergeant felt sorry for her. She seemed so defenseless. It was obvious that she had never been in a police station before and he was sure its strangeness added to her stress.

Raynie waited with one officer who nervously sat across the table from her while several others peered through the one-way glass. The whole department was holding their breath while the young beauty sat silently in the small interrogation room. As for Raynie she was unaware of anyone. Her mind was focused on the tragic image that was burned into her memory forever. It played over and over, just the way it did on the video camera. She had only viewed a few seconds of the film before she ran out of the house, but now she knew how the blood and hair became dry on the corner of the desk. She groaned then bent over and grabbed her stomach. This image was making her feel ill, but she couldn't stop it from rolling over and over and over again. She asked herself, *should I ask to use the bathroom, I think I'm going to throw up.*

It seemed like forever, yet it was less than an hour later when Simon hurried through the door with her father right behind him. Their concern for her was all over their faces and this suddenly brought the nightmare to its reality once again. She could tell by their expressions that the officers had already filled them in on what the camera had recorded.

Carmen was full of indecision after she peered through the peephole for several seconds. Laden with suspicion she eventually opened the door slowly.... then peeked around the edge. She and Jessie had feared for days that something awful had happened to Mrs. Aleut. Now here stood several uniformed policemen and she wasn't sure whether she wanted to hear what they had to say. She said nothing to the policemen after she opened the door, she just stood there as she mumbled to herself and made a cross from her head, to chest and shoulders. "Oh Jesus, dear Lord, I know ta mans are here ta tell me that our Mrs. is dead. Please make it no so."

When the door was finally closed behind the two officers that Carmen finally asked in, one immediately tried to calm the obviously distraught maid with a friendly smile when he stated, "We're sorry to bother you, Miss." Then he asked in a more serious voice, "Is Mr. Aleut at home?"

Carmen nodded sadly, and said, "He be asleep, Mr." She stepped aside and they moved further inside the hallway.

The taller of the men asked, "Can you please wake him? We need to speak with him immediately."

Carmen moved sluggishly down the hall, yet instead of heading upstairs where the officers assumed the bedrooms to be, the maid headed for the living-room. When she looked back, she could see the confusion on both policemen's face and stated, "He sleepen on da couch. I think he be drinkin too much whisky again."

The two officers immediately moved to Carmen's side and followed her into the lavish room where they saw the sleeping Dan. Unemotionally, they watched Carmen as she attempted to wake him. When it was apparent that he was passed out and not just asleep, they picked him up by the arms and pulled him off the couch and hauled him out the door. One of the men stopped long enough to lay a search warrant on the table near the doorway, along with the authorization for Dan's detainment for questioning.

At this same time, several other officers entered the house along with a man in a dark suit. All hurriedly flashed their badges and asked where the library was. Behind them came two plain clothed detectives. Both also quickly flashed their badges and one said, "We have some questions. We'll need the staff to step into the living room or somewhere where we can speak privately?"

"Living ro...room," answered the scared Carmen as she stuttered, if ta...tat be o...kay, sir?"

"Can you get them all together;" he asked?"

"Yas, Sir."

Carmen held Jesse who was frightened. She whispered, "it okay, Jesse." And they clung closer together. Neither said anything more while they watched the house fill and swarm with people within minutes. After they acknowledged the detective's last request both women stood frozen, so he asked once more, "Please can you get everyone together? They simply nodded a yes and scooted away to assemble their coworkers.

Confused, Kenny, Jessie and Carmen maneuvered their way to the prescribed area. Around them was a mass of confusion which frightened Jesse even more. They were ordered by several different officers to not touch anything. After several minutes, the staff was finally seated on the sofa with two officers gaping down at them. Each looked more frightened than the next as they waited with uncertainty.

The large blond detective moved forward and introduced himself and his partner. "Hi, I'm Detective Lou Volfensberger and this is my partner, Detective Harry Gonzales. We only have a few questions to ask you about Mr. and Mrs. Aleut."

From the start, Jessie was not eager to answer any questions. Especially about her new employer, Mr. Dan Aleut. But the handyman, on the other hand was even more closed mouth. Although once he heard about Mr. Aleut's alleged drunkenness on that last day when the two maids seen him coming home on their way out, he began to open up some.

Kenny sat awkwardly on the couch with his large frame straight upward. His manner was rigid, almost impermeably defiant. Though Volfensberger could hear he held a lot of respect for, Mrs. Aleut. Each question he answered his voice was full of regard and filled with concern for the lady's safety. His first question proved the Detective's theory correct when Kenny apprehensively asked, "Did he hurt her? She's not dead, is she?"

Volfensberger eagerly questioned, "Why would you presume that Mr. Aleut would hurt Mrs. Aleut?" Ahhh...," The detective looked down at his pad and added, "Kenny?"

The handyman stood up respectfully and muttered, "Ya, it's Kenny. Kenny Stewart. I've been with Mrs. Aleut a long time." He hesitated, not saying anything more as he self-consciously looked at each face in the room.

Gonzales cut in and asked, "Can you please answer the question, Sir? Why do you assume that Mr. Aleut, would hurt Mrs. Aleut?"

Kenny shuffled back to his seat; it was obvious that he was uncomfortable with the situation. Cautiously he evaluated the question longer than necessary before answering, "Well, I guess... cause at times he's simply on the mean side."

"Why do you say that... Kenny?"

"Well, I really got no reason, only what I see in his actions and the way he treats her. That's all. Especially when he's been drinkin."

Volfensberger jumped in to ask, "What do you mean the way he treats her?"

"Well, Mrs. Dey, ah...I mean, Mrs. Aleut, she's really a good person. She takes really good care of her own, if ya know what I mean? She rarely sees the bad in people and there's times when she's taken advantage of."

"Are you saying Mr. Aleut took advantage of her?"

"Ahh well, I guess what I'm sayin is, Mrs. Aleut really loved Mr. Aleut and so she didn't see no bad in him." Kenny wavered. He really didn't like talking about his employers. But on the other hand, he felt an immense loyalty to Mrs. Aleut. Swiping his hand over his forehead, he continued... "Well, Mr. Aleut, he seems... to have a roven eye. He was always lookin. Especially for the pretty young things and from what I'd seen...um... when drivin him around town a few times, was that it didn't always stop at lookin."

"Are you saying that Mr. Aleut cheated on his wife, Kenny?"

"Well, yes, Sir..., I'd say so."

"Are you sure about that, Kenny?"

Kenny studied both detectives, as he answered in his slow Texas drawl, "Well Detectives, I guess I'd have to say, as sure as I can be without seein the actual act with my own two eyes."

Volfensberger glanced over to where detective Gonzales stood, and their eyes locked in a smile. He then moved his eyes to look directly at Carmen and asked. "You, you said you saw them arguing on the last day you saw Mrs. Aleut? Can you tell me about it?"

Carmen didn't like being in the center of attention. She was shy and usually stayed in the background and let Jessie handle any narrative, but this time Jessie was in a frightened state. Stumbling, she mumbled, "M...me, sir?"

Detective Volfensberger nodded and answered, "Yes you... Carmen."

"Ya...Yas, me and JJJessie we both..., we both, we see him come back. Heee was real mamad and he was screamin for the Mrs."

"What did he say? Did you notice if he had been drinking?"

"He always be drinkin, sir." She hesitated then moved on, "He was cussin and yellin for...for her. We did-an't hear no more, cuz we go. Mrs. say go, take off day."

"Was he drunk?"

"I donno if he be drunk, but he was real mad."

"What about you Kenny? Did you hear anything?"

"No, no sir, I waudn't around. I was runnin errands."

"What about you, Jessie?"

"Jest whaat Carmen say. Thats all, sir."

Gonzales started to say, "You guys can leave...," then stopped in mid-sentence when he remembered something Kenny had said earlier. "Kenny, you said Aleut got meaner when he drank? I noticed he was well gone now. Is this something that happens often? Is that something routine, him getting drunk?" Gonzales looked at the ladies then added, "Have you notice he drinks a lot?"

They all looked at one another. Jessie bravely answered for the group, "Jest lately, he use ta not drink soo much. Now he drinks a lot and all ta time, just like Carmen say."

"Thank you for your time. If we have any further questions, we will contact you. Is this number here good or do you have another number?" After getting both maids home phone numbers, and Kenny's, who said he lived over the garage, Detective Volfensberger excused all three. He said their work was done for the day so they could leave.

Once everyone scattered Carmen returned to where the officers were going over and discussing their notes. Carmen approach the officers cautiously and said, "Excuse me, sirs, I not go."

She informed them that she refused to go. She chose to stay in case there was something they needed. She said, "I owe da Mrs. much. She always be good ta me, so I stay and give you help. I make coffee and bring cookies, maybe lounch and dinar."

The Detectives smiled and welcomed both cookies and lunch since neither have had time to eat thus far on this hectic day.

CHAPTER TWENTY-FOUR

When Detectives Volfensberger and Gonzales arrived back at the precinct, they were told that Aleut was awake and pissed off. He wanted a lawyer and said he was going to sue the ass off the whole damn department if they did not release him immediately.

They all laughed but looked at each other in exasperation. With this kind of attitude so early on, meant that Aleut was going to be a jackass and not easy to work with.

Gonzales asked, "Did someone read him his rights?"

"Yeah, he's been read his rights. I think that's what sent him off in the first place."

An hour later, both Aleut and his lawyer sat across the table glaring at Gonzales. Volfensberger was in the corner near the stenographer; there he could view the suspect and not distract him. He had always liked to evaluate a defendant on his own terms, which included no eye contact at the time of interrogation. This gave them less chance of playing on his sympathy. Early on in his career he realized he had a bleeding heart and tended to go soft when the suspects played the, *I'm blameless and have been treat badly my entire life.* He chalked this up to his mistreatment as a child. So, at the time, he came up with a theory that by merely watching a suspect's body movements, you can learn a hell of a lot more than by listening to their unreliable jargon. So, he usually chose to stand to the side looking bored and disinterested while Gonzales did the questioning.

From the get-go, Dan came across as righteous and was furious that the cops had brought him in for questioning. Almost immediately after the first couple of basic questions, Dan lost his temper completely. He jumped up and launched into what Volfensberger later labeled as, *a dramatic performance.* "It was very entertaining, if not convincing," was what he had told his fellow officers. "The best part he said was when Dan ended it with a loud roar, "You have no right to break into my house and drag me off to this shithole station for questioning! I have my rights and every one of you are going to pay fucken big-time for this blunder. My lawyer here is going to see to it personally. We're going to sue every ass in this city, right down to the fucken janitor who scrubs your stinking urinals. I'll show you; you can't do this to respectable tax paying citizens and get away with it. Especially not to someone like me. I own Aleut Productions; do you know what that means? It means I have connections and you will all be sorry once I'm done with you. This kind of involvement can ruin my career and you can't get away with it. Do you hear me fuck-heads, you can't get away with it?"

Arrogantly, Dan threw himself back in his chair. It was easy to see he was quite pleased with himself and his presentation.

Gonzales sat calmly and said nothing to acknowledge Dan's lengthy hysterics. Instead, he dispassionately looked directly at his lawyer, at which point he pleasantly acknowledged, "Good afternoon, Mr. Drake. It's nice to see you again. It's been a while. I take it; you're representing, Mr. Aleut?"

"You can, Detective Gonzales and I would appreciate if you will tell me and my client, what he's being arrested for."

"Mr. Drake, Mr. Aleut is in here for questioning only. As of yet, no charges have been filed."

At that moment, Gonzales moved his gaze over to Dan. His dislike for the man was apparent. He did not care for his insolent attitude, but he made the effort to ask him as politely as possible, "Mr. Aleut can I bring you some coffee or water before we get started?"

Dan said nothing and Gonzales continued without hesitation, "Mr. Aleut; where is your wife?"

Without any indecision Dan shot back, "How the hell should I know?"

"We have a report...here..," Gonzales shuffled through a stack of papers that lay on the table in front of him, "that...says she's been missing for over a week and you're not concerned?"

"Why should I be? And who said she's missing? She just took a little trip that's all."

"Oh! So, you can tell us where to find her?"

"NO! Hell, no! I'm not her keeper."

"When was the last time you saw your wife, Mr. Aleut?"

"Like you said, about a damn week ago."

"That last day, being... say May seventeenth?"

"Could be, I don't remember."

"Did you two have a fight that day?"

"Nope!"

"No?"

"You heard me, N O!" Under his breath Dan muttered, "Damn idiot cop."

"What? I didn't quite get that last part, Mr. Aleut."

"Nothing."

"Are you sure, Mr. Aleut?

Dan folded his arms and his eyes glared spitfire at them.

The detective studied him for a minute or two, before he said, "Well, Mr. Aleut, before you answer again, maybe you should stop and rethink the last day you saw Mrs. Aleut and if you two argued or not?"

Dan immediately gave the detective a snide unconcerned grin and remarked, "*YES*, officer, I'm quite sure we didn't argue. I don't need to rethink anything."

"Oh, really Mr. Aleut?"

"Yes, you see Mr. Detective, we're newlyweds; you know like madly in love and all. Damn it's like we're still on our honeymoon if you get my drift. In any case, we never argue, Mr. Detective, never."

"Really..., Mr. Aleut? That's very strange since we've heard otherwise. And we... me and my partner over there..." he smiled deviously and glanced in Volfensbergers direction in hopes to insinuate the two shared a secret.... "Well, you see we've come across some evidence that shows otherwise. So why don't you answer me one more time? Mr. Aleut, did you and your wife have an argument the last time you were together?"

Dan's face and demeanor changed and suddenly his head snapped in the direction of Mr. Drake. Gonzales could easily read the fear in Dan's eyes and the question on Drake's face.

Dan and his lawyer peered at one another for several seconds before Mr. Drake nervously muttered, "Ah, gentlemen...um...if you don't mind, I think I need a few minutes alone with my client?" Will that be okay?

Detectives Gonzales and Volfensberger exchanged glances before Volfensberger answered, "Sure, take all the time you need. We're not in no hurry."

"Yeah, we're not going anywhere soon," added Gonzales. Both Detectives chuckled and strolled leisurely toward the door. Their eyes were glued on their perp who was now wringing his hands anxiously.

Mr. Drake could unquestionably see the detective's air of confidence when they moved slowly towards the door. He could tell they thought they had an open and shut case. This thought scared the hell out of him, since he knew he wasn't that good of a lawyer. If his instincts are correct and if Dan continued to insist that he represent him, Dan could be a dead man. All and all, he had little experience in matters like this. He mostly dealt with corporate law. He hardly knew anything about criminal law. Wearily Mr. Drake studied Dan's cynical face. At the same time, he searched his mind for words of support while he moved his eyes around the room to assure himself that they were alone. Tautly he coughed into his hand before he nervously said, "Dan, if you confess right now, they'll probably go easier on you. Maybe we can do a plea bargain." He saw Dan's astonished expression so he quickly added, "or maybe you can plead temporary insanity? It's done often and people do get away with murd...."

At once Mr. Drake recognized the distaste in Dan's eyes and decided it was best if he said nothing else for the time being. Besides, it was plain to see his client had no intention of co-operating. Abashed, he closed his briefcase and they sat in silence while they waited for Detectives Gonzales and Volfensberger to return.

For the next two hours Dan denied wholeheartedly that he killed his wife. At first, he continued to deny the fact that he even hit her. That was until Detective Gonzales revealed that there was proof to the contrary. That they held in evidence a tape that showed an attack against, Mrs. Aleut. At that point everything changed, and Dan incoherently uttered under his breath, "That bitch, that damn fucken bitch. She set me up."

Gonzales asked, "What did you say, Mr. Aleut?"

"I didn't say anything."

"What did you mean by, she set you up?"

Dan crossed his arms, sat back, and said nothing. By now he was beginning to see the big picture. Jackie had outwitted him. He could only guess what was on the tape. Either way it would be incriminating, but how incriminating was the question.

Once Dan came to terms with this fact, he began to grasp the seriousness of his plight. Suddenly panic sat in and he began to shout angrily, "I didn't kill Jackie! I didn't and if you really have a tape, you'd see that. You'd see that I only hit her, that's all. She's fine. Just a few bruises, that's all."

"Okay, I see..., I take it you didn't realize the camera was rolling throughout your argument, Mr. Aleut."

"It wasn't. I mean if it was you would've seen that she wasn't dead. Jackie was still alive when I left the library." Dan's eyes suddenly grew large and Gonzales could see a new notion excited him, and he jumped up and added, "Maybe the camera ran out of tape or something, that happens."

"Yes, that could be a possibility, Mr. Aleut. Or, more probable, when Mrs. Aleut struck her head on the desk the camera was knocked over. Maybe that's when it stopped filming the actual act of you killing your wife, Mr. Aleut."

"I didn't kill my wife;" he shot back, "she's not dead."

"Then you tell us where to find her," demanded Gonzales?

Volfensberger for the first time threw out, "If she not dead, how do you, account for her disappearance? No one's seen her since that night."

Dan sat back and stared. His eyes filled with uncertainty and his face showed a new fear. He had no answers, and it was plain to see he was scared. At this point he didn't know what he should say or not say. He had already decided that his lawyer was useless, since he advised him to co-operate and confess to the murder before the cops even suggested there was one. Dan's mind searched frantically to picture everything that he could remember that might be on the tape. Unconsciously his body trembled when he decided he was a dead man. Yes, that little bitch she really got him good, she deserved to be dead.

All of a sudden, another thought came to him and he started rambling eager to put blame on someone else. "It's those guys. It's the loan sharks. They killed her... It had to be them. See they wanted to ruin me, so they killed Jackie. They already took my production company. Don't you see? It's because of the money I owed them. They have to be the ones who killed her."

Gonzales laughed, "Ooh..., I see. Sorta like the cop show on TV. The Fugitive and the one-armed man theory. Aye, come on Mr. Aleut, you can do better than that, can't you? I mean you being in the movies and all, I would've expected more."

Dan's mouth flew open with an answer he assumed would put an end to the Detectives suspicions.

Mr. Drake interrupted him abruptly with, "Mr. Aleut, maybe you better not say anything more right now. I think we need to talk first. Detectives, can you give us ten?"

Dan turned on his lawyer and overdramatically yelled, "I didn't do anything. I'm not going down for a murder I didn't commit. Can't you see, it's Paulo and Vicente. They did this, and I'm probably next? I need protection! Not harassment!"

Detective Gonzales' face hinted a, not too well-hidden smile, when he glanced over to where Detective Volfensberger stood and nodded. Without further conversation both detectives headed for the door. When Volfensberger turned to close it behind them Gonzales whispered, "You know if this wasn't so serious, it'd be funny."

Sometime later after they had resumed their interrogation, Volfensberger was still in the background and had remained mostly silent as he had from the get-go. As for Dan, he was still proclaiming his innocence and Gonzales was beginning to ask the same questions all over again.

Detective Volfensberger could see by Dan's body language, that he was far more nervous than an innocent man should be. His intuition told him Dan was a viper and couldn't be trusted, but right now they were going in circles and not getting the answers they needed. With this in mind, he stepped out of the shadows and faced Dan.

"So, you think you've been framed?" He asked the question nonchalantly, then added as an afterthought; "but.... Dan, if this is true, how does that account for the forged checks? Mrs. Aleut referred to forged checks on the tape? If I recall correctly, there was also an attempted rape mentioned. Mr. Aleut, are you also innocent of these crimes?"

Deflated Dan sat back in his chair; this was the first time he had nothing to say. His anger was abandoned and replaced by new fear. He coughed in his hand, and whispered harshly, "I want to talk with my lawyer. I need to speak with him alone."

"First," Gonzales said as he stood up. "I have one more question; then you can go Mr. Aleut. Can you tell us how drunk you were on the night of May 17th? The night your wife taped this argument?"

Dan glared at both detectives but said nothing more. His mouth was clamped shut like a steel grip and the detectives knew it was useless. It was obvious that Dan Aleut had no intention of answering any more of their questions.

Gonzales looked over at Volfensberger and the detective shook his head letting Gonzales know he had nothing more to ask. Gonzales turned and said, "Mr. Drake your client can leave. I suggest that he stays in town and available for more questions at a later date."

It was extremely late by the time the cab finally drove Dan through the gates of Jackie's estate. He was exhausted and ready for a drink. He grumbled a couple of curse words at the cabbie and threw him a $20.

When he stepped up to the front entrance of the house, he noticed the yellow police tape blocking the entrance. He was immediately approached by an officer who informed him, "Sorry sir, the house is a crime scene and in lockdown. The residence has not been released yet. You can't go in until the department informs us that it's clear."

"What...what the f...."

"Sorry sir, you're not permitted inside until we get those orders."

By now Dan's disposition was weary and his anger returned with a vengeance and he was ready to strike out at anyone, including the cop standing between him and the entrance to his house. He stood there seething while he decided what to do. For an instant, he thought about knocking the cop aside. Finally, he decided he needed a drink far more than the pleasure of the attack, so he hurled a few despicable curse words in the cops' direction and stomped off.

Angrily he plopped his frame onto the seat of the Mercedes. He sat there for a moment trying to determine where he should go. Indecisively he slammed the car door and immediately threw the car in gear as he headed for the nearest bar.

As soon as Dan entered the lounge, he loudly ordered a bottle of vodka. Impatient, he grabbed the bottle from the bartenders' grip and slugged down a huge swig and sat down on the nearest barstool. He still couldn't believe that Jackie was that crafty. He knew she was smart, but this...she set this whole thing up and was going to use the tape against him. He ran his fingers through his hair as he asked himself, 'Now what the fuck am I going do?'

He drank while he continued to curse the day, he met her. He drank until the bartender finally said it was closing time. He be-grudgingly walked lamely out of the bar and back to his ill-parked car. At this time, he realized he didn't have any place to go. He couldn't go to the office, that was no longer his. His foggy mind thought of Mike and he decided that was his best bet.

When Dan pulled up in front of the house he was surprised. For some reason, the place looked different. He sat looking at it for several minutes before realizing where he was. He was at his and Mike's old residence. Now it belonged to someone else and they had painted and changed some of its exterior. Suddenly, a light flickered, and stayed on up-stairs. Without further deliberation, he put the car in to gear and headed for Mike's new home.

Within the first mile he remembered it was also Louis Carver's house, but this fact did not slow him down. In truth it fueled his de-termination, and he stomped on the gas pedal as he shouted several curse words. Afterwards he felt a gratifying surge of satisfaction and shouted one last, "FUCK YOU, CARVER!"

Dan leaned heavily against the door while he rang the bell five or six times. It was several minutes before a maid dressed in a che-nille bath robe opened the door. When she saw who it was, she be-came frightened and backed away which left the door wide-open and free for entry.

Snickering Dan started to take a step forward and suddenly a voice from nowhere said, "You can stop right there, Aleut."

Startled by Louis's command, which emitted a sharp and embit-tered resonance, Dan halted his step in midstride, and instead took a shaky step backward. He was immediately embarrassed by his action, and promptly became agitated. Craver's intrusion was enough to set him off again and he shouted, "This has nothing to do with you, Carver. I want to see Mike."

"When there's a cold day in hell, Aleut, which, I imagine you'll probably be aware of long before any of us. And, according to what I've just learned from the police, that's exactly where you belong."

"Fuck you, Carver. No! No on second thought never mind, because you'd probably like that, wouldn't you? So just knock off the bull and go tell Mike I want to see him."

"Sorry, no can do. You see Mike doesn't ever want to see you again. Frankly, I can't blame him especially after all the shit you've been dishing out lately. Who would?"

"You just tell him to get his skinny little dick down here or I'm gonna kick his fucken ass. What the fuck does he think he's up to anyway? He's always been there when I needed him. I'm his best friend and he's not gonna turn on me now. What kind of fucken friend would do that, huuh, Carver, huh?"

Suddenly Dan saw Louis's face as he stepped out of the shadow into the moonlight; it was full of contempt and determination. Instinctively Dan took several steps back, before he started to stumble but then caught himself just before he hit the ledge. However, this gave Louis time enough to leap forward and grasp him by the collar of his shirt. Angrily Louis shoved and pushed Dan against his car and snarled, "You bastard, that man upstairs was the best thing that ever happened to you. He gave you more than friendship. He gave you everything and you gave him nothing in return. You're a filthy snake, a user, and a simple nobody. You've abused every relationship you've ever had, but right here and now, it stops. Do you hear me, Aleut? I want to make sure you completely understand. Mike's love for you is gone. It's in the past, never to be again. Yes, Aleut, there was a time when he would've died for you, but now your venom is finally out of his system, and I promise you, you will never hurt him again."

By this time, Dan's alarm was replaced by a staggering anger and he struck back with a renewed strength as well as debasing assertion, "HURT! ME, HURT MIKE? How the fuck does one hurt a queer and a male whore, a gigolo? Tell me Doctor, do people like you have feelings like normal people?"

Louis's hatred for this man rose as fast as his fist did. Dan closed his eyes and braced himself for the blow that never came. When he finally opened his eyes again, he could see Mike standing behind Louis holding back the fixed swing. Instantly his self-confidence returned, and a sarcastic grin covered his face. He knew Mike wouldn't let him down; he knew he could always count on him and his loyalty.

A second later Dan felt the hard-piercing blow across his jaw, soon followed by a sharp jab in the stomach. The surge to throw up engulfed him and he heard Mike's words as he fell forward, "Sorry Louis, but this one was for me."

Louis released his hold and Dan crumpled the rest of the way to the ground at which time Dan felt one sharper blow. It stung his face just before the coldness of the cement did. Mike's face twisted as he grimaced and muttered, "Now, get the hell out of here before we do what we should've done in the first place... shoot you as an intruder."

Dan tried to focus, yet everything was blurred and seemed to be in slow motion. He could barely make out the two men in front of him. He wanted to speak but nothing came. He watched their synchronized movements as they glanced at each other than back towards Dan. Together they gave him one last disgusted look before both turned and walked hand and hand back into the house. The slam of the door was loud when Louis swung it close. The bang echoed throughout the darkness and it rang in Dan's ears for several seconds before the echoing stopped.

At last, Dan sat alone stunned and disheveled in a heap by the side of his car. He cursed loudly as he stood up, staggered, then stumbled his way to the driver's side of the car. It took several minutes before he was able to put his thoughts together, but once his shock had diffused, he became enraged again and howled, "Fuck you, Mike. Fuck all of you." He shoved the car in reverse and felt a sudden thud. He had struck and knocked over a huge planter that stood in front of the house. Laughing he threw the gear in first and sped off.

From the living room where Mike stood, he could hear Dan shifting and jamming the car into the wrong gear. He could also hear when he tried to jerk it back, likely without using the clutch since the gear made such a loud jarring sound. Mike had no doubt its screeching could be heard for blocks. Mike listened until he couldn't hear anything except silence. After a moment of complete quiet he moved closer to the window and mouthed silently, "Sorry, Dan."

Dan stepped on the gas harder and harder as he drove away from his attackers. For blocks he cursed them out loud while he weaved the rest of the way back to his estate. There he finally slept off his inebriated state in the back seat of his car.

CHAPTER TWENTY-FIVE

Late the next morning Dan was finally allowed back in the house. He cleaned himself up and ate a hardy lunch that Carmen begrudgingly made for him.

Later that afternoon when the phone rang it made a loud eerie shrill that vibrated throughout the quiet house. Carmen apprehensively but politely answered the call. She then as easily became rude. She almost threw the phone on the desk as she muttered to Dan, "It's for you," and hurried away.

Dan's entire body tensed when he heard, "Good morning, shithead. I've heard you've had quite the night. Been having a little trouble with the local authorities, huh? But then again, I'm sure with the recent demise of your lovely wife, life itself must be terribly stressful for you. Nevertheless, with all this grief you have to cope with, I hope you still remember what day it is."

Paulo hesitated then sniggered, "Aleut, if I were you, I'd keep in mind how much time you have left to get the rest of our money to us." He snickered again and added," Wouldn't want a double funeral, would ya?"

Dan hung on every word Paulo said and when he threatened one last, "You better not fuck with us, Aleut." Dan quickly grumbled his reassurances, "No, no, you don't have to worry. There's no problem, you don't have to worry about the money. You'll have it, no problem."

After he hung up, he hurried into the library and pulled out Jackie's leather-bound checkbook. His hands shook when he wrote another check. A half an hour later he was still feeling a bit unstrung when he irritably gathered the papers and check he had written earlier. He needed a drink but changed his mind. He wanted to have a clear head when he withdrew the exorbitant amount from the bank.

As soon as he handed the check through the window to the teller, a puzzled look replaced the practiced smile that she had pasted on her face only seconds before. He could tell at once something wasn't right. She caught her breath and threw him a taut grimace as she mumbled a quick, "Excuse me for a moment... please," before she bolted in the direction of the manager's office.

Dan stood there bewildered and nervously he stepped from one foot to the other until he saw her move back in his direction. The manager, who now carried the check in her hand, held it as far from her body as her arm would allow. It looked as though she thought the paper was hot or contaminated. As soon she reached the window where he stood, she quickly shoved the check back towards him like she needed to be rid of it as fast as possible.

Dan stood there bewildered and started to request an explanation when the manager abruptly cut in, "Sorry, Mr. Aleut, but we can not help you. We can no longer cash any checks against, Mrs. Aleut's account."

"What do you mean, you can't cash it? Why...I?"

"All of her accounts have been frozen, Mr. Aleut. I'm sorry, sir, but it's out of our hands." She smiled a false smile and without further explanation turned and walked away.

Dan stood there dumbfounded. He looked at the teller and the check in his hand. He didn't know what to do. He needed the cash right now. Even though the loan sharks had taken his production company, they still wanted to be paid the rest of their original loan. He needed a quarter of a million dollars by the end of week. He had figured he'd write several checks, and nobody would be the wiser. He grumbled out loud, "Damn assholes."

Several people were startled by his words and behavior. They quickly moved away as they watched him shove a lady aside and pushed the door so hard it barely missed an entering customer.

"Now what? Shit," he cursed. "Jesus...Christ... my life is falling apart." He thought, *I have to get the money or I'm a dead man. Damn... this whole mess is all Jackie's fault. She should've been the wife she promised to be. She should've helped me like she said she would, then none of this would be happening. What am I going do, who can I turn to?*

Who has that kind of money laying around? Maybe he could hock some of Jackie's jewelry, maybe sell her cars. Dammit, he's gotta do something and now.' Instantly he thought of her other bank accounts, then as quickly realized they too would be frozen. "Dammit. Damn you, Jackie."

CHAPTER-TWENTY-SIX

T he attendant, Helena; knocked on the door twice as she pushed it open and entered the room. Her guest was still laying on the lounge contentedly sipping her morning coffee, while she was casually surveying the birds in the garden, as they happily skittered and bounced around the densely shaded Koi pond and garden. The attendant smiled and said, "Good morning Miss. Isn't it a lovely day?" Then setting the breakfast tray on the table in the center of the room along with today's newspapers. She said, "Here's the, L.A. Times you requested, plus the local newspaper. I'll run you some bath water and set everything up for your ten o'clock massage. Will there be anything else?"

The guest shook her head and went back to her coffee and her meditation. When she heard the first splashes of bath water running, she stood and walked over to the chair and seated herself at the table. Tearing apart and nibbling on a piece of raisin toast, she aimlessly began leafing through the pages of the local newspaper. There didn't seem to be too much going on locally which is usually the case. That's why she requested the L.A. Times yesterday. After a couple more glances, she threw the pages to the floor and reached for the Times.

The attendant laid the soft ivory towels next to the folding work-table where the masseuse would be working during the rub down. She quickly glanced around the room to make sure all things were in place and that everything that was needed for her charge was available. She understood it was of the utmost importance that she met all her client's needs. Especially for this particular client. It wasn't so much that Helena thought the lady was a difficult guest. It was just that she was a little more demanding than most. But since she always tipped so very, very, well, nobody at the resort re-ally minded the extra diligence it took to please her many whims.

All of a sudden without warning, Helena became startled when she heard what sounded like a loud spontaneous scream and a panic-stricken screech, then laughter. The sound conveyed a ring of hysteria to it and Helena turned to run towards the hullabaloo and to see if she could help. At the same time she ran she grumbled, "Oh no, I bet it's another one of those ugly desert-lizards. It must have gotten into the room and it's frightening the city lady."

But before she entered the room to see what all the hysteria was about, she heard bellowing laughter, then another, even louder hoot. It immediately began to change to an incredulous, "Ooh my.... Oh my, God, this couldn't be. It's just toooo good. This is just sim-ply delicious. This couldn't possibly be any better than if I'd planned it myself."

Helena stood silently watching Jackie dance around the room laughing and kicking up her heels like a madwoman. After a minute or two she asked in a timid voice, "Ma'am? Are you all right..., Miss? Can I get you some water or something stronger? Do you need a doctor?"

Still laughing Jackie stopped her dance long enough to answer the bewildered keeper. "No, no, no Helena, I don't need a thing. Ev-erything is marvelous and life is wonderful. However, you are a sweetheart for asking. But thanks to the heavens above my life couldn't be any better."

Jackie ran over to her dressing table and grabbed a handful of bills. She rushed back to where the stunned service maid stood and thrust the bills out and pushed them into Helena's hands as she giddily announced, "Thank you for everything, Helena. You have taken wonderful care of me, but I will not need anything more. I'll be leaving today." Jackie pushed the puzzled Helena towards the door as she giggled with open delight. "Thank you, Helena. Ask the bellhop to pick up my bags in an hour.

The way Jackie was acting, and her announcement of an early departure further bewildered the maid. She asked, "Are you sure, Miss?"

Jackie slammed the door without answering and ran back to where she had tossed the Los Angeles Times. She reread what she'd read earlier and gave another hoot. With one hand, she turned the page to where the rest of the story was located. When she started to close the first page, she stopped and reread the headline. Then reread it again. She wanted to be sure of what she had read and that she had interpreted it correctly before going on.

She was still stunned when she reread it for the sixth time, **Producer Found Dead, Apparent Suicide**. Finally, she turned the page and started reading. Almost immediately she became astonished by what was written. **'Movie Producer, Dan Aleut, was found dead early Wednesday morning. It appeared Mr. Aleut drove his car off Topanga Canyon Road in a successful suicide attempt. Investigators say there were several reports that Mr. Aleut, who was under investigation for the disappearance and alleged murder of his socialite wife, Jacqueline Dey Aleut, had been despondent for weeks. There are also reports that since the recent loss of his production company, he had been drinking heavily. Mrs. Aleut, who has been missing since a taped altercation with her husband on May Seventeenth... is presumed dead. Her body, as of yet, has not been found.'**

Jackie couldn't believe what she was reading. She'd forgotten about the tape. Everyone thought she was dead. Why? Why would they think that? It seems the tape would have shown that she was alive. Unless the camera ran out of film and didn't record what happened after she hit her head on the edge of the desk. Maybe it didn't show Dan reaching for her and shaking her back to consciousness.

Suddenly Jackie shuddered at the awful memory. When she had finally become conscious, she couldn't believe how Dan hadn't shown any kind of concern for her wellbeing. Instead he went on with his barrage of cursing her. He even hit her again..., twice, before he finally stormed out of the room, leaving her alone and bleeding, but... still very much alive.

Again, she cringed at the memories of that late afternoon. These same scenes had flickered across her mind over and over these past few weeks. Each time the overwhelming visions rolled passed her eyes, they were like silhouettes on a movie screen and she felt ill and angry. They were unforgettable and she struggled to deal with them, yet they still gave her the same ill feelings. The knowledge that she had made so many ridiculous mistakes in the recent months added to her anxiety. She was smarted than this, yet here she was hiding from a mad man.

She moaned as she fell back in time, and once again she was home on the floor in the library. She had been extremely frightened by Dan and his violent temper that day. So much so, that she waited a long time before she felt safe enough to leave the room. It wasn't until after darkness came and she heard nothing stirring, she stood and crept towards the door. Jackie shivered when she recalled how cold she had felt. The only light in the room was from the evening moon which gave the room an unfamiliar presence. Her legs felt weak and she moved slowly out of the room into the hallway. When she saw no one, she moved her way purposefully up the stairs to her bedroom. She feared that Dan was somewhere in the shadows. She was so very relieved when he was nowhere to be seen. Once safely locked behind her bedroom doors, Jackie cried.

At last she walked over and stared at the vision in the mirror. When she focused on her face she was horrified, and her legs buckled, and she fell onto the loveseat nearby. Her face was unbelievable, it was a mass of swollen cuts and bruised to the point of nonrecognition. Her head ached and her hair was dark red on one side and she felt a sharp pain when she touched it.

She sat there and stared at her blood-stained hair and swollen face for a long time. Finally, she came to the conclusion that she had to do something. This was unforgivable; she needed to call the police. Then she thought of Raynie and decided she didn't want her to see her like this. It would break her daughter's heart. It was selfish but she couldn't stand the thought of Raynie knowing how stupid she was. Her whole plan had backfired. What had she been thinking, taking on a madman by herself? What did she think Dan would do? She was taking away his only true loves, his company and access to her money. Still, she never dreamed he'd beat her like he did.

She looked once again into the mirror and for the first time faced the eyes of degradation. She realized she couldn't endure the publicity that a common domestic squabble would bring. Not only for her, but also for all the people she cared for. She didn't need this plastered all over the papers to get her divorce. She had her videotape. That, would secure her money and her divorce from Dan.

After Jackie had reached her decision, she studied her face a moment longer. Her resolve was written all over her bruised face and her new determination gave her energy. Quickly and swiftly she moved her pain-racked body around the room. Erratically she grabbed a few clothes from the closet and bureau and shoved them all into an overnight case and zipped it closed. Moving to her bathroom she washed her face and did a touchup job on the bruises. Hurriedly she called a cab, then snatched her bag and several items off her desk. Finally, she tiptoed as quietly as possible down the stairs. She was still frightened and didn't want to chance meeting Dan in the hallway. As she passed the living-room she noticed that he was asleep or passed out on the sofa. She prayed that she wouldn't wake him from his snoring slumber. She held her breath as she hurried across the hall to the doorway and out the entry. There she waited in the shadows until the cab came.

When Jackie leaned back against the seat, she sighed her first breathe of relief. But couldn't think of where to tell the cab driver to take her. She was certain she didn't want anyone to see her in this condition. In the end, she shrieked, "Just drive."

At last she made a decision and asked him to drive her to the airport. On the way there, she shakily wrote a note to Raynie so she wouldn't worry. At that time Jackie was still distraught, and her mind was going in every direction. She could not think straight and had absolutely no idea of where she was headed, just away from Dan. Consequently, she couldn't give her daughter a phone number to where she could be reached. Ultimately, she decided she'd call Raynie later and let her know her whereabouts. Unfortunately, she never got around to that call.

When Jackie got out of the cab, she realized she had forgotten her purse at home. Thankfully, when she was packing, she had thrown a wad of cash in her overnight bag. She was still dazed, and her swollen eyes would hardly open, but she handed the Cabby a bill from the stack and mumbled, "Keep the change." By his response of a jubilant, "Thanks, lady," she assumed it was a large enough bill.

Heading into the terminal she dropped the note she had written to Raynie in the mailbox outside the entrance. She had no stamp with her but hoped the post card would get to her daughter, marked postage due.

Once inside the terminal Jackie halted and stood frozen. She didn't know in which direction she should move. At this time of night, the airport was at a standstill and no attendants were at their assigned stations. At last she saw that one location was open and she rushed towards the lady behind the desk.

Jackie realized how strange her appearance must have looked to the young woman. But she left the sunglasses on along with the scarf that covered most of her face. She hoped the woman would think she was some eccentric starlet who wanted to hide her identity.

Jackie's mouth ached when she asked, "When is the next available flight? And where is it headed? She was immediately relieved when the answer was, "Arizona." Right away she snapped, "I'll take it."

As soon as Jackie received her ticket, she hurried to the nearest phone and called Marilyn at the Golden Door and pleaded, "Please get me a room. Anything will do."

Jackie couldn't believe her good fortune when Marilyn said, "No problem, Honey. I'll put you in your favorite suite."

The Golden Door Health Spa will be a perfect place for her to hide while her broken and bruised body mended. Smiling, Jackie exhaled as she sighed, "And to think," she laughed. "All the while I've been basking in the Arizona sun, healing my battered flesh, everyone thought I was dead."

Almost immediately after her last remark she squealed, "Oh my, God, my poor Raynie. She thinks I'm dead."

Jackie rushed to the phone and dialed her daughter's number. The answering machine picked up on the first ring. Jackie returned the phone to its cradle; she didn't want to leave a message. She waited a minute and then decided to call Ray.

Kelsey answered on the third rang and as soon as Jackie said who it was, Kelsey screamed into the phone. For a second, she regretted her announcement, because she feared Kelsey was going to die of a heart attack right then and there.

She attempted to calm the woman by quickly and briefly explaining her whereabouts, then asked "Can I please speak with, Ray?"

But the overwrought Kelsey said, "Sorry, but no. He's in court and from there, I don't know what his plans are. When he left, he told me that he wasn't coming back to the office today." Breathlessly, Kelsey asked, "Have you talked with Raynie? Does she know you're okay? Oh God, Jackie. She's been beside herself with despair. She's been blaming herself."

"My poor baby," replied Jackie, "But, no I haven't talked with her yet. I tried to call, but she wasn't at home."

"Oh, that's right she's staying at Simon's place." Jackie heard a shuffle of papers before Kelsey continued, "Here let me give you his number."

Once Jackie hung up the phone, she considered Raynie and her relationship with Simon. It certainly appears to have progressed rapidly. She had no idea that they were so involved.' "Not that I'm complaining," she whispered. "I'm merely pleasantly surprised." She smiled to herself. Delighted, she reached for the phone and pushed the digits as she thoughtfully resolved, "Well, at least one of the Dey women made a good choice."

Ray was sitting alone at his desk in his home office. He continued to tap the pen that Jackie had given him for Christmas against the vase that sat next to the telephone. His mind went over the past week's events for the umpteenth time. He still couldn't believe that Jackie was gone; she had always been so vibrant. She was the essence of life and the center of his universe. He inhaled a deep disheartened breath and released it slowly. Suddenly he became aware of how quiet the house was; he was sure a person could hear a feather drop. Once again, he sighed sadly. There was never a time in all the years of marriage to Jackie that their house was ever remotely as quiet as this. Jackie always had something going on; that was just the way she was. Suddenly he started to chuckle when he thought of what she always said about idleness. '*When a woman stops and does nothing at all, at least ten gray hairs has time to catch up and sprout, along with a few new wrinkles.*' "God, I loved that woman. But who wouldn't, she was everything a woman should be?" Unfortunately, for him, he wasn't what she wanted.

The high-pitched ring of the phone brought him back to the here and now and reality. He grabbed it and answered with a sharp, "Hello." He listened, then answered, "Yes. Good. That's, damn good. Yes, the papers this morning said that at first; they did suspect foul play. But later, after considering the situation, along with his psychotic behavior lately, they penned it as a suicide. Wasn't that fortunate? Yes, that's right. So, I take it there should be no surprises?" He waited then moved on. "Great! We can wash our hands of the situation and bid a good riddance to bad rubbish. That's terrific and thanks for a crackerjack job." Still smiling, Ray laid the phone down as he whispered, "Touché, Aleut. Touché."

CHAPTER TWENTY-SEVEN

Mike set the paper aside when he heard Louis's footsteps draw closer to the breakfast room. He stood and walked over to the grand quadrangular window that looked out onto the flower garden. Life was blossoming everywhere.

A tear touched the corner of Mike's eye when he felt the soft tenderness of Louis's hand lay upon his shoulder. After a few minutes, Louis whispered, "The world will be a much nicer place to live, now that it doesn't have someone like Dan roaming its spheres."

Mike knew Louis was right. However, he still couldn't help but mournfully remember some of the good times, even though those times seemed so long ago. God, life holds so many surprises. His own life wound up being nothing like he thought it would be or with whom he thought it would be with. He realized it was wrong to feel bad for what life hadn't given him. Especially since his turned out far better than Jackie's did. He felt an intense stab of guilt and thought, *I'll always blame myself for her death.*

When Mike tried to speak his voice held a controlled sob. He turned to face Louis and laid his head on his shoulder while Louis tried to comfort him. Finally, Mike choked, "Poor...Jackie. Louis, she never saw the corrupt evil in Dan. Maybe...if she had more information..., but, but.... I didn't I warn her. Louis, why didn't I warn her? I should have. And since I didn't, I'm partly to blame for her death. Oh, why Louis, why didn't I warn her? Why was I such a coward?"

Louis tried to console him, but soon he realized it was useless when Mike cried out, "How can I make this up to Raynie? How...how can I ever make something up like...this, I... I took her mother away." Mike pictured Raynie's exquisite heart shaped face, and suddenly broke down and cried hopelessly. *Yes,* he thought, *I deserved to carry this burden of guilt for the rest of my life.*

Raynie pulled the covers back and slowly opened her eyes. The room was bright, and she could see the shimmering specks of dust flickering in the sunlight. She smiled briefly before the first thought of her mother entered her mind. This was the same every morning since she learned of her mother's death. She had come to believe that her life will never be the same. Her mother had always been the core of her world and now each day she had to wake to the memory that she was no longer a part of it.

She pushed herself over to lay on her back and felt the warmth of Simon's body. This brought another smile to her face, and a thought fluttered across her mind, *Mother would be complete, if she knew that Simon was such a big part of my life.*

She felt Simon's arm move slowly and encircled her waist as he rolled gently over on top of her. He kissed her softly, then more ardently as his need grew obvious. Raynie eagerly kissed him back and held him as close to her as the strength in her arms would allow. She needed to feel him close. She wanted to savor their bodies as they intermingled and gradually merged...S*he hoped forever.*

Out of nowhere a loud boisterous knock at the door echoed throughout the chamber. Quickly they jumped and pulled apart. Each looked at the other, then at the door. At the same time another earsplitting call came from the outer hall, "Simon! Simon! Raynie ere yau awake? It tis the telly. A rightful important call, it tis. A vary, vary, important call." Yula's knocks grew louder and harder with urgency with each continuous bang.

Finally, Simon leaped out of bed, grabbed his robe, and bellowed, "Yes Nanna. We are coming."

Nanna was a name Simon called Yula when he was relaxed, and his phraseology was not guarded. At those times he spoke less formal and relaxed. Raynie grinned, she loved the idea that he felt so secure with her.

Simon pulled the door slightly open and observed a wide eyed Yula. She frantically rushed past him and stopped abruptly just inside the entrance of the room. She was soon followed by the rapid steps of another wide-eyed maid who carried a breakfast tray. Raynie hurriedly tied her robe to cover her nakedness as she watched the servant set the tray on the table near the bed. At the same time, she attempted to observe Yula and Simon while not appearing to be ease dropping. She couldn't guess what was upsetting Yula this early in the morning.

Yula was frantic as she murmured quietly in Simon's ear. Suddenly they stopped and looked at Raynie. Yula nervously shooed the other maid out of the room and quickly followed right after. Raynie thought, *they're both acting awful strange.* With a question on her lips, she turned her eyes to Simon for an answer.

Simon turned to close the door but stood with his back to her for several minutes after Yula left the room. Slowly he turned to face her. Instinctively fear gripped her, and she became apprehensive. The strange expression that now replaced Simon's earlier smile frightened her and she braced herself for bad news. She wanted to ask but her questions refused to be spoken.

Simon realized that his actions were frightening her, and he hurried back to her side. At once she saw that his eyes sparkled with excitement. He suddenly became wild with energy when he grabbed and hugged her close to him while he swung her around happily. Finally, he cried out, "Raynie, I love you and honey I have the most marvelous news for you. Though at first, I'm sure you're not going to believe it. He stopped then thoughtfully added, "As a matter of fact, I think you better sit down."

Simon watched her expressions as they changed from disbelief then directly moved to shock, and then merriment. Ultimately her mood shifted to sheer giddiness and her hands flew to her mouth to contain a scream. He thought her excitement made her look even more breathtakingly beautiful and when her arms fluttered about wildly, they both began to laugh with absolute joy.

Raynie vaulted from her chair and ran to the other side of the room and grabbed the phone off its hook. She jumped up and down as she eagerly gasped into the mouthpiece, "Mother, Mother, mother is it really you? Are you there, Mother?" She fell silent and heaving a loud sigh of relief she fell heavily onto the settee next to desk that held the phone. She listened intently to every word her mother spoke. All of a sudden, her laughter burst forth and she began speaking excitedly with her mother. Her mother, who not only minutes before she thought was lost to her forever.

Simon leaned back against the pillow and poured himself a cup of coffee. Lovingly he watched her high-spirited commotion before he withdrew his gaze and opened the newspaper. He read several articles before he suddenly bolted upright and quickly glanced towards Raynie. Unconsciously he muttered to himself, "Bloody hell, not now."

He watched Raynie for a full minute then recognized that so far it appeared that she knew nothing about the newspaper article. If Jackie was aware of it, she must have felt it was not important enough to intrude on her and her daughters' joyful reunion.

Vacillating Simon watched Raynie for several minutes more, then went back to the newspaper's contents and reread word for word, every detail. After he read the majority of the article, he began to relax. The officer in charge indicated that there would be no further investigation of the crash or Dan's death. Once reading this, his worry lessened. He observed Raynie from across the room and smiled at her happiness. Instantly his feelings soared. Soon after they increased even more when he read that Dan's death was deemed a suicide. Apparently the first two officers who arrived on the scene after the car plunged from the cliff had had several questions about the circumstances. But soon, they both ruled out foul-play. This information brought about an immediate surge of satisfaction.

As he pondered this Simon laid the newspaper aside. Again, he thoughtfully viewed Raynie who was still happily in conversation with her mother. Immediately he dismissed the question should I tell now? Right now, Raynie is happy that's all that matters. As for Dan, the festering fool finally got what was coming to him and deservedly so. Thank God, he didn't succeed in his attempt to kill Jackie.

Simon heard Raynie say, "Goodbye, Mother." Then another, "Mother, I love you! I absolutely love you. I can't wait to see you."

Instinctively Simon reached for the newspaper and shoved it under the breakfast tray. He was keenly aware that what he was about to do was wrong, but for now he would do anything to protect Raynie and her newfound happiness. In any event, as far as he saw it, things were as they should be. Dan's death was rated low on his list of minor disturbances. Purely a trifling distraction, and he hoped it would be the same for Raynie.

Raynie brimming with vitality ran over and threw her arms around Simon's neck and cried, "Ooh Simon! Simon! Simon! I have never been happier in my entire life. I love you, my darling, Simon. I absolutely love you. Matter of fact, I love the whole world! Simon, I can't believe I still have my mother. She's back Simon, she's back. Thank you, thank you, thank you!"

He grinned and a sound that almost sounded like a chuckle escaped his lips. Embarrassed at being so school-boyish, he immediately pulled her arms from around his neck and kissed her lovely lips firmly. Once he felt some control returning, he pushed her slightly away so he could see her beaming face. While he viewed her loveliness, his body instantly filled with pleasure and his spirits rose, as a fresh new excitement began to develop. He was thankful that she knew nothing of Dan's ill-fated departure and hoped he could keep the news away as long as possible.

Hastily he kissed her broad smile and said, "First I must set the record straight. Sweetheart, as much as I would like to be the hero in this story and take all the credit for your mother's resurrection, I just can't. However, there is one thing I can do for you. That is, if you let me..., and, of course I understand nothing can be as wonderful as the news you just received, mind you. Though, I dare say, you can consider this indeed a sanctification of my love..."

Raynie slipped her hand over his month so he could not say another word and grinned as her eyes dropped to get a full view of Simon's silk pajamas. Suggestively she whispered, "And what, pray-tell, can that possibly be, Simon?" She attempted to tickle his stomach with her lips as she asked, "Come on, Simon, tell me my love, what do you have for me?" Her eyes had taken in what was obvious and she whispered once again, "If you tell me my sweet, Simon, I'll see what I can do to make your wishes come true and your ardor be deemed."

Simon chuckled and murmured between kisses, "That's exactly what I was hoping for. Yet sadly that will have to wait. You see my dear with all that has been going on, I forgot to tell you that I have to go to England. I have some business that needs my attention and regretfully it cannot wait."

"What! Oh, Simon, no, no, not now. When do you leave?"

"Today, my love. My plane will be fueled and ready to go in a couple of hours."

Her smile changed to a pout and she whispered a sullen, "Oh, I see."

Instead of looking dismal, Simon laughed at her gloominess and briskly continued, "Raynie, I love you, I love you deeply and I want to marry you.Will you please be my wife? Simon nervously wrung his hands together, and asked, "Will you, please... go to England with me today?"

Startled by his last question Raynie pulled further away and peered into his eyes. He could see that she was assessing his questions. Her hesitation brought an immediate rush of fear. Maybe he was moving too fast. Could she be having cold feet? All this ran rapidly through his mind which soon followed by an even worse fear. Maybe she did not feel the same as he did. With that thought, his heart instantly stopped beating and he ceased breathing for several seconds while he waited for her answer. He lingered in panic before he caught a glimpse of mischievousness in her eyes. His doubt vanished just seconds after her laughter burst out. Immediately he could feel the weakness in his knees as he sucked in a deep breath of relief.

Raynie jumped up and waved arms in the air as she danced around the room for the second time. A minute later she jumped back into his arms and kissed his face, lips, and every part of his body she had access too. As she giggled and declared, "Of course, of course I will! I'll marry you. I absolutely adore you, Simon! Abruptly she stopped and claimed, "But, but I can't. I can't Simon."

Raynie could read his sudden alarm, so she hurriedly corrected her declaration, "I mean I can't go to England with you. Not now anyway. My mother she's coming home, she'll be here today, and she'll need me. I can't just leave her here alone to face Dan and all her marital concerns."

Simon's face was full of disappointment and Raynie hurried on, "Simon, please understand, she needs me. I can't just abandon her in her time of need."

Rapidly Simon leaped in, "Yes, yes, I do understand, Raynie. Please listen to me. You can go with me, I have it all planned. Of course, you are absolutely correct. Your mother is going to need you. But she will also need a place to flee to when the media and all of its undesired attention, overcomes her. You know honey, like a refuge, a place to get away and hide from all the cameras and journalists. You know they will no doubt be hounding her endlessly."

Simon took a deep breath then continued, "So you see Raynie, my plan is that you come and stay at my estate in England. It is very well guarded twenty-four hours a day and Jackie will have the security of knowing you are safe and out of arms reach of the pa-

parazzi. She will also be aware that she has a safe haven. A place she can run to as soon as she needs it."

"Simon all that sounds good, but I need to be here for her...while she's going through all the insanity."

"Darling, you may need that, but does your mother need that? You know very well that she will have your father to lean on while she's dealing with the police, divorce and whatever... I know your father, Raynie. And he will do whatever it takes to help Jackie get her life back in order."

Simon could see that his arguments were not getting through the barrier of concern Raynie held for her mother's welfare. Hastily he added, "Believe me Raynie, Jackie will feel much better, if she does not have to worry about you while all this is going on."

She studied him indecisively. Unhappily, she pushed him away as she asked; "Do you really think so?" All at once she slapped her forehead, "What the hell am I saying? Of course, you're right. My mother hates it when I worry about her. Knowing her, she'll be so anxiety-ridden about the press hounding me, she won't spend a minute of time protecting herself from those hungry barbarians." Raynie turned to face Simon. "Simon you are completely right. I am being self-indulgent. I must think about what's best for mother. Mother comes first."

"Sweetheart, you are simply afraid to let her out of your sight. That is completely understandable with all that has transpired these past few weeks."

Smiling Raynie whispered, "Simon, I love you. I would love to go with you. Above all I can hardly wait to be your bride."

"I love you too, Raynie. Together in England we can start to plan our wedding while we wait for your mother to join us. You will see, this will be best for all concerned."

"Lightheartedly Raynie teased, "Yes, and if I know my mother, the expectation of my wedding alone, will give her peace of mind and the passion to get on with her life." She paused while her last flicker of doubt succumbed, then asked, "So when do we leave?"

Excited Simon kissed her ferociously, before he turned her towards the bathroom and said, "Well soon to be, Mrs. Charles. I love you and will venture to say probably far more than you will ever know. Nonetheless, I do plan to remind you often enough. And ... the answer to your question is, we leave immediately. As of this minute, I will say you have less than two hours to throw a few things in a tote, so I would advise that you get a move on." Laughing he guided her towards the shower and added as he turned to leave her to her tasks, "Get a move on young lady. We have a plane to catch."

As soon as Raynie closed the door to the bathroom and he heard the shower water beginning to run, he grabbed the breakfast tray along with the newspaper and set it outside the bedroom door. Next, he called the maid and told her to pick it up promptly and trash the paper. Not until he heard the clatter of the trays being collected and carted off, did he breathe his first sigh of relief.

"Now;" he said. "To put this plan in order, we need to be as far away from the States as we could get before, I inform Raynie of Dan's luckless demise." He hoped Raynie would forgive his controlling manner, but this he knew was best for all concerned.

After a minute or so of guilt-ridden self-deliberation, Simon swiftly grabbed the phone and dialed his pilot. He needed to inform him of the flight so he could prepare for the eleven o'clock take off.

Sometime after he spoke with his pilot, he decided he had one more important call to make before joining his lovely fiancée in the shower. He smiled at the thought, while another vision came to him, and he picked up the house phone and called Yula.

When Yula laid the phone down she scratched and shook her head. For the life of her she couldn't guess why anyone would want a pile of red rose peddles two inches thick pitched across every inch of their bed. But that's exactly what Simon had ordered for his bed in England.

His last remark was, "Yula, *please* make sure there is not a single thorn left within them." She lifted the receiver to alert the staff in England of their arrival and muttered to herself, "Whaat a buunch a balderdash." Yet she grinned ear to ear with delight... her Simon was happier than she could ever remember.

Simon took a deep breath to calm himself as he reached for the phone to make his last call. He dialed slowly and inhaled several deep breaths as Raymond Dey's private number began to ring. Nervously he waited while the phone rang a number of times. He was excited as well anxious for he intended to properly ask for Raynie's hand in marriage. He also wanted to thank Ray for arranging and making things right.

Four weeks later:

After all the guests had walked away, Jackie began to struggle with her own resolutions. Her long black veil continued to slap against her face, and she reached for the lace and held the fabric next to her cheek. The material had been fluttering up and down with each gust of the Santa Ana wind throughout the entire service. It had been quite irritating, but she was utterly thankful that it had not lifted high enough for anyone to see her face or the brilliant smile she wore during most of the ritual.

Jackie was fully conscious that she looked frail as she stood motionless amongst the flowers that now encompassed Dan's grave. She waited silently while the news cameras snapped their final shots. At last they walked away, and she stepped closer towards the headstone. She studied it then thought, *for some reason it looks out of place.* When she first picked the slab, she thought the marble was beautiful, but now...it sat so ominous alongside his grave site. After she regarded it for several minutes, she bowed her head ever so slightly and reread the name and dates with immense satisfaction. They were printed in the bold script she had chosen, and the calligraphy really did look rather lovely. Her eyes immediately fell to the poem she had written for him and she giggled lightly. The words were all for her, not one syllable was for Dan and she will take joy in reading them each and every time she visits his grave. Disdainfully she whispered, "That is.... until I weary of playing the grieving widow."

Jackie reached out and casually caressed the engraved marble and felt the first hint of release as she read to herself.

> *Say where to thee, but not to me.*
> *For I am gone, but not beyond,*
> *Just out of reach, of you, my sweet.*

At the end of the poem she grimaced as she recalled the fear she had felt when she had fled her abuser. She pulled her wrap closer for protection from the memories and the wind as it continued to blow. She stepped nearer, and in a voice so low that it could scarcely be heard she asked, "Dan I wish you could tell me; I really would like to know? Is death as difficult for you, as life itself was? Moreover, I especially would like to know, did you go to purgatory or straight to hell?"

Her lips held a slight smile and a vibrant glee flowed in each of the words she had spoken when she asked the questions. By this point she was not in any way trying to hide her bliss or the reparation that she was genuinely feeling within. She winked, smiled then briefly paused before she turned and hurried towards the waiting car.

Eight Weeks later

These past weeks have flown by and Jackie had genuinely enjoyed her widowhood.

With her help, Simon had convinced Raynie to return and stay in England until she herself could join them to make their blissful wedding plans. Ray and Pamala will fly out next week to meet Simon's impressive family.

She herself had flown to England before the funeral and spent a wonderful two weeks meeting Simon's kin. She especially enjoyed the company of Simon's handsome and very wealthy uncle, Arthur Henry. She smiled as she hugged herself and thought, *she and Arthur will make a striking couple.*

Jackie sighed, as she considered their secret courtship. She could hardly wait to begin their open love affair. But that must wait. Yes, of course they have to wait, there has to be a proper waiting period. She heard a year was the standard mourning period. After that time, they can openly be seen together without the gossip columns going crazy with nonsense. Especially with Dan's supposed suicide she certainly didn't want to add to that speculation. Her body quivered as she remembered some of the articles printed about Dan's and her marriage. Along with the many absurd reports on how he really died. She laughed at the memory then shook her head as she hugged herself again. Oh, Raynie, she will be so utterly happy for her and Arthur. This time there will be no silly jealously or competition between the two. Yes, life is rich and so unpredictable.

THE END

ELLEN'S BIO

For Ellen the urge to write had started long before her first book, with poems and miscellaneous writings. Her first effort was a short story named Kathleen/Catherine. To prove her dedication to the written word the story was typed out on a small portable Smith Corona typewriter, no computer screen, no spell check, no correction key or save or print key. She had gotten a response from Red Book indicating they liked her story but would preferer something more towards women's rights.

As the years rolled by Ellen authored Kathleen/Catherine, One for the Money, and Murder by Proxy, and in a different genre CeeCee Shades of Black. A prominent New York Agent was excited about her work and was eager to guide her through the publishing process when 9/11 happened and the publishing industry and her writing went on hold.

Today once again she is looking forward to marketing her manuscripts to the public.

OTHER WORKS BY ELLEN M. FOSS

Murder by Proxy
CeeCee Shades of Black
One For The Money

Coming soon
Kathleen/Catherine

www.ellenmfoss.com